PRAISE FOR DENISE WELLS

Denise Wells did an excellent job balancing out the different emotions you experience while reading this book.

— GOODREADS

My first read by Denise, but it won't be my last.

— GOODREADS

It is a fresh premise that Denise Wells did beautifully!

— GOODREADS

I HEART MASON CARTWRIGHT

A ROMANTIC COMEDY

DENISE WELLS

Cover Design: Kristie, Vanilla Lily Designs

Editing: Missy Borucki

Proofreading: Judy's Proofreading

Publicity: Linda Russell, Foreword PR

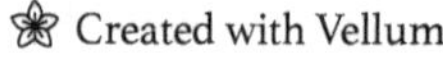 Created with Vellum

For BW - who I heart every single day.

In memory of :

Norman Eugene Lampman

October 21, 1949 - April 21, 2019

I miss you, Daddy.

Nothing that I wouldn't do

Go to the ends of the earth for you

To make you feel my love

— BOB DYLAN

ALSO BY DENISE WELLS

<u>STANDALONES</u>

The One I Can't Have, a steamy age-gap novella in **AB Worlds Age-Gap series**

The Three Way, a steamy novella in the **AB Worlds Valentine's Day Series**

Forever Wicked, a steamy novella in the **AB Worlds Halloween Party Series**

Summer Shivers, a romantic thriller in the **Summers in Seaside Collection**

Overdrive, a steamy enemies to lovers romance **in KB WORLDS - DRIVEN COLLECTION**

Pour Decisions, a romantic comedy novella in the **Girl Power Collection**

How to Ruin Your Ex's Wedding, a steamy romantic comedy

I Heart Mason Cartwright, a steamy romantic comedy

Love Off The Rocks, a romantic comedy short

Rebel without a Claus, a steamy, gay romantic short

Breaking Dylan, a coming of age story

<u>AGENTS AND ASSASSINS TRILOGY</u>

Fearless - Book One, a steamy romantic thriller

Careless - Book Two, a steamy romantic thriller

Ruthless - Book Three, a steamy romantic thriller

<u>SAN SOLOMAN</u>

Keeping Kat, a steamy second-chance firefighter romance

Romancing Remi, a steamy enemies to lovers romance

Loving Lexie, a steamy cowboy enemies to lovers romance

Seducing Sadie, a steamy firefighter romance

Trusting Tenley, an emotional second-chance at love romance

ANTHOLOGIES

High EX-Pectations, a romantic comedy short in the **Imperfect Date Anthology**

CAUGHT UNDER THE MISTLETOE - **A Holiday Affair to Remember,** a romantic comedy holiday short

STORYBOOK PUB CHRISTMAS WISHES - **Mistle Oh-No,** a romantic comedy holiday short

STORYBOOK PUB - **Breezy Like Sunday Morning,** a romantic comedy short

LIMITED RELEASES

GIRLS JUST WANNA HAVE FUNDAMENTAL RIGHTS - Charity Anthology

SEEDS OF LOVE A Charity Romance Anthology to benefit Ukraine - Charity Anthology

HOT AS F$#K SUMMER ROMANCE ANTHOLOGY - SULTRY SUMMER NIGHTS

LOCKED AND LOVED: An Isolated Romance Collection

SUMMER WITH YOU: Summer Shorts Collection

JUST A LICK Collection

LOVE LETTERS Collection

STOCKING STUFFERS Anthology

INTRODUCTION

MASON

Wrong place, wrong time? No good deed goes unpunished?

There's probably a million ways to describe being black-mailed into a fake engagement. With the most accurate being: Sucker.

WILLOW

Words I never thought I would hear my sister say: "Mason, meet my sister, Willow. Willow, this is my fiancé, Mason Cartwright."

With model worthy hair, sparkling brown eyes and a scruffy salt-and-pepper jawline that begged to be kissed, I was trapped in his swirling vortex of charisma.

Oh, Holy Hell's balls.

Good thing I don't believe in love at first sight. 'Cause if I did, I'd be booty over bean in love with Mason Cartwright.

I HEART MASON CARTWRIGHT

1

—————

MASON

The hotel bar I've parked myself at has been quiet for the last hour of the two I've been here. Which is why I'm surprised when I hear, "Wanna buy me a drink?"

It's close to midnight and the little blonde who is asking is a little too dressed up to be a casual, late-night drinker.

"Why not," I say.

"Great! I need it. It's been a hell of a day." She settles on to the bar stool next to me. Her short satin skirt rides up her thighs in the process. Way up. I try really hard not to notice. I'm not successful.

She tries (not) very hard to pull it down.

And is also not successful.

"What're you having?" I ask.

"I'll take a lemon drop martini, please." She bats her eyelashes at me. A trick I'm ashamed to say works every time. I'm a sucker for . . . well shit, there's not really one particular thing I'm a sucker for when it comes to women. I'm just a sucker for women.

This one has big blue eyes and full berry-colored lips. Her eyes are a little bloodshot, but it's hard to tell whether that's from crying or drinking.

I order her drink and introduce myself. "Mason." She takes my offered hand in hers. Her grasp is firm, her fingers small, and skin cool to the touch.

"AshLynn, it's nice to meet you." She smiles.

"The pleasure is mine, AshLynn. You from around here?"

"No. I live in Southlake, Texas. I'm only in Washington, or here in Leavenworth, for a wedding. One of my sorority sisters got married this afternoon. God, it was not a fun day. I can't believe I wasted my time. What about you?"

"My buddy's fortieth birthday party was earlier tonight. He and his wife live over in Wenatchee, but she threw the party here. We all got rooms for the night. Why wasn't the wedding fun? I thought all girls liked weddings."

The bartender sets her drink in front of her.

She takes a sip and looks up at him. "It's a bit tart, don't you think? I guess it will have to do." She turns to me. "Girls like weddings when it's their own. Otherwise, it's just a bitchy bride lording it over everyone else that she's married and you're not."

"Ouch," I say, and not just because she's a little harsh.

"Exactly. And my boyfriend was supposed to propose at the reception. It's all I've been talking about for weeks. Instead, we got in a fight and he left me here, stranded. Can you believe it?"

"Uh, no?" I don't mean to ask it as a question, but I don't really know her, so I have no idea why he wouldn't have proposed. Or left her stranded.

"When I asked him why he didn't propose he said it was too soon. As if." She takes a large sip of her drink.

I nod and look for the bartender hoping he'll join the conversation. This is not how I thought it was going to go down when she first asked me to buy her a drink. I think I liked the silence better.

The area behind the bar is empty and I can tell by the reflection in the mirror on the wall that he's not in the general seating area either.

Where did he go?

So, I keep talking to her. "Is it too soon?"

"Pfft. No. And he knows this was the best time in my schedule for an engagement. I can't believe he didn't do it. It was humiliating to say the least."

"Busy schedule, huh?"

"Very. You have no idea."

Please don't tell me.

"I won't bore you with the details," she says.

Thank god.

"But suffice it to say," she continues, "that I'm in demand and on the go. Like, all the time."

"I get it," I say. Even though I really don't. She looks more like a pageant queen than an in-demand woman on the go. But, hey, what do I know?

"Plus, he knew he was supposed to do it now so that I could upstage Whitney, the bride. Because she has been such a monumental bitch through this whole wedding-planning thing. Now I look like an idiot because he didn't do it."

"That's tough." Saying something is tough, or using the word ouch as a response, about maxes out my ability to be empathetic, so I hope she's about talked out.

"He's ruined everything." She pouts. But it's a pretty pout, I get the impression she has perfected it over time. In a mirror.

She sees the obnoxious button still pinned to my shirt from my buddy's party that says *First-Rate, Fuck-able, and Forty.* His wife made everyone wear them in honor of his birthday.

"You don't look like you're forty," she says touching my forearm and nodding to the pin.

"I'm not." I laugh.

She looks at me, eyes narrowed. "Hmmm. I'm guessing maybe twenty-eight."

She aims low on purpose, I'm sure to flatter me.

It works.

"Thirty-five," I correct her. Then I guess at her age. "And you are ... twenty-three?"

"How'd you know?" She takes a larger sip of her drink and shudders a bit as she swallows.

I wink. "Lucky guess." And it was, with me deciding to be nice even though she's a bit bitchy.

She looks down at her lap, then back at me. "Where do you go after this?"

"You always this inquisitive?" I ask.

"Of course," she says. "I'm rarely denied anything when I ask." Then grabs her drink and repeats the swallow and shudder. Almost half her drink is finished now. I look down at the scotch I've been nursing for half an hour, I still have most of it left.

"Well," I say. "To answer your question, I plan to head out tomorrow sometime. I'm renting a car and driving down to Seattle."

"What's in Seattle? Wife? Girlfriend?"

"Mom," I say. She's kind of cutely annoying with her subtle questions.

"So, you're single then?" As well as her not-so-subtle questions.

"Happily."

"You guys doing okay here?" the bartender asks her cleavage. Not that I blame him.

"I'm good," I say. "You?" I ask AshLynn.

"I'd like another, but with more sugar this time." She downs the remainder of her drink and hands the empty glass to the bartender. I wonder if I'm paying for this one too.

"So, AshLynn, where are you headed after this?" I ask.

"Since Brian, that's my boyfriend, abandoned me, I suppose I could go to my sister's house in Seattle tomorrow, but I don't know how I'm going to get there. I'm stuck." She pouts and looks at me with eyes wide.

Shit.

"I can give you a ride," I say before I can stop myself. Because I'm an idiot. An idiot who just invited a stranger to join me on a two-and-a-half-hour drive.

"Really?" she squeaks. "Ohmigod, that would be amazing. Thank you so much! You are a lifesaver." She leans in and gives me a hug, then kisses me on the cheek.

"Yeah, no problem. Happy to."

The bartender sets down her second drink.

"Cheers!" She raises her glass and I clink mine with hers hoping I didn't just get myself into trouble somehow.

I'D TOLD AshLynn to meet me in the lobby at ten o'clock in the morning. At ten minutes after the hour, I ring her hotel room to let her know I've got the car and have checked out of the hotel. She says she'll be down in five minutes. I take a seat in the lobby to wait.

Twenty minutes later I ring her room again.

No answer.

I walk around the lobby to see if I've missed her somehow, but don't see her. I grab a cup of coffee and sit back down. She finally exits the elevator, as I'm finishing my coffee. Two large suitcases in tow plus a garment bag and a purse. I move to help.

"How long have you been here?" I take one suitcase and the garment bag.

"I don't know, three days or so," she says.

"Isn't this a lot for three days?"

"No. One suitcase is just for shoes and irons."

That must be why it's so heavy.

"You know the hotel supplies an iron, right?" I smile.

She scoffs. "Hair irons. Flat iron, curling iron, wave iron, and my round rod."

"You use all of those for your hair?"

"Not at the same time, obvi. But I never know what mood I'm going to be in or what the weather is going to be like, so I don't know how I'll want to style my hair."

"Which one did you use today?" I ask to be polite.

"The wave iron," she says. "What do you think?" She poufs her hair on one side and does a little pose.

"Looks great," I say. "I hate to tell you this, but I got a convertible."

"But it still has a roof over it, right?"

"No, the *top* is down. Hence the convertible part."

"Well, you'll have to put it up. It took me over an hour to get my hair like this."

I open my mouth to rebut and realize this is my penance for being a nice guy. Because no good deed goes unpunished, right?

What's the word for more of a sucker than just a sucker?

Idiot? Moron? Nincompoop?

We reach the rental car and she leaves the suitcase and garment bag near the trunk for me to load into the car. I would have done it anyway, but it grates a little to have her expect it.

"Where's the button to put the top up?" she asks from the passenger seat.

"The car has to be on for it to work."

"There's air-conditioning, right? Can you start the car? It's hot."

I take a deep breath and count to ten before getting in the car.

You offered. Suck it up like a big boy.

Twenty minutes into the drive she asks to stop and use the restroom.

"Can you wait like ten more minutes?"

"I don't think so."

"Don't Change" by INXS comes on the radio and I turn it up and sing along.

"Ohmigod, now I know you're old," she says.

"What?" I turn to look at her. "I was born *after* this song came out."

"Yeah, but you know the words." She snickers.

"Because it's a great song."

She shrugs.

"Do you know the words to I Will Survive?" I ask.

"Of course I do." She rolls her eyes.

"That's older than my song, so what does that make you?"

"A modern woman."

"The song I Will Survive makes you a modern woman?"

"Yes." She draws out the word and upswings at the end.

"Okay, fine, other than that song, what kind of music does a modern woman listen to?"

"Do you have any Taylor Swift?" she asks.

"Nope."

"Shawn Mendes?"

"Negative."

"Ariana Grande?" Her eyebrows rise so high they are close to her hairline.

"No."

"Jonas Brothers?"

"Definitely not."

"Well, what do you have that's not like fifty years old?"

"Everything I have is *not like fifty years old*," I sigh. "How about Post Malone? I think I have his latest in here somewhere." I hand her my phone, which has most of my music downloaded on it. She begins scrolling through, mumbling criticism as she goes.

"You have a lot of old-people music in here."

"You mean a lot of classics?"

"Um, I guess if you consider Bob Seger classic."

"Hell fucking yes, Bob Seger is classic."

"Ugh, you should meet my sister. She loves all that crap. Do you like Journey? Oh, yep, there's a ton of Journey in here."

"Because Journey is the greatest band in the whole world," I say.

She makes a gagging face at me with her finger in her mouth.

"Given the list you just asked me about, I'm not exactly going to trust your taste in music."

"Oh! Oh! Rest area. Can we stop please?"

I pull off the freeway to the rest area, she's out of the car on her way to the restroom almost before I've parked.

I guess she really did have to go.

Her phone rings from the passenger seat. I look over at the screen. MOM. The ringing stops and immediately starts again. MOM. I wonder if I should bring it to her? Just yell into the bathroom that her mom is calling. The third time in a row MOM calls, I answer it.

"This is AshLynn's phone, she's just stepped away for a second, but I can have her call you right back."

"Who is this?"

"This is Mason. I'm—"

"Where is AshLynn?"

"She's—"

"Are you aware you've caused her to miss the Southlake's Finest Pageant? I hope whatever you're off doing is important. Because for her to shirk her responsibilities like this is inexcusable."

"I didn't—"

"Oh for god's sake, where are the two of you?"

"A rest area just outside Leavenworth."

"Where is Leavenworth?" she asks.

"Washington. State."

"Washington? Oh good lord." She puts her hand over the phone to speak with someone else, but I can still hear her but not the other person. "Jonathan, she's in Washington . . . I don't know . . . this is just, I can't believe she would do this . . . she is? When did Willow move to Seattle? . . ."

"Young man, how far are you from Seattle?"

"We are heading there now. We are about ninety miles out, maybe two hours."

She covers the phone again. "They are two hours away. When is the next flight? . . . Okay." I hear some rustling, then she comes back to the phone. "Listen," she says to me.

I don't hear what she says next because AshLynn is approaching the car. I hold the phone out to her. "It's your mom."

"My mom?" Both her mouth and eyes widen. "And you answered it?"

"I'm sorry. She called three times in a row, I thought it was an emergency. I only answered to tell her you'd call right back and then she started talking."

AshLynn takes the phone. I can hear her mom still talking.

"Mommy?"

Her mom's voice rises considerably. AshLynn talks over her. "Why do you need to know that . . . he's very nice . . . you don't need to . . . I do not . . . fine . . . Of course I did, I said I would, didn't I? . . . fine. I'll see you there." She disconnects the call and screams. Loud. The couple from a neighboring car looks over. I wave and smile. They look away.

AshLynn looks at me. "Can we go now? I need to be in Seattle like yesterday."

Whatever you say, Your Highness.

2

WILLOW

I STUDY THE PICTURE IN MY BIG ORANGE HOME IMPROVEMENT book one last time before doing a semi-crawl-with-a-long-leaning-type maneuver back under my kitchen sink to turn the handle for the water thingie to make it come back on. I'd like to say I'm not worried about what's going to happen, but that's not true.

I'm totally worried, I've never done this before. I take a deep breath and hold it while I grab the rounded knob that will make water magically reappear at the sink faucet and twist.

And twist.

Nothing happens. I look back at the pictures. They did one full turn. Maybe two. I'm over four turns now. I don't think it should rotate this much.

Did I go in the wrong direction?

I crank it a few times in the other direction.

Nothing happens.

It feels loose. Maybe too loose? I fling it down on one side with my finger and watch as the handle spins freely.

This can't be good.

The book doesn't say anything about what to do if the knob spins freely or won't stop turning. I crawl back out of the cabinet and stand, wiping my hands on the sides of my jeans, and try to decide if I should try the faucet again. Princess Tinkerbell, P-Tink for short, my ever-faithful Husky puppy (and canine home improvement assistant), whimpers at my feet.

"I know, I think you're right. But let's think positive thoughts," I mumble to her. She closes her eyes and sighs.

I raise the handle on the kitchen sink faucet. The pipes respond with a loud groan. The faucet rattles in protest, a brownish sludge drips to the sink bottom and stays there. I raise the handle a bit more and lean in to watch what happens. The rattling intensifies, the sludge clears in color a bit, and then the entire apparatus catapults off its base on the counter, clipping me on the forehead as it flies through the air. Water follows, spouting every which way at least three feet in the air.

"Aaah!" I cough-snort as the tinny-tasting stream shoots up my nose and down my throat. "Dammit, Janet! That freaking hurts!" I mutter my favorite curse phrase from one of my favorite movies.

I duck and move to the side to get out from under the rusty-colored spray, rubbing at the sore spot on my forehead. P-Tink barks and hops back and forth on either side of the spattering shower, trying to bite the streams of water as they flow to the floor.

I watch the dirty brown water drench everything in sight and try not to cry. I knew when I bought this old fixer-upper that the kitchen would need replacing, but I'd hoped it would last a little longer than this. Especially since I'll now need a new floor once this one warps.

Flooding.

Oh crud, I've got to get the water off the floor.

Wait. I've got to get the water turned off.

"Oh! P-Tink, crap!"

I move back in, squeezing my eyes shut against the deluge and blindly try to staunch the flow with outstretched hands. I get my hands clasped over the top of the pipe, then grab the nearest thing I can find to use as a stopper. My favorite hoodie I'd laid on the counter earlier. I shove the edge of the sleeve into the pipe opening, then fold the material in on itself to create a thicker barrier. I already know I'll never wear it again after seeing the color of that water. No matter how many times I wash it.

I look around for something to weigh the hoodie/water stopper down. My home improvement book is the only thing in reach.

Sigh.

I lodge it between the backstop of the sink and the folded hoodie material to hold it in place over the pipe. I haven't stalled the flow of water completely, but the hoodie has definitely lessened the raging spout to more of a dribble; with most of the water going back into the sink and down the drain.

I'm a freakin' home maintenance MacGyver!

I check the floor-plan-map-thing the realtor drew for me to identify where certain things are located: breaker box, electric meter, main water shut-off valve, sprinkler controls— the kind of stuff that home renovators need to know. Since I'm now a home renovator, I need to know these things. I could hire people to do this. I have the money.

My grandmother, Granny Violet, recently passed away and she and I were close. She left me some money. And by some, I mean a lot. Like, I never need to work if I don't want to. Neither do my kids. Even if I have ten of them. Which I won't. Because that would be crazy. I could never handle ten kids. I can barely handle one dog.

But I don't want to hire people. I remind myself of that as I try to find the main water shutoff valve for the house. Luckily, this one is a lever that only goes in one direction. I get it switched to off, and slog back to the house where P-Tink is slurping water off the floor.

"Good girl, just go ahead and get it all while you're at it," I tell her. She makes a wooing sound in response. She totally gets me.

IT's obvious the man in the orange apron is trying not to laugh at me. Only, he's not very successful. His lips purse and his chest shakes as he listens to me tell him what happened. Which is crazy since he *must* hear stories like mine all the time—home repairs gone awry—he works in the plumbing aisle at a hardware store for goodness' sake.

I want to smack him across his chubby smirk-filled face with my new home improvement book that I'm getting to replace the waterlogged one at home. But this is my year to become responsible since I'm a homeowner now, and something tells me responsible people don't hit one another over the head with three-inch-thick books.

"Okay." He clears his throat, his mirth in check. "So, you were trying to repair a leaking kitchen faucet, and the water shutoff valve under the sink just kept spinning?"

I nod. I see from the handwriting on his apron that his name is *Bill* and he specializes in plumbing. I'd introduce myself, but don't see a need for us to be on a first-name basis.

Though, if I did, I'd introduce myself as Willow who specializes in being responsible. And I would tell him it's not polite to laugh at another's misfortune.

"And it was round? It didn't look like this?" He holds up a silver almond-shaped knob thing. I return my attention to Bill.

"Yes, and it didn't," I say. "Because apparently nothing that is actually in my stupid new old house looks like the pictures in this damn book."

"And that's when the faucet flew off and hit you in the head?" Bill confirms.

"It didn't just fly off; it was like a freakin' missile with a water rocket chaser. I needed *two* bandages!" I point to them on my forehead to enunciate my point. "And don't forget the weird engine revving sound the pipes made when I tried the faucet. And how everything rattled."

"Okay, well, that's common in some of these older fixer-upper homes. Especially those built by the waterfront, where things rust much faster than inland homes do," he says.

"What about the water being brown?" I ask. Because I *know* that can't be normal.

"That sounds like sedentary water, just needs to be flushed out. It should turn clear after running it a while. If not, you may have a hole in the pipes somewhere underground, maybe leaking mud into your supply line."

Huh. Okay.

He keeps talking. "Okay, well this is a . . ."

I tune him out as he holds up the part I need to buy and then tells me how to install it. I know I should be listening to what he says, or else I'll have questions later, or worse, more exploding house parts. But I don't want to care about valves and levers and stuff. I just want to go home and get the water working again so I can shower somewhere other than the gym.

Now, I know that listening to him would only help me in fixing the problem, but it's boring. Bill is boring. My mind just automatically wanders to things more interesting to me, like the olive green crossbody bag that woman in the return line has and where she bought it.

This illustrates my main problem in life. I don't stay interested in anything for too long. I can't. I gloss over what's now, so I can get to what's next. It's why I figured tackling a large project like renovating an old house would be perfect since there is always something different to do. If I get bored, I can bounce around from repair to repair.

What I did not consider was how long each task might take to complete. And how some things, like a plumbing leak, can't just be left incomplete. *And* have to be cleaned up. So far, everything outside of choosing a new front entry mat is super hard, takes knowledge I don't have, and an insane amount of time to finish.

I rub the spot behind my left ear with my thumb. Then put the new levers and flex pipes from Bill in my cart next to the wet/dry vac he also told me to buy, and head to the next section to find a new faucet.

I video call my best friend, Zach, from the faucet aisle to get his opinion. He's got a great eye for interior design.

"Yes, dear?" he answers, the camera remarkably close to his handsome face. So close in fact, I can see how perfect his skin is.

It's like he has no pores. Just flawless, pore-less skin that radiates beauty. If he wasn't my best friend, I would hate him. He's almost too pretty for his own good. Stylized golden-brown hair, glasses that make him look both smart and handsome, a sculpted jawline, thick eyelashes. It's like if you cross a young Brad Pitt with that super smart kid from Criminal Minds, you'd get Zach Thornton.

"Z, I need your help picking out a faucet."

He rolls his big green eyes. "Of course you do. Show me."

I turn the phone and show him the three that I've narrowed it down to.

"The middle one," he says.

"Are you sure? I was thinking the one on the left."

"Then why did you call me?"

"To make sure I was right."

"You aren't. Get the middle one, hire some hunky man to help you install it. We can make mai tais and watch him."

"I'm the one installing it."

He pretend yawns. "So boring. Is that all?"

"Yeah, why, do you have somewhere to be?"

"If you must know," he says. "I have someone here with me."

I gasp. "Are you in bed, is that why the camera is so close to your face? Wait, did you just get a facial? Why does your skin look so good?"

"No, I did not just get a facial. I'm always this pretty. But I am in bed. Because one of us should be getting laid, and I vote me. I have that post-sex glow."

"Nicely done, Mister Thornton. Is he cute? Do you like him? Is he your new boyfriend?" I ask my questions rapidly, knowing he plans to disconnect the call at any moment.

He turns the phone, bringing a large hairy man with a gag over his mouth into view.

"This is William," Zach says. "William, this is my one true love, Willow. You may say hello." He pans the camera to William's hands, both of which are tied to the bed post. William wiggles his fingers at me. I wiggle mine back.

"Go back to what you were doing. Thank you for taking my call. Sorry for interrupting. Love you," I say as I hit end. I grab both the middle and the faucet from the left side and put them in my cart. Then head toward the check-out lines.

3
____

MASON

I DECIDE TO GET TO KNOW MY TRAVEL COMPANION A LITTLE better. Especially since we still have another ninety minutes on the road and time is dragging.

"I just realized, I don't even know your last name," I say.

"It's Brooks. You?"

"Cartwright," I say. "So, what do you do for work?"

"I'm too busy to have a job," she says.

"How can someone be too busy to have a job?"

"I told you, I have a lot to do."

"Like what?"

"Oh, where do I start? Okay, well for starters I'm the president of my sorority's alumni chapter—go Deltas! I co-chair the Southlake Women for Functional Change, I've got my Daughters of the Republic of Texas work that I do, plus I panel three different pageants."

I'm not surprised to hear she's a pageant girl.

"And," she continues, "since I won the Southlake's Finest Pageant and the Miss Bluebird Pageant, plus was a runner-up in the Queen of the Lone Star Pageant, I'm always relied upon for my opinion on various causes and issues. Not to mention upcoming pageants. I have to mentor other pageant girls, teach them the ropes, help them shop. And, I'm the Southlake Representative of the Friendship Ambassadors for the state. Plus, Mommy just signed us up to judge a beautification contest in some poor neighborhood. It's exhausting how much I am responsible for."

She doesn't stop there. She just keeps talking.

"We have the fundraisers that we plan, and there's the big gala at the club every year for the orphans, I think. Or, that might be the one for the kids with learning disabilities. Not that it matters which it is, I suppose. Anyway, we have quite a few that we help with. We aren't the only ones who do it. There are a lot of women who use their time to give back."

"But you don't get paid for any of that?" I ask.

"No, it's giving back. That's what giving back means. It's free for the people."

That's not quite what it means.

A song that I like comes on the radio and I turn it up. She sighs. Loudly. And turns her body away from me.

I guess we're finished talking. Which I'm fairly certain I am fine with.

I sing along with Gary Clark, Jr., my favorite blues musician, and take in the scenery. This has to be one of the most beautiful stretches of freeway I've ever been on. Huge trees blanket the sides of the roads, the snowcapped mountains off in the distance, wild grasses growing in the center divider separating the north and southbound lanes. The air smells clean, the sun is shining, there's not a lot of traffic. I've made this drive quite a few times before, but I don't remember taking the time to enjoy it like I am now.

It helps that AshLynn is actually being quiet for a moment, and we've still got a way to go before we are even close to the Port of Seattle. With any luck at all, the rest of the drive will be this nice.

AshLynn spends a lot of time on her phone. Texting, scrolling social media, posting selfies, and declining phone calls.

After the fourth time, I say something about it.

"It's just my parents," she says in response to my question. "They want to make sure I'm still headed to Seattle to see my sister. I've texted them already. That should be enough."

"Maybe they are just worried because you are in the car with a stranger," I suggest.

"No. I told them you . . . were a good guy."

"I sense some hesitation in your answer." I state the obvious. "Why'd you hesitate? Is that not really what you said?"

"Of course it's what I said. Besides, I never would have gotten in to the car with you if I hadn't been sure of your intentions. I'm good at reading people."

If she was that good, she would have known there was a point last night that I just wanted to bail at three in the morning and leave her chatty ass behind.

We drive along in silence for a while, finally exiting the freeway toward downtown Seattle. According to AshLynn, her sister, Willow, recently moved to Bainbridge Island, bought a big fixer-upper on the sound, and is renovating it herself. As someone who has renovated many a home in the past, I'm excited to see what she's doing with it.

Traffic is heavy, and it takes us a while to get from the freeway exit to the ferry terminal. AshLynn gets more agitated the closer we get. By the time we arrive, she's sighing intermittently while also looking at her phone continuously. To top off her mood, it's a twenty-minute wait until boarding for the next ferry.

"I can't believe it took so long to get here. This is ridiculous. And traffic is boring," AshLynn says. "Which makes me bored. Let's go already!" she yells.

"We're almost there. Aren't you excited to go on a ferry?" I ask.

She shrugs.

"To see your sister?"

She shrugs again.

"Are the two of you close?" I ask.

"No, not really. We were when I was young, but we drifted apart over time. She's a lot older than I am, with her own life and I was just an annoyance."

"How much is a lot older?" I ask, picturing someone in their forties.

"She's thirty-four."

"I thought you said you were twenty-three?" I ask.

"I did."

"That's only eleven years difference."

"I know, see?"

Somehow, I don't think we are at all on the same wavelength here. I wait a minute to see if she'll say anything else. She remains quiet, so I keep talking.

"What about your parents?"

"What about them?"

"You said they were meeting you there. Are you excited to see them?"

"God, no."

So, why are we rushing to get there?

"How far into the island does your sister live? Do you know?"

"No, I still need to get her address and let her know we're coming."

"She doesn't know you're coming?"

"No. But, it's fine. She loves it when we visit. It's why she bought such a big house, so she'd have room for us all." She sounds funny when she tells me that. Almost like she's saying what she wishes it was like, instead of how it actually is.

Her sister doesn't answer the first time, so AshLynn calls right back. I'm starting to see a pattern with this family and their inability to leave voicemails and wait for a call back.

Willow answers the second time around and their conversation is brief.

"You know that we are much closer to her than an hour, right?" I ask in relation to how far out she told her sister we were.

"Well, then it will be a surprise when we arrive sooner." She waves her hand in the air dismissively.

"Does your sister like surprises?"

"Not really, no."

I put the top down after we exit the ferry despite AshLynn's protests; the sun is just going down and it's still warm enough for it. It doesn't take us long to reach Willow's house. Large, mature trees line each side of the long driveway making it feel incredibly private. The effect is isolating and peaceful at the same time.

The drive curves slightly and I see the house ahead. From the outside it's a bit reminiscent of a log cabin with its redwood siding and brick-colored trim. The rounded drive circles a huge sugar maple tree surrounded by a low brick wall. A detached multicar garage sits off to the right of the main house shadowed by more large trees. If it weren't for the sun setting on the horizon above the single-story home, it would be impossible to tell the home was on the waterfront.

A stone walkway leads to the front porch in one direction and the garage in the other. From the exterior, the home appears to be in decent shape. It is well lit on the inside, but even from the car I can see the dated interior through the windows in the front. Nevertheless, the structure looks to be a ranch-style home—one of my favorites to renovate.

A tall woman comes out to the front porch, a small Husky puppy by her side. She's dressed in cut-off shorts and a tank top. Curly red hair pulled into a messy bun on top of her head. My heart beats a little faster, which seems odd since I've yet to even meet her. Though, I've always had a weakness for redheads. And I find myself inexplicably drawn to this one.

"By the way," AshLynn says as she steps out of the car. "I may have to introduce you as my fiancé since Brian fucked everything up. It won't be for long. Just go with it. Otherwise, I'll tell everyone you assaulted me on the drive here. And I'm a really good actress."

4

———

WILLOW

THREE HOURS EARLIER

I decide on the middle faucet. Mostly because Zach is always right. It takes me just over three hours to install it and the new water shutoff levers under the kitchen sink. The book said it would take a novice thirty to forty minutes. The man at the hardware store said it would take no more than an hour. Neither one of them mentioned the need for Teflon tape. Nor the number of times I would return to said hardware store for the correct sizes of completely random stuff that no normal human being ever knew went in to making water mysteriously come out of the faucet.

I am now convinced that plumbing is just straight-up magic. I have no idea how water travels up the pipes. Or how it stops running just because I turn a knob. And why doesn't it then back up and explode from the pressure when I stop it from flowing? I mean, it exploded earlier when I barely did anything.

I wipe my hands on my pants and slosh through the remaining water on the floor to grab a diet soda from the fridge, holding the cold can against my warmed cheeks. I can feel the grit on my face from lying under the sink. Which is another thing that no one tells you: grit gets everywhere during home renovations. I don't even know what grit is, but I know I have it everywhere on my body. Layers upon layers of dirt and grit blended with the sweat on my face. So much so, the bandage slides right off my forehead.

I sit down on an overturned bucket and crack open my soda, draining most of it in one large gulp. Then wait for the burp. One of P-Tink's party tricks. If we ever had parties that is. When you burp, she will launch herself into the air in front of you, bite at nothingness, and catch the burp. It's super fun when it's just me and her after a few beers.

She does not disappoint, the minute I burp, she launches and catches. Yelps in satisfaction, turns in a circle four times, and settles in beside me on the floor. Happy to lie in and lap up the water at the same time.

"What would Granny Violet think if she could see us now, P-Tink?" I ask my dog. She barks in response. She and Granny Violet never met, but they are a lot alike in personality: tenacious, loyal, nosey, and vocal. I like to think that if reincarnation exists, Granny Violet has come back to me by way of Princess Tinkerbell—though Granny passed over a year ago and P-Tink and I have only been together a little over a month.

A local rescue was holding an adoption event outside a grocery store a few days after I'd moved to Bainbridge Island and I happened to be out of diet soda. P-Tink was being paraded around amongst a bevy of admirers, standing tall, with her shiny coat, bushy tail, and big blue eyes. Part Siberian Husky, part diva; I looked at her, she looked at me, and that's all it took. She slipped her collar, glued herself to my side, and we've not been apart since.

I finish off my soda and toss my can toward the recycle bin. It bounces off the edge and lands on the floor. P-Tink hustles over to pick it up and drops it neatly in the bin. That's her only other party trick. Which is convenient since I'm a poor shot when tossing things at the trash and recycle bins.

My phone buzzes with a call. It's my half sister, AshLynn. I can't imagine what she wants with me, we aren't very close and we definitely don't talk much.

I send it to voicemail.

She calls right back.

What if something is wrong with my dad?

I answer. "Hey, Ash. I'm surprised—"

"Willow, I'm so glad you answered! Are you at home?"

"Uh, yeah."

"Great, I'm coming to visit, text me your address."

"What? Why? When?" I rub the spot behind my left ear.

"Soon, silly. We're just outside of Seattle."

"We?"

"Mason and me. Text me! See you soon!"

"Who's Mas—"

She disconnects the call. I look at my phone, willing it to go back in time, to before I answered. Better yet, to a time when I send the second call to voicemail as well. It's not so much that AshLynn and I don't get along . . . actually that's exactly what it is.

I'm sure it's the same for AshLynn, she doesn't need me, she's got plenty of friends. I can't imagine why she would come to visit me. Plus, the whole Granny Violet inheritance issue turned my whole family against me, but that's a story for another time. Besides, our family doesn't do impromptu visits. We do scheduled visits, planned weeks in advance. Months even. To give us all plenty of time to agonize over the fact we'll have to see one another and be civil. Or maybe that's just me.

Regardless, what's AshLynn up to?

"I guess we'll know when she gets here, huh, P-Tink?" She wags her tail, slapping it in the water on the floor.

If they are just getting into Seattle, I should have an hour or so of sanity left depending on the ferry schedule.

And who the hell is Mason?

This is not a good time for a visit.

I should call her back and say no. I need to get the water off the kitchen floor. I can smell myself, so I know I need a shower.

But she reached out to you, Willow. She never does that. The least you can do is reciprocate.

Gah! I hate my inner self sometimes.

Against my better judgement, I text her my address, then survey my surroundings. I glance over at the wet/dry vac I bought. It's supposed to suck up the standing water, but I have my doubts. First, anything involving electricity combined with water is never good. I don't even trust the underwater lights in swimming pools. So, the idea of vacuuming water scares the ever-lovin' crap out of me.

I got as far as taking it out of the box, but I haven't plugged it in or moved it anywhere near the kitchen yet. Instead, I've thrown as many bath towels, blankets, and dirty clothes I could find on the floor to mop it up. P-Tink is picking up sopping towels from the floor and shaking them in her mouth to create random sprays of water, which she then tries to chase. There are so many times I wish I were a dog. If for no other reason than to be entertained by creating and chasing water sprays that I will never catch.

She takes a break to lap up water pooling between the articles of bedding and clothing. "Good girl, P-Tink. Just go ahead and get it all up while you're at it," I tell her. "That way I won't have to vacuum." She makes a wooing sound back at me. I pick up random wet things and wring them out in the sink, then throw them back on the floor to continue cleanup. There's got to be two inches still in here.

How can one sink have so much water?

P-Tink's ears perk up and she runs to the low windows in the living room to investigate; I follow.

"Just getting to Seattle, my ass." A red convertible pulls to a stop, dangerously close to my front flower bed. Or what will be a flower bed once I plant flowers in it. Right now, it's just dirt surrounded by brick. I open the front door and step onto the porch, P-Tink at the ready by my side. At least I think she's at the ready. It occurs to me that I don't really know if she will protect me from bad guys or not.

What I do know is that she loves everyone and everything at the hardware store. Outside of that, she doesn't seem to appreciate strangers, big trucks, anyone wearing a Fedora, or the sound of flip-flops. So, the odds are in my favor here. Or maybe it's just hard to tell.

The passenger door flings open and AshLynn emerges, large sunglasses covering her face, mid-riff halter-style top, and a flowy A-line skirt, looking like a modern-day slutty Grace Kelly.

"Willow!" she cries, opening her arms and skipping toward me with a wide smile on her face.

I've got half a mind to turn around to try and find this other Willow that she's so happy to see. I let her hug me and ooh and ahh over the house and how good I look and how great it is to see me. Then she turns and motions toward the car. "Mason, come meet my sister!"

All I can see over the frame of the windshield is the top of a baseball cap. The driver's side door opens, and Mason unfolds himself from the car, straightening to his full, impressive height. He comes toward us, measuring in at what must be six foot three inches tall. I'm five foot nine inches, and he towers over me.

He takes off his baseball cap and runs his hand through his tousled brown hair; bright brown eyes sparkle in my direction, and his scruffy salt-and-pepper jawline begs to be kissed. AshLynn grabs his hand and squeals with excitement.

"Mason Cartwright, meet my sister, Willow Brooks. Willow, this is my fiancé, Mason."

A trill races through me as I shake Mason's hand. His eyes widen at my touch, making me wonder if he feels it too.

Oh, Holy Hells Balls.

All I have to say is, it's a damn good thing I don't believe in love at first sight. 'Cause if I did, I'd be booty over bean in love with Mason Cartwright.

5

———

MASON

I SHAKE MY HEAD.

Uh, what the fuck just happened?

Did she just say assault?

For fuck's sake.

You couldn't just keep your mouth shut when the damsel in distress needed a ride, could you, Mason.

Idiot.

AshLynn exits the car with a cry and runs toward her sister. I stretch my sore muscles and try to temper my hair under my cap as the women embrace. AshLynn comes back and grabs my hand, pulling me toward the house to introduce me to her sister, Willow.

AshLynn makes the introductions, talking fast, moving fast, making me wonder if she's nervous.

I look back and forth between the two sisters as I hold my hand out to shake Willow's. She shocks the hell out of me when we do.

Literally.

What feels like an electric current runs from her body to mine and zaps me. She pulls her hand away quickly and cradles it to her chest, then keeps an eye on me as she ushers us inside.

"Bathroom. Now!" AshLynn demands. Willow points toward a doorway just off the hall, AshLynn run-walks toward it leaving her sister and me alone.

She looks at me. I look at her. She looks away.

I look at her. She looks at me. She looks away.

It's obvious I make her uncomfortable.

She is far more gorgeous up close than when I saw her from the car. My dick stirs in my shorts.

She clears her throat. "Well, welcome, I guess." She ends the sentence on an up note, like she's asking me a question. Then sticks her hands in her pockets and rocks to and fro on her feet from heel to ball and back again.

What the hell is AshLynn doing?

"Uh." I pause to clear my own throat. "Thanks. Should be a fun time."

Should be a fun time?

Jeez, Mason. Get it together, man. She's going to think you're a dork.

"So." I clap my hands once in front of me and rub them together while I glance around. "I hear you're renovating the whole place?"

"Yeah. I am." She turns in a slow circle, looking at the room. "It's a much larger project than I thought it was going to be. But I'm enjoying it so far. I think. Sorry it's such a mess, I had a pipe break earlier, and water went everywhere—"

"What happened with the pipe?" I interrupt, sensing I may be able to impress the pretty redhead and fix this for her, thus making a good first impression. I'm better with my hands than I am my words.

"Oh." She shakes her head. "The faucet was leaking. When I went to shut off the water, the valve broke. Before I could shut it off at the main, the faucet exploded. Water everywhere and this goose-egg on my forehead." She points to the cut on her forehead.

"You should have that looked at," I say gesturing to her head.

AshLynn comes back in the room. "So, you don't have running water, Willow?"

"No. I mean yes." Willow takes a breath and lets it out in a huff. "I have running water; I just had to turn it off because of the issue in the kitchen. But it should be back on. Maybe there's a delay in—"

AshLynn makes her way toward the kitchen. "Ohmigod, Willow, what happened? I think I'm going to throw up. Is that—" She makes a gagging noise. "Is that poo water?"

"What?" Willow exclaims rushing to her side. "No, it's just sediment. The water hadn't been used in a long time. That's the way it comes out at first."

"Ohmigod, so gross," AshLynn says. "It looks like it smells."

"It doesn't smell," Willow says. "Smell it."

"No. Ugh. Gag. Get me out of here." AshLynn goes out the front, letting the screen door slam shut behind her. I notice a brand-new wet/dry vac off to the side, grab it, and look for an outlet to plug it in.

I find one just as Willow says, "Oh, I'd be careful with that—"

I power it on and start suctioning up the water from the floor. When I glance back at Willow, she has her eyes shut with her hands over her face, but I'm not sure why.

Willow spreads her fingers to peek through them after a minute, her mouth moves but I can't hear what she's saying. I hold my hand up to my ear to show her that I don't know what she's saying. All I hear are the sounds of water being sucked through the hose into the vacuum canister. Willow waves her hand to show it was nothing and smiles big.

She's got a nice smile.

I set the hose on the floor to let it do its thing and start picking up all the sodden clothes and blankets to wring them out in the sink. Willow watches, eyes wide and mouth agape. It takes me less than fifteen minutes to get all the water off the floor and the garments and things used to wipe it up hung out to dry.

"Ohmigod! You're my hero!" Willow says once I've turned off the wet/dry vac. "I can't believe you just walked in and did that. You're amazing. Thank you so much. Just so you know, I really wanted to help you, but I'm not entirely convinced I won't be electrocuted by walking in water with a vacuum. Or really anything that's powered by a plug and outlet. I mean, obviously you're still alive, but let's face it, you could have some random magic electricity juju that wards off evil volts of death charges."

I laugh. "I know a thing or two about home renovation."

"Mason is *great* with his hands," AshLynn trills as she reenters the room. I'm tempted to puff my chest out. There's something about when a girl gushes over you in front of another girl that makes a guy feel like he's invincible.

Until I remember that AshLynn doesn't know how I am with my hands. And that she introduced me as her fiancé. Which I need to find out the reason for. Just as soon as I'm finished losing my mind over her sister.

"Anyway, thank you, so much," Willow says. "The vacuum scared me with the water, and even though the hardware store man said it was safe, I just . . ." She trails off and looks to the ground, cheeks turning pink.

"Oooohhh, why are you blushing, Willow? Who's the hardware store man?" AshLynn asks the question I was thinking. "Do you have a crush?"

Please don't have a crush.

"Hardly." She scoffs. "It's the worker at the hardware store. He's older than Dad and allergic to dogs."

I hide my relief at her lack of a crush by kneeling to pet the dog sniffing at my feet. "What is this beautiful baby's name, by the way?"

"Princess Tinkerbell," Willow says. "P-Tink for short. Part Siberian Husky, part diva. She can catch a burp in the air, makes sure the trash and recycling always make it in the bins, loves long walks on the beach, and is a Capricorn."

I stand. "She's beautiful," I say looking Willow directly in the eye. She blushes slightly and looks down.

"Thank you."

I could get used to that blush. I like it.

"Oh, that's so cute," AshLynn says of Princess Tinkerbell, but oddly not looking at or even trying to pet her.

P-Tink nudges her head under my hand so I lean over to pet her some. Her tail wags with satisfaction and I swear I hear her sigh. "She's awesome."

"You don't burp at her, do you?" AshLynn asks. "That's so gross."

"Duh. Watch." Willow grabs a diet soda from the fridge and takes a couple long swigs. After a few seconds she burps. On cue, P-Tink leaps through the air in front of her, clapping her jaws open and shut as she goes. She barks and runs in a circle after she lands, then sits looking up at Willow, proud as can be. "Good girl," she tells her as she rubs her head.

I hold my hand out for her can of soda, wanting to try it for myself. Liking that I'm about to place my lips where hers just were. She hands it to me and watches as I take a long drink, which results in a large burp. P-Tink is up and in the air in front of me before it's over. I'm impressed and praise the dog accordingly. It's not a trick that serves a purpose, but, damn, she'd be great at parties.

"Now that it's all cleaned up, you going to give us a tour?" AshLynn asks.

"Actually, AshLynn, can I talk to you outside first?" I look at her pointedly.

She avoids my gaze. "Of course, right after the tour."

Goddammit.

Willow wasn't kidding when she said it was a fixer-upper. This place is a bit of a dump. But the bulk of the floor plan takes full advantage of the view of the sound. Which is incredible.

The house is laid out in sort of a long rectangle, and only two rooms and a bathroom don't face the sound with a water view.

To one side is the master suite, which faces both the front of the house on one side, and the sound on the other. It's a huge room. But the bathroom is small and closed in. Making me wonder if it was added at some point just as a convenience and not truly an en suite.

The other side has another four rooms with a hallway in between. Two rooms and a bath on the sound side and two rooms and a bath on the front side. The living room is open, but a couple partial walls close off the dining room and kitchen.

"These walls have got to be opened," I mutter to myself as I turn back into the living room after the tour.

"Right?" Willow says appearing next to me. "That's what I think too. I would love to open this entire room actually."

I would kill for a place like this. Why have I never thought about renovating on one of the islands before? Shit, I would kill just to work on a house like this. Not that the structure itself is that fantastic, but what you could turn it into is fabulous. And it wouldn't take much. Creating a master bathroom, combining two of the smaller guest rooms to make one larger room with an en suite and closet. Knock down some walls, add a skylight or three, redo the kitchen, and voila. You'd have yourself a straight-up masterpiece. I want to talk to her more about it. I want to know her ideas, who she's working with, what her master plan is. I want to know everything inside that gorgeous head of hers.

"This is a disaster, Willow," AshLynn says. "Why don't you just hire people to do this and stay in a hotel? So you can live a normal life."

Willow starts telling her how she's missed the point. AshLynn argues about something else unrelated, so Willow counters with something equally unrelated. And soon it's a cacophony of screechy female voices trying to outdo one another. I tune them out and kneel to pet P-Tink. Right now, I think she might be the only rational girl in the house.

6

———

WILLOW

"I'm not going to argue with you about this, AshLynn. I don't care whether you agree," I say.

"What. Ever."

"All right, subject change," I say. "So, how long are you in town for?"

"Uh . . ." AshLynn looks to Mason.

"Not long," he says. Though it sounds more like a question than an answer.

"Where are you going next? Back to Texas?"

"Yes," AshLynn says at the same time Mason says, "Oh no, I live here."

"Oh." I look at them, brow furrowed. That kind of surprises me. "I just assumed you were from Southlake, as well?"

Mason looks confused.

"Southlake, Texas," I explain.

"Oh, yeah, no. I'm not," he says.

AshLynn glares at him.

"AshLynn," he says. "Can I, uh, talk to you now? Outside?"

"I thought it would be nice if we talked to my sister for a bit. Willow, do you have any place to sit?"

I gesture toward the kitchen on the west end of the house. "On the patio."

"Let's go," AshLynn says.

We take a seat on the back deck. The air has started to cool slightly as the sun begins its slow descent.

"Wow, this is incredible," Mason says.

"Thanks. I am really happy with my choice."

Mason walks to the edge of the deck to see the view. I wait until he's out of earshot before turning to AshLynn to ask, "Where are you going to live after you get married?"

She shrugs. "Don't know."

"Clearly, you've discussed your future with this man, AshLynn. Nice job."

"We've discussed enough," she says.

"Yet, you're engaged," I mumble. But I passive-aggressively make it loud enough for her to hear. That's just the kind of girl I am.

"Don't be that way, Wills," AshLynn pouts.

"What way? The practical way where you actually know someone's favorite color before taking their last name. Do you even know his last name?" I'm pissed off by this latest act of impetuous immaturity on her part.

"Now you're just taking all the fun out of it," AshLynn says.

"When is the big day, anyway?" I ask.

"A few weeks." AshLynn smiles big. "If you're nice to me, I might even let you be my maid of honor."

"I can barely contain my excitement." I roll my eyes. If she thinks I'm going to be her maid of honor, she is sorely mistaken.

That's a lie. If she asked, I would totally do it. I would die a little bit inside. But I would do it. I talk a big game, but rarely back it up with action where my family is concerned.

Mason returns and sits down with us.

"So," I ask, mostly of AshLynn. "Do your parents know you're engaged?"

"About that—" Mason says.

"They know." AshLynn shrugs her shoulders.

"Wait, I thought you were sisters?" Mason asks.

"Half," I say at the same time AshLynn says, "We are."

"Different mothers," I add. He nods.

"They aren't going to be happy about this," I scold.

"It's not their decision now is it?" AshLynn says.

I scoff at that. Because once again she's thought nothing through all the way. I'm willing to bet she has no plan.

"Have you thought this through?" I ask, looking at both of them. Then, just at Mason. "You don't know this about her yet, but she never thinks anything through. She just assumes everyone around her will bend to make sure everything works out."

"Me?" AshLynn looks affronted. "What about you?"

"I think things through," I say.

"Oh yeah, what about buying this house? Did you think that one through? You don't even have any furniture, Wills. What the hell?"

She has a point.

Not that I'm going to tell her that.

"How about we table this discussion and maybe grab some dinner?" Mason makes an attempt at peace. I want to laugh at how naive that is. AshLynn and I have sibling rivalry down to an art form. We've been practicing her entire life. If there was a Super Bowl of bickering, we would win it.

AshLynn's phone rings. I can tell by the look on her face that it's her mother, Cassandra.

"I'll be right back," she says to us. And then into the phone, "Hi, Mommy."

She steps into the house, closing the door behind her. I can see her through the windows, pacing in my empty kitchen.

"I'd offer you something to eat," I say to Mason. "But all I really have is diet soda and chips."

"That's okay." He meets my eyes and smiles, like an apology and an invitation at the same time.

I want to swoon. He could power a small city with that smile, it's that electric.

Oh, and I'm that corny.

Jesus. Get a grip, Willow. It's your sister's fiancé.

Half sister.

"Is it, uh, is it hard being engaged long distance?" I ask.

His eyes widen.

"Uh," he starts.

"I'm sorry. I don't mean to put you on the spot. I'm just making conversation. Stupid conversation. Until AshLynn gets back. You don't need to answer that."

"No, it's fine. I just, you're right, I hadn't really expected the question. Caught me off guard is all."

I smile. And wait for him to answer my question.

"Oh." He startles. As if just remembering I'd asked one. "Right. Um, it is *not* hard being long distance. No."

"That's good."

"Yeah."

AshLynn opens the front door and comes back in. "So, did we say we wanted to have dinner?"

"I thought we had to go," Mason says standing. His stomach growls loudly. "Although, I guess I am hungry."

"Don't include me in your plans. You guys go ahead," I say, standing to go back in the house. "I'm hitting the shower, ordering a pizza, and then there's a Walking Dead marathon on Netflix with my name on it."

They follow me inside. "When will your furniture be back?" AshLynn asks at the same time Mason says, "Now that sounds like a good evening."

Again, I'm not sure which one I should respond to first. I go with AshLynn. "I don't have any furniture."

"Well, where are you living then?" Her brow is furrowed, and a small frown mars her face.

"Here."

"With no furniture?"

"I have a bed."

"That's it?"

"Yeah, I didn't want to get furniture until I knew what the house wanted, what felt right. Plus, I still need to redo the floors and paint the walls."

"When will that be finished?" AshLynn asks.

"When I finish it," I say.

"Don't you have people to do that?" AshLynn asks.

I laugh. "No. That's the whole point of renovating the house myself."

"How do you know what to do?"

"I don't. Not really. But I have my book." I point to the big orange home improvement how-to book. "And if I really get in a bind, there's YouTube and the hardware store."

"Wow," AshLynn says. "I thought Daddy was kidding when he said you were doing this."

"Nope." I swear I grow two feet taller when I say this, because I am proud as peaches of myself for doing this.

"That's awesome," Mason says at the same time AshLynn says, "You're crazy."

"You guys should take that act on the road," I tell them. Mason laughs. AshLynn stays confused.

"Okay, well, we might need to stay just a little bit longer than I thought," AshLynn hedges.

"How long?" I ask.

"Maybe overnight." She squeaks the last part of the sentence.

"Excuse me?" I say at the same time Mason says, "AshLynn, what the hell?"

7

————

MASON

She ignores us both. "So, which room is ours?" she asks instead.

"You're not staying here," Willow says at the same time I say, "I'm not staying here."

"Wait," AshLynn says to me, holding her palm up to my face. She turns to Willow. "You don't have a guest room for us to stay in?"

"AshLynn, I don't have any furniture!"

"You have a bed."

"For me!" Willow says.

This, whatever it is, has gone on long enough. I grab AshLynn's upper arm and spin her to face me. "You want to tell me what the hell is going on, AshLynn?" I ask gruffly, my body uncomfortably close to hers.

"We need to be here when . . ." She trails off, not finishing her sentence.

"When what, AshLynn?" Willow asks stepping almost in between us, glaring at her sister.

AshLynn avoids looking at us both.

She stays silent. I look at her. Then at Willow, who is also looking at her. Then back at her. She looks up finally, her eyes flit between the two of us.

"For when Mommy and Daddy get here," she mumbles.

"What the?" Willow says at the same time I say, "You've got to be fucking kidding me."

"Why are your parents—" Willow starts.

"Our parents," AshLynn interrupts.

"Our father, your mother." Willow sighs. "Why are they coming?"

"To meet Mason."

Willow nods slowly.

"No. Absolutely not. No way," I say.

"Hang on, Mason," AshLynn says.

I try my best to absorb this added information without losing my shit. "When are they coming?" I ask, ignoring her request to *hang on*.

"Now."

"AshLynn! You did this on purpose," Willow yells.

"Did what?" AshLynn asks.

"You arranged to be here at my house when they first meet him, on purpose, so I could act as a buffer for when they blow up at you." Willow is still yelling.

AshLynn at least has the decency to look ashamed. "No, I didn't."

I almost believe her.

Almost.

"I can't believe you, AshLynn," Willow continues yelling. "You do this all the time to me. I'm not your safety net when you're about to get in trouble. You are a grown woman, take responsibility for your actions."

"How could I possibly know we would end up here?" AshLynn lifts her chin and narrows her eyes.

"Because you called me and asked if you could come here," Willow says, narrowing her eyes back.

I see it all clearly now. AshLynn set this entire mother fucking thing up. She set me up, she set Willow up, and she just expects that we will all go through with it and bend to her will.

Which is exactly what you are doing.

I'm not sure if I'm angrier at myself or AshLynn.

She grabs at the front of my shirt. "Please," she whispers. "I'm so sorry. It's just, well, then they said they were coming to meet you and—"

"Coming to meet me?" I hiss. "This was just a ri—"

"I know, I'm sorry." To her credit, AshLynn does look sorry. "Please, just give me an hour."

I look to Willow. She is just as upset by this as I am.

"Fine." I flick my hand in the air and begin to pace the room. Willow does the same at the opposite end. Every few feet, we pass and she rolls her eyes or huffs at me.

"Look, would you guys chill?" AshLynn looks at Willow, then me, then Willow again. "It's no big deal. They are just coming to meet Mason. Anyway, I thought we were going to order pizza. Mason, didn't you suggest pizza?"

"Unbelievable." Willow shakes her head and sighs, giving AshLynn a dirty look. Then grabs her phone to order pizza. She asks for my favorite toppings.

"That sounds disgusting." She wrinkles her nose when I tell her. It's cute.

"Just trust me. I promise. If you don't like it, I will bring you your favorite pizza every day for a year."

She looks at me, brow furrowed, lips scrunched to the side. "Okay. I'll trust you."

I smile.

She smiles back. It's like the clouds part and for a moment the world is clear and sunny and bright. Her smile makes that much of an impact.

Jesus, Mason. You fucking sap. Get it together.

I volunteer to take P-Tink outside to get a minute to myself. It's one thing to be tricked into getting fake engaged on the spur of the moment, but it's a whole other thing to then start meeting someone's family as the fake fiancé.

I take a deep breath and let it out slowly at the same time a large sigh escapes P-Tink lounging next to me. She and I are sitting on the edge of the deck watching the water. I get the oddest feeling she is picking up on my mood. I've heard animals can do that, be in-tune to and match their owners' frames of mind. Except that I'm not her owner and I've just met this dog a couple hours ago, but I feel it anyway.

P-Tink yelps in response to my thoughts then shoves her head under my hand so I can pet her, completely validating everything I was just thinking. Sure enough, after petting her for a few minutes, I feel better about meeting the parents. And almost calm about this entire situation.

To say that Willow was pissed when AshLynn said her parents were coming is an understatement. The woman is clearly a force to be reckoned with as it is. But mad? She scared even me, and I've got a good five inches and eighty pounds on her.

But goddamn if she isn't sexy as fuck when she's mad.

Ease up on the sex thoughts, buddy.

The last thing I need is to get in between two sisters. Especially with parents on the way. I sigh heavily, amazed that I've let myself be dragged into this. P-Tink drops a squeaky ball at my feet.

"You want to fetch, girl?" I ask. She wags her tail in response. I throw the ball down the beach; she turns and races after it. But comes back a short time later with no ball.

"Where's your ball?" She looks at me, then paws at my thigh. "What's the matter? Can't find it?" She paws at my thigh again and yelps. "Okay, let's go get it." I walk down the beach in the direction I threw the ball. We find it quickly and I throw it back toward the house, P-Tink races after it again.

I turn to follow, glancing briefly at the house, and my world gets rocked.

Hard.

From this angle on the beach, I can see right into Willow's bedroom. The sheer drapes over her windows don't do much in the way of privacy. She's putting lotion on her naked body.

My feet won't move. Every thought in my brain is telling my feet to move, but they refuse to cooperate. My feet and my dick are in cahoots, both wanting to stay and watch the beautiful woman with the amazing body run her hands all over it. My cock hardens. I reach down to re-situate and have a strong impulse to leave my hand there and give myself a little rub.

Willow is long and lean. Oh, and flexible. Wow. I wouldn't have to bend half my body to kiss her. Or fuck her. She could wear heels and be right at eye level, or damn close. She is graceful when she walks around the room. I can't tell what she's doing, but I get alternate side and back views. That ass makes me want to kiss it and smack it simultaneously.

I watch her until she dresses.

This woman is going to kill me. In a good way.

Even though I don't get a front view, I know that I'll be dreaming of that body tonight. And quite a few more to come.

"What are you doing?"

I jump a good foot in the air and shriek like a little girl. AshLynn has her arms crossed over her chest looking at me with eyes narrowed.

"Uh," I say, still breathless from my voyeuristic jaunt. "We lost Princess Tinkerbell's ball."

"And, you thought you'd find it looking in my sister's bedroom?"

"Um." *Think, Mason, think.*

"Was it a good show, perv?"

Fuck.

"The pizza is here." She turns and walks back toward the house. I whistle for P-Tink and follow.

"Guess what Mason did?" AshLynn asks once we get inside.

Fuck. Fuck. Fuck.

"I—" I start.

"He lost the dog's ball." AshLynn smirks.

"Oh no, did you find it?" Willow asks.

I nod dumbly.

"Thank god," she continues. "She loves that thing. I don't know what we'd do if she lost it. I need to find a spare as backup just in case." P-Tink goes to stand beside her, Willow pets her head. The dog winks at me.

At least I think that's what happened. I must be more tired than I thought. I run my hand over my face.

Now what is AshLynn up to?

Willow is already taking a bite when I open the box.

She moans.

It's carnal.

"Sorry, I didn't realize I was so hungry," she says out of the side of her mouth.

The impact her moan has on me, on top of seeing her naked, moves me. Literally. Like my dick hardens, my heart swells, and suddenly having to pretend to be engaged to AshLynn just to spend time with Willow is totally worth it.

"Ohmigod, this is incredible. I love you for making me try it. I will never doubt you again. Marry me instead."

When she jokes that she loves me I want to say it back. When she teases with the marriage proposal, I want to shout yes. Which makes me an asshole of the highest degree. Lusting after the sister that you are *not* pretend engaged to does not sound like the beginnings of a story that will end well.

Fuck.

I need to come clean. Like now.

AshLynn yells that I'm already engaged.

Which might make this the perfect time to interject with the truth.

"Actually—" I start.

"Mason, want a beer?" AshLynn interrupts, wedging herself between Willow and me, and holding up a beer. The look on her face an odd combination of murderous and pleading.

Don't be stupid, Mason. What's another hour of this ruse for her parents? You've already come this far.

I nod, take the beer and three pieces of pizza to start. Then grab a seat outside to try and eat my rage and sexual frustration before her parents arrive.

8

WILLOW

There's nothing even remotely positive about my father and his wife coming to visit when my house is in disarray.

At least Mason cleaned up all the water.

I eat my pizza standing at the kitchen counter. Mason was right, it's a fantastic combination of toppings. I look around my house as I chew, trying to see it through my father's critical eye. It's not that he will disapprove per se. Oh hell, who am I kidding? That's exactly what it is. My dad likes things a certain way. And that way is typically finished and pretty. Rather, not in progress. So, for him, the idea that I am living in a house that has not already been renovated and remodeled is not an attractive one. Couple that with me doing the work myself and it's an abomination.

Daddy is all about the image. The better things look, the better they are. The more expensive something looks, the more money you must have. And he wants it all yesterday. Effort + time = results is not an equation he subscribes to. He likes the quick buck. The easy money. The quicker and easier the better. He was lucky to have married my mother, she had money to burn. So he did. Burn through it that is.

She loved him enough to believe in each of his ideas and schemes. Her faith in him never faltered. And it's not like every idea he has fails. Plenty have made him a lot of money. But per the law of averages, plenty of them have not. What has saved him financially is being the sole beneficiary of my mom's estate when she passed. A separate trust was set up for me, but he is the trustee. So, that's the money that he spent first. It's the primary way he has supported himself. That and his business dealings.

He likes to buy old buildings, shopping centers, stadiums, etc., tear them down and rebuild something newer and better. It's all about progression and gentrification. He justi-fies using my trust fund by saying it's in my benefit to accu-mulate more funds. Which is what his investments do. At least in theory they do. I've since learned that most of his actions were borderline, if not completely, illegal. Not that I'll do anything about it.

My thought is Granny Violet knew what he was doing and that's why she left me so much money herself. I never have to touch the money from my mom, my dad can keep it. Neither do my kids or my grandkids. But it angers both my father and Cassandra that Granny Violet didn't leave anything to AshLynn. Even though they were no relation. My father took my mother's name when they married because it was the more prestigious of the two. Plus, it made my mother's family happy. Especially Granny Violet (Brooks), my maternal grandmother. Since my mom's family was the one with all the money, my dad would do anything to make them happy.

All of which makes him sound like a bad guy, and he's not. I had a great childhood filled with fun times and happy parents. We did everything together. Right up until the day my mom died. Because that changed everything. As death tends to do, I suppose. Shortly after that is when my dad became more frenetic with his ministrations. No matter what he did, how much he made, how successful he was, it wasn't enough. He became obsessed with money, and at the same time more reckless with it. Taking chances that he never would have before. And he was way risky before. I feel sorry for him. I may not know what the hell I'm doing with my life, but at least I'm not living it on the edge and finding everything lacking.

As if summoned by the devil himself, I glance up as P-Tink barks and see a black town car coming up the drive. I look around the empty room out of habit, trying to find ahead of time whatever it will be that my stepmother will find fault with.

Hah! Nothing! The house is empty.

My father holds Cassandra's elbow as they walk up the front step, her heels click-click-clicking. Like a big segmented metal door coming down, slowly closing me off from the rest of my sanity and patience. They must have come straight from the airport, that's the only way to get here so fast. Before I'm ready for it, the doorbell rings.

"It's showtime, P-Tink." She yelps in response. I swear the dog understands me.

My father, as always, is dressed in a golf shirt and khakis. With Cassandra in what I consider to be typical Southlake second-wife attire: brightly colored, knee-length, skin-tight dress, flashy jewelry, designer bag, killer heels, and a hair weave.

My father enters the house. "There's my Willsy." Calling me by a nickname he hasn't used in years. It's bittersweet hearing it come from his lips now. He holds his arms out and I walk into his embrace for a hug. Which I cut short.

AshLynn squeals from behind me. "Daddy!" She, on the other hand, runs into his arms.

"Oh, my little girl is all grown up now. Engaged and everything. Where's the lucky guy?"

I look around for Mason, but don't see him anywhere.

"I think he's on the patio," I say. "I'll get him."

AshLynn and Cassandra immediately begin to titter about wedding-type things. And I slip outside.

"You are being summoned," I tell Mason.

He groans in response.

"They aren't so bad," I lie.

"It's just"—he pauses as if to gather his thoughts—"I was not expecting this, is all. And I feel blindsided."

"Well, that's AshLynn for you. If it helps, this happens to her all the time. Men lose their minds around her and are always at her beck and call."

God, why did I say that? There I go talking without thinking. Again. Way to insult the man and imply his fiancée is always surrounded by men.

She is always surrounded by men.

Not the point, Willow.

"I didn't—" he starts.

"I'm sorry," I interrupt. "I didn't mean for that to sound like she has been with a ton of men."

He waves his hand in the air. "It's fine. Don't worry about it. Really."

Mason stands and follows me into the house.

"There he is," Cassandra trills. "Oh, he's older than I thought, but still very good looking. Goodness, AshLynn, your kids are going to be beautiful." She rushes toward Mason and pulls him into her arms. He stands there stiffly, not returning the embrace.

"It is so lovely to meet you," Cassandra says.

Note to self, new guy is not much of a hugger.

My dad is up next. He too pulls Mason in for a hug. "Welcome to the family, son."

"Thank you, sir." Mason's face looks tortured from over my dad's shoulder, at this angle I'm the only one who can see him.

We stand there and look at one another in that awkward way that only family can manage. My father strolls around the room, taking everything in, then peeks down the hall.

"Gotta say, it's a cool house, kid," my father says as he comes back in the room. "You done good."

"Thanks."

"Looks like a lot of work, though." He grimaces.

"I got time." I smile.

"You always were the strong one," he says. "Just like your mother."

"Thanks, Dad." My heart warms when he says that. It's not often I get a compliment from him. Let alone one that means so much to me.

Cassandra bristles. She always does when my father mentions my mom, who died when I was eight years old. I was in the car with her when it happened, riding in the backseat. We were on our way home from dinner and a movie. My father had met us at the restaurant straight from work and was in his own car behind us. We'd gone to a French restaurant and then to see the movie *Madeline*, my favorite book series.

We did it at least once a month, dinner and a movie with a theme. The night before my father had brought home berets for all of us to wear. As an adult, looking back I know my parents were awesome for giving me such experiences. As an eight-year-old at the time I just remember feeling fancy and sophisticated.

My mom and I were hit by a drunk driver in a head-on collision. She died in minutes, all the while telling me not to worry and that she loved me. I walked away without a scratch. Physically anyway. It took fifteen years of therapy to be able to talk about it without breathing into a paper bag. Which is why AshLynn likes to call me broken. And maybe I am. I know pieces of both my father and me died that night with my mom.

Dad married Cassandra two years later. A year after that AshLynn was born. At first it was great, but it didn't take long for me to realize I was a hurtful reminder to my father of the great love he had lost. It started with matching dresses for *his three girls*. I hated it. Cassandra and AshLynn loved it. They'd still do it to this day if they could get away with it. Now they can't even wear the same dress twice, let alone the same dress as each other.

Then came the slip-ups, when he would call me AshLynn. Or bring me her favorite ice cream as a treat instead of mine. Or buy the two of them presents because they *were easier to buy for* than I was, and I could just pick something out of a catalog, right? I let it all slide, because grown-ups make mistakes. And my dad had faced a horrible loss, same as me.

But when he told me I had to celebrate Mother's Day with Cassandra instead of going with my Granny Violet to my mother's gravesite, I about lost my mind. It took the paramedics twice the recommended dosage of Ativan to get my panic attack under control enough to get me to the hospital.

After that, my father loosened up a bit about pushing Cassandra and AshLynn on me. But Cassandra hadn't *signed up* for a moody tween who didn't want her around. So, she made her preference of her own daughter exceedingly clear. I responded in kind and got a little lost in the shuffle. We've been a messed-up family ever since.

"Willow, do you have coffee?" Cassandra asks.

"I made some fresh, right before you arrived," I tell her, proud of myself for remembering.

"I see there are no furnishings, do you at least have mugs?"

"In the kitchen. Cupboard to the left of the fridge."

"Would you like a cup, Jonathan?" she asks my father. He nods in response.

Cassandra gets their coffee and comes back in to the room. "Let's talk about this engagement, shall we? Willow, a place to sit, please?"

Because I can conjure this stuff up with my Magic 8 Ball?

"I've got patio furniture," I say, gesturing toward the back patio.

"We're going to sit on the patio?" Cassandra asks.

"That's where I've got places to sit," I tell her.

"Are the seats . . . clean?" she asks.

"Do you mean free of dirt, or something else?" I smirk.

"It will be fine," my dad interjects. "I'll grab one of those towels and lay it down for you, Cassandra."

I refrain from telling Cassandra that she'll be sitting on a towel that mopped up dirty water from an equally dirty floor. That'll be my little secret. Which makes me smile.

9

———

MASON

WE FILE OUTSIDE, FOLLOWING MRS. BROOKS' NOT-SO-SUBTLE suggestion. Willow has some kick-ass patio furniture, I'll give her that. All teak wood with big soft cushions, and hella comfortable. We sit at an umbrella-covered table for six. The chair I choose is a rocker, giving me the opportunity to lean back slightly, which is always nice since inevitably my legs will hit the person across from me when sitting at a table such as this.

I've gathered from earlier conversation that her name is Cassandra and his is Jonathan. And that I should have already known that somehow.

"Okay, so I took the liberty of making a list on our way here of everything that needs to get done before the wedding," Cassandra says. "I found a website online that is just fantastic for things like this. And they have a countdown with deadlines of when all those things should be finished by before the big day."

Uh, excuse me?

"Now, I would have done a mock-up of the invitations, but I didn't know Brian's last name," Cassandra continues.

Brian? Wait, is she pretend marrying me or pretend marrying her ex? Or is he her boyfriend? What do you call the guy who refuses to propose and then strands you at a hotel two thousand miles from home?

"His name is Mason," AshLynn corrects Cassandra.

"You said his name was Brian," Cassandra says.

"Why would I say his name was Brian when his name is Mason?" AshLynn asks. "Maybe Daddy got it confused and then told you wrong."

"Well, that does sound like something I would do," Mr. Brooks says. "Sorry, Bri— err, Mason."

I nod. "Are invitations necessary?" I ask the table at large.

"Well, of course," Cassandra says. "Time is of the essence. We don't have a minute to waste. The invitations have to go out immediately."

"And why is that exactly?" I ask.

"People could already have plans. And we want as many people there as possible."

"Right." I draw out the word.

"You didn't give us a lot of time to prepare," Cassandra says.

"And how much time is that?" My voice sounds strained.

"Three weeks," Cassandra says.

My head spins. I want to throw up.

I scoot my chair back and put my head between my knees.

"That's so cute that he's got the jitterbugs. Isn't that cute, AshLynn?"

"Yep, that's my Mason for you," AshLynn says.

"Uh, AshLynn, can I talk to you a moment?" I ask weakly.

"But we have so much to discuss here, with my parents," she says.

I clear my throat and straighten. "Now, please."

She nods and follows me into the house and out the front door. I force her to sit on the brick planter surrounding the big maple tree and begin to pace.

"What—" I've got to get my thoughts together before I just start firing questions. She had to have a good reason for doing all of this. Right?

"I can't—" I don't finish that thought either. So, I just ask the hardest question first.

"Why are you doing this, AshLynn?"

"Doing what?"

I pinch the bridge of my nose and squeeze my eyes shut. I'm not going to yell. But I am going to get some fucking answers.

"Why are you pretending that I am your fiancé and why does your family think we are getting married in three weeks?"

She sighs. Like my questions are a huge inconvenience to her.

"Because that's what I told them happened."

"I get that part," I say. "Why did you tell them that?"

She shrugs. "That's what they were expecting to hear."

What in the actual fuck?

"Okay, let me try this a different way," I say. "Why am I involved in this?"

"Where is it that you're confused, Mason? I told them we were engaged and getting married in three weeks."

"Why?"

"I told you, I'd thought Brian was going to propose, it's all I'd been talking about, so they were expecting it."

"And they hadn't met Brian before?"

"No. I met Brian in Cabo at Hildy's bachelor/bachelorette weekend."

"Cabo San Lucas? As in Mexico?"

"Is there another Cabo?" She blinks her eyes at me as though I'm the poor communicator here.

"So, you met him in Cabo, and then he went to the wedding with you?"

"He was in the wedding, same as me."

"And when were you in Cabo?"

"Two weeks ago."

"Let me get this straight." I take a deep breath to calm myself. Because surely, I've just entered another dimension into the Twilight Zone. Either that or someone is playing one hell of a practical joke. Those can be the only explanations.

Close my eyes. Count to ten. Continue. "You met a guy—"

"Brian."

"You met Brian two weeks ago in Cabo during a party weekend."

"Yes."

"And you thought he was going to propose at the wedding you were both in after two weeks?"

"Now you sound like that bitch bridesmaid, Marci. She said the same thing. You don't get it. We were into each other. Like, big-time. I spent the last two weeks with him. I went home after Cabo for a couple days, told my parents we'd fallen in love, and that he was going to propose at Hildy's wedding. Then packed all my stuff and flew out to surprise him."

"And he was okay with that?"

"He loved it. I'm telling you. Into. Each. Other."

"So, why did he leave you at the wedding?"

She waves her hand in the air. "He said I needed to go home. That it was too soon."

I think I'm starting to understand. The whole family is fuck-nuts crazy.

Except for Willow.

I hope.

"Which is where I come in?" I confirm.

"Yes," she says with a huff.

"You understand I have no intention of marrying you, right?"

"Duh. And gross. You're . . . old." She looks repulsed.

And enjoy your moment of humility there, Mason.

"So, how do you see this playing out then?"

She shrugs. "We'll break up."

"When?"

She looks around and shrugs again. "I don't know, soon?"

"And what happens tonight?"

"We'll probably go to a hotel." She could have easily added a *duh* at the end of that sentence as well.

"And stay in the same room?"

"I don't know. I guess." She huffs again. "I don't have all the answers here. It's no big deal."

I nod. Still not quite believing I'm in this situation.

"Staying in the same room is no big deal?" I confirm.

She nods.

"I'm not doing this, AshLynn. It's ridiculous. I agreed to give you a ride to Seattle and this has already gone *way* beyond that."

"Oh, you're doing this, Mason."

"What makes you think—"

"Otherwise, I'll tell my family right now that you were spying on Willow when she was naked in her room. Pretty sure that's a felony when I tell them you were also rubbing one out at the same time."

"I was not!"

"Maybe. But who are they going to believe?"

Fuck.

Fuck.

And fuck.

"Fine. How long do I have to do this for?"

"Until I break up with you for cheating on me."

"I don't cheat."

"Of course you do."

"I draw the line there, AshLynn."

She sighs and rolls her eyes. "How about still in love with your ex?"

"How about we just decided it was too soon?"

She flicks her hand in the air. "Fine. Whatever."

"How long are we continuing this?" I ask. "By that I mean a literal deadline, how many days?"

"A couple days at most."

I nod. "Next time you want to uproot my life like this, could you give me some warning?"

"There won't be a next time." She pauses a moment. "Are we through?"

"Yes. By all means, let's go back in there so we can keep planning the pretend fucking wedding."

"Great."

I follow her back through the house and out to the deck.

"Did you two sneak away for a little alone time?" Cassandra gives us a simpering smile.

"He can't keep his hands off me," AshLynn says.

"Okay, well, while you were gone, I found a couple venues I want to show you and I emailed that caterer we used for the gala last year, do you remember the one that was so good?"

"Oh, yes, I loved their food." AshLynn nods.

I sit back and let the ladies continue with their drivel. Indulging in a quick little flashback to Willow putting lotion on. I peek at her from under my lashes. She has her eyes shut. In fact, if I'm not mistaken, she's asleep. Her head does that quick dip before snapping back up. She opens her eyes and looks around. Only to shut them again.

Watching her makes me smile.

I grab my phone and check my email while we're waiting. I have a buddy looking for some help on a renovation he's doing, I make a note to answer him later. I have a group of friends and we all renovate homes either to keep for investment, or to flip. We do the work ourselves and will often get together to help one another if a project is large. Somehow it ends up being an equal exchange amongst us, or if it's not, no one has complained about it.

I won the Washington State Lottery when I was nineteen. Not the super big one, but I still walked away with about seven hundred thousand in cash. A friend of my mom's gave me the best advice of my life. He said, *Give yourself five percent to fuck around with and put the rest away for six months. Then use it to acquire appreciating assets. Only. Live off the income; you'll never work a day in your life.*

So, after I quickly blew ten thousand fucking around with my friends, I bought a motorcycle, and socked away the rest, not even blowing the full five percent. I sat on it for months, making plan after plan, running through scenario after scenario. Ultimately deciding after six months to buy the old building my mom's bookstore was in. One, so she no longer had to pay rent, and two, so I could collect rent from others. Three stories with two commercial spaces on the ground floor and four residential spaces split between the second and third floors.

It took me a long time to fix up the apartments, one at a time with a huge learning curve and a lot of trial and error. Unlike what Mom's friend had said, it was hard fucking work. But I enjoyed it and as I finished renovating each living space, they rented fast.

Second thing I did was buy the house I grew up in just outside of Seattle, WA, and moved my mom to an upscale condominium with a water view. Once I finished renovating the commercial building, I fixed up the house, and sold it at a nice profit. Which allowed me to buy two more houses and do the same thing. And so on.

I got lucky. I bought a lot of property in a down market and I took my time renovating, some I sold and some I kept. But the result is, I own nine single-family homes and three commercial buildings free and clear, all of which I rent out. All are around the Seattle area, near my mom, and thanks to the city's popularity I make a decent profit. I live modestly and invest soundly. Which allows me to travel most of the time when I'm not working. Recently, I was in Los Angeles for five months renovating a triplex with a buddy of mine.

Which is how I find myself free as a bird and homeless now. The only reason why AshLynn is able to blackmail me into this.

I have nowhere else to be.

10

WILLOW

AshLynn and Cassandra prattle on about wedding things for another half an hour. My dad sits silently sipping his coffee, which has to be cold by now, Mason is doing something on his phone, and I am falling asleep in my chair.

"Can we pick this riveting conversation back up in the morning?" I ask the table at large. "I've had a long day and I'm really tired."

"Well, sure, because you are the only one who has a bed," AshLynn says. "What are the rest of us supposed to do?"

"There are a few hotels in the area. And more over in Seattle."

"I'd like us to meet in the morning. There's a club just down the way, I'm sure they have a nice sit-down brunch. And probably, sister hotels. I'll make a couple calls," my dad says standing and going into the house.

I sneak my phone out of my pocket to text Zach.

ME: I've been ambushed.

ZACH: My god, what has happened?

ME: My family is here.

ZACH: Define "family" ...

ME: Dad, Cassandra, AshLynn, AND her fiancé.

My phone buzzes in my hand.

Zach.

"Hang on," I say. I step out to the beach and down a bit from the house so I won't be overheard. P-Tink follows close behind me.

"Hey," I answer.

"Oh, it's worse than I thought," he says.

"No. It's fine. I'm just surprised is all."

"Liar."

"How do you do that?"

"I know you, Willicent, better than you know yourself."

I sigh. Mostly because he's right.

"I'm a little shook up about AshLynn getting married."

"Oh, lord have mercy, the poor man."

"That's about what I said."

"So, who is he? A Palmer? A Lynch? One of the Abbott boys?" he asks, naming a few of the more affluent families from our area of Texas. "Oh no, please tell me it isn't that slimy, but hot, Campbell boy that she used to date?"

"I still can't believe you thought he was good looking."

"Sweetheart, *everyone* but you found him attractive."

"Hmm. Well, not him either. This is a new guy. Someone she just met."

"Ah, to be young and impulsive again. Tell me, is this new man pleasing to the eye?"

"He's okay."

He gasps dramatically. "You want to bone him."

"Girls don't bone."

"You want him to bone you."

"No, I don't."

"Oh, Willicent, don't lie to me. It's a waste of breath."

"You know I hate the name Willicent. Willow, Wills, Willsy, all fine. Willicent is weird."

"Not true, you like it because I'm the only one who uses it. That and Willimena. Plus, your family calls you both Wills and Willsy and you hate it."

"Not when my dad uses it."

"Agree to disagree."

I can picture him flicking his hand in the air to disregard my response.

"Now," he continues, "describe the man you want to bone you. Leave no luscious detail out."

"I never said I want him to bone me."

"It was implied."

"Can we stop using the word bone?"

"When's the last time you got laid, again?"

"Point taken."

I hate that he knows me so well.

"Thank you. Now, tell Zachy all about the pretty boy."

"Tall. Like still four or five inches taller than me."

"And you're an Amazon."

"Exactly. Brown hair, that looks a little tousled. Brown eyes, huge smile, salt-and-pepper beard, broad shoulders, muscles everywhere."

"Yummy. Is he older?"

"I don't think so. I got the impression he's early to mid-thirties with premature gray in the facial hair."

"Full head of hair?"

"Yes."

"Is he a bear? Maybe I should take him?"

"I haven't seen him shirtless. I don't know. And it doesn't matter because he's engaged to my sister—"

"Half sister."

"And therefore, off-limits to us both."

"Things could get sticky if you lust after your sister's husband. What was that movie where the man was having an affair with his son's wife?"

"Fiancée."

"Not you, the movie."

"In the movie, it was the son's fiancée, not wife."

"Oh."

"Damage."

"That's right! Juliette Binoche. That woman is almost enough to make a gay man want to be straight."

"Can we focus, please?"

"Yes."

"They are all spending the night on the island. And my dad wants us to meet for brunch at *the club* in the morning."

"You have a club?"

"He can sniff those places out with remarkable accuracy."

"Hmm. Not a talent I'd want, but not a bad talent to have I suppose."

"So, I'm going to need you to go with us." I lower the proverbial hammer hoping Zach is in a generous mood.

"I'm pretty sure I'm busy tomorrow. Really busy."

"Come on, Zach, please?"

Silence.

"Don't make me go alone. Please. I'm begging you."

More silence.

"I'll be a fifth wheel if you don't come. And you know how much I hate being any numbered wheel."

"Fine. But you owe me."

"Thank you! Thank you! Thank you! I'll do anything, just name it."

"Perfect. You're my new tango partner on Tuesday nights."

Shit. Next to electricity, the only other thing I avoid at all costs is dancing.

Just. Kill. Me. Now.

"Shall I take a water taxi over now or in the morning?" he asks.

"Morning is fine. But first thing, okay?"

"First thing," he repeats.

"Thank you, Zach. You are the best friend a girl could ever hope to have."

"I know."

We disconnect the call and I make my way back to my deck.

"There you are," my dad says. "We have a couple rooms just down the way as well as brunch reservations at ten o'clock. Does that work?"

"Yes," I say. "I'll meet you there."

We say our goodbyes and within a few minutes, I am blissfully alone.

I turn to switch off the lights and see Mason's baseball cap on the kitchen counter. I pick it up. Of course, it's a Seattle Seahawks hat. The people in Seattle are crazy about their Seahawks. And not even just Seattle, it's all the surrounding areas and counties as well. I place it on my head, it drops low over my eyes.

He has a big head.

Which makes me think maybe his *other head* is big too, making me giggle.

And that is how Mason walks in on me when he returns for his hat.

"Oh." I pull the hat from my head. "I was just—"

Just what, Willow?

"Stealing my hat?" He smiles. My face heats. "You a fan?" he asks.

"I'm not much of a Seahawks fan, I'm afraid."

He gasps and places his hand over his heart. "If not the 'hawks, then who?"

"Um, no one, really."

"You don't watch football?" he asks.

"I don't really understand it, to be honest."

"I'll explain it to you."

"Now?"

Because I'd be fine with that. You can stay.

"No." He laughs again. "Next home game, we'll get nachos and beer and I'll teach you the ropes. What do you say?"

I say yes!

Wait—is he asking me out?

"AshLynn isn't really one for sports," I say.

His face falls.

If I'm not mistaken, I think he forgot about her.

A car horn sounds from outside.

"Speak of the devil," he mumbles.

I hand him his hat. His fingers brush against mine as he takes it from me. A shiver runs through me.

"I'd better go," he says. "I'll, uh, see you tomorrow?"

"See you tomorrow."

P-Tink follows him to the door and whimpers after he leaves.

"I know what you mean, P-Tink. I feel the same way."

11

MASON

"Do you know if your dad got us a room with two beds?" I ask AshLynn.

"I don't know why he would," she says.

"I'm not sleeping in the same bed as you, AshLynn."

"As if I would even let you."

"You say that like you are taking the bed if there's only one."

"I am."

"You don't automatically get the bed."

"Of course I do."

"We can flip for it."

"My dad is paying for it."

She has a point.

"I can just as easily pay for it."

She shrugs. Which seems to be her favorite reaction to most things I say. Her version of: *Fuck you, Mason. No one cares what you think.*

We reach the hotel and check in. Say goodnight to her parents, and head to our room.

With one bed.

Fuck.

But there is an armchair with a footstool, so I'm in luck. If you consider sleeping on a chair to be lucky. I brush my teeth, find the extra blankets, and settle in to my chair.

Meanwhile, AshLynn is still unpacking her bathroom supplies. The girl has more bottles of lotions and potions than I've ever seen. It takes her almost thirty minutes to prepare for bed. I'm nearly asleep when she exits the bathroom and turns all the lights back on to get into bed.

"Did you need to turn them all on?" I ask squinting.

"Yes, I did. I don't want to trip over anything. Now close your eyes, I'm taking my robe off. I already know how much you like to perv on naked girls."

Don't comment, Mason. Just keep quiet.

I do as instructed, waiting until the lights are off to open them. "I go for a run first thing in the morning, just so you know."

"If you wake me, I will kill you."

"Then who would you have to blackmail into being your fake fiancé?"

"Fine, I'll make your life hell then."

"Already accomplished, *dear*."

"Well, then my work here is mostly done. I hope you don't sleep well, Mason."

"Ditto, AshLynn. Ditto."

I SLEEP RELATIVELY WELL CONSIDERING I was in a chair all night. But I definitely wake up feeling sore and cramped everywhere. AshLynn, on the other hand, is completely spread out in the king-size bed, sleep mask over her eyes, ear plugs in, and one of those nasal strips over her nose.

I grab my bag and tiptoe into the bathroom to change. I looked up running routes last night on an app I have, and there's a three-mile trail just down the way. It loops around close to Willow's house—not that I expect to see her, but one can only hope. I grab a bottle of water and slip out of the room, stretching in the hall before heading out.

The run to the trail doesn't take long, and it's quiet. There aren't any people out on the streets yet, the sun is barely up. I feel my muscles start to loosen as my body warms. I put my earbuds in and find a playlist to run to. Metal is my favorite on mornings like this when I have a lot of angst and frustration to work through.

I checked and Ashlynn is right, it is a felony to spy on someone for sexual interest or gratification in the state of Washington. If she says she caught me jacking off, I'm screwed. It doesn't get any more "sexually interested" than that. I'm not entirely sure how she would prove it. But she's also not someone I'd want to go up against not knowing that. Practicality is not her strong point.

I reach the trails and pick up my pace. My average is a six-minute mile, but I go a little slower since I'm not familiar with this trail and I don't want to trip on a branch or rock. One song bleeds into another as I find my groove. Sweat dripping from my face and body, my lungs expanding, legs pumping. It's times like this I wish I had a dog. Maybe it's time to get one, no reason why I couldn't bring it to jobsites with me.

P-Tink would love this trail.

Get the dog and its owner out of your mind.

But—

Doesn't matter. You already perved your way out of a chance with her. She thinks you're engaged to her sister.

Half sister.

Like it matters.

I slow to a walk to get some water before starting up again. While I enjoy these little talks with myself, I know that I'm right in that I don't stand a chance with Willow. The sooner I accept that, the better off I will be.

Sprint.

Sprints will clear your head.

I check the app, I have another mile and a half of the trail before turning back.

I sprint the remainder of the way to the end of the trail before pausing to catch my breath. There's a small clearing at the end, surrounded by trees, with a couple benches for people to rest on. I walk in small circles so I stay moving, get some water, pull my shirt off to wipe the sweat from my face and tuck it into the band of my shorts instead of putting it back on.

I take the route back at an easier pace if for no other reason than to prolong my time out here alone. It's quiet and relaxing, which makes it easy to think. I've yet to come up with a way to get myself out of this mess aside from blackmailing AshLynn back with something. She said that we'd be breaking up soon, so I'm hopeful that by soon she means today.

I'm not at all interested in meeting them for breakfast except that it will be a way to see Willow again.

My god, man. You've got it bad for this girl.

I don't know that I have it bad so much as she intrigues me. I want to know everything there is about her. I want to know her thoughts and dreams, the music she likes, her favorite foods, what makes her happy and more importantly what makes her sad. I want to count the freckles on her face. Hell, I want to count the freckles on her body. I want to know if she sunburns easily, her favorite ice cream flavor, if she likes flowers or chocolate better as an impromptu gift.

Otherwise known as having it bad.

I want to find out if she moans during sex the way she did with the pizza. How she tastes, what gets her off . . .

Slow down, tiger. You're sporting wood.

Shit, difficult as fuck to jog with a hard-on.

Mom. Taxes. Roadkill.

I think of things to expel any sexual interest coursing through my body.

It works.

I'm a short distance from the beginning of the trail when I hear howling. Followed by something crashing through the brush. I stop and look around, but don't see anything. Including the dog that flies through the air and hits me at the chest, knocking us both to the ground, before it proceeds to lick my face.

"P-Tink?"

12

WILLOW

Morning comes early. P-Tink drags me out of bed as the sun is coming up so we can go on our morning walk/run. I run, she walks. But only because my running pace is still too slow for her. There are trails near the house that we go to, which she loves. I'd let her run free, but I don't yet trust her with squirrels or other such wildlife that we may encounter along the way.

We reach the path and she immediately begins howling.

"P-Tink, quiet!" I tug on her leash to get her attention. The last thing I need is her waking all the neighbors at oh dark thirty. She stops howling and pauses to sniff at a tree. I use the time to adjust my earbuds and change the music I'm listening to. The leash slips. P-Tink takes off running, howling as she goes.

"Dammit, Janet!" I take off after her, going as fast as I can without killing myself.

I round a corner in the trail and run smack-dab into a wall of sweaty flesh.

"Ooof!" I bounce back. Strong arms prevent me from falling on my butt. P-Tink bounces around me yelping. My hands rest on the chest in front of me. The bare chest of minimal hair and maximum muscle. I look up the chest, to the neck, and finally the face.

"Mason?"

"You okay?" he asks, his hands still on my arms. My bare arms. My hands are on his bare chest, his hands are on my bare arms. All I can think about is how good it would feel if everything were bare. All of him with all of me, bare skin against bare skin, my body warms from the middle and up.

"Willow?" he asks again, using one hand to push the loosened hair from my face, his eyes search mine. "Are you okay?"

I nod, not looking away.

"What are you doing here?" I ask finally.

"I was running until P-Tink came in for a blind tackle," he laughs.

That shakes me out of my brief fantasy.

"Oh gosh, are you okay?" I ask, looking him up and then down.

Big mistake.

His torso is long, and his shorts are not. He has something close to a six-pack with a light trail of hair leading down into his shorts. Those v-things that only guys in movies have mirror one another on either side of his hips. I can see the outline of his penis in his shorts. And his legs are beautiful.

Lean with perfectly shaped calves, big muscular thighs, light smatterings of hair.

My god, is nothing on this man flawed? My mouth waters. Literally.

Why does AshLynn get the good ones?

Ha—not nearly enough body hair to interest Zach. I smirk to myself.

"Fell on my ass, I'm fine," he says.

"Oh no, are you sure you're okay, let me see?" I spin him around and am brushing dirt and leaves from his bare back and covered bottom before I realize what I'm doing. I gasp, step back, cover my mouth with my hand, and close my eyes.

I hear him turn, but I keep my eyes closed. Which he mistakes for something else.

"You sure *you're* okay?" he asks.

"Uh huh, yep, just groped my sister's fiancé, but hey, no biggie, right."

"Half sister," he says.

I open my eyes, he's smiling. So, I do too. "Half sister," I repeat.

"It will be our little secret," he says.

I nod.

"You want some company on your walk?" Mason asks.

"Oh, uh, I should probably get back," I say.

"Weren't you just starting your walk?"

"Yeah, but we've got brunch, and I don't want to be late . . ."

He looks at his watch. "Not for another three and a half hours. Come on, I'll walk with you, but you have to let me hold the leash." He winks.

I blush.

We walk in silence for a while. It's a comfortable silence. Just enjoying the sound of the breeze in the leaves and the birds in the trees. P-Tink is back and forth across the path sniffing and pawing different things, her tail wagging constantly. Every so often, his arm brushes against mine. I like the way it feels.

You are playing with fire, Willow.

I can hear both Zach and my inner critic chastising me. So, I silence them both and continue on with my walk. We reach the end of the trail and take a seat for a minute on the benches.

"You already reached this part once today, huh?" I ask him.

"Yeah, but it's okay, I need the extra exercise."

"I don't see why," I scoff, gesturing to his body.

"My muscles were all cramped this morning and needed loosening. A nice walk after a run is perfect for that."

"Wear yourself out last night, huh?" I pretend to joke and elbow him. Regretting immediately that I've said anything. I don't want to know if he wore himself out. Maybe he and AshLynn aren't sleeping together. That would be the best scenario.

For who?

For me, duh.

"No, I slept in a chair."

Oh, thank god.

Wait, why would he sleep in a chair?

I look at him, brow furrowed. "Why did you sleep in a chair?"

He looks guilty. "Uh," he starts but doesn't finish his thought.

"Did you guys get in a fight?" I ask hoping that's not the case.

Actually, that's a lie, I totally hope that's the case.

"Yeah," he says. "We got into a fight."

Yes!

"Sorry," I say not meaning a word of it. "Is everything better now that it's morning?"

"She wasn't awake when I left, so I'm not sure."

"Do you want to talk about it?" I ask.

Please say no. I don't want to give you advice about AshLynn.

"I appreciate it, but no. I'd rather talk about you."

"Me?" My voice squeaks slightly, I clear my throat. "Or, we could talk about you."

"I'm boring," he says.

"I doubt that," I tell him.

"My idea of a good time is hanging out at home, making a nice dinner, and maybe watching a movie."

"Mine too!"

"No way," he says with a small smile.

"What's your favorite dinner to make?" I ask.

"I grill."

"He grills," I mimic in a baritone.

"Anything you want I can figure out a way to grill or smoke."

"Anything?"

He nods.

"Pasta?"

"I do a mean mac-n-cheese in the smoker."

"No way, how?"

"Trade secret." He winks.

My panties flood.

Must maintain distance from this irresistible man.

Right. Okay.

I stand and prepare to head back. "We should go back, I guess. Right?"

He looks disappointed. "Uh, sure. I guess."

Then, much to my dismay, puts his shirt back on. We take our time walking back to the trailhead, I savor every minute.

Zach is at my house when I get back. He's made a pot of coffee and is sitting on the back deck sipping a cup. P-Tink runs to say hello to him.

"How's my beautiful baby?" he coos to her. She yelps in return and rolls on her back, so he can rub her belly.

"Did you guys go for a walk?" he asks before looking at me.

"Yep." I take a seat next to him with my own cup of coffee.

He looks over at me. "Ohmigod. What did you do?"

"Nothing. What do you mean? We went for a walk."

He studies me. "No, something else happened."

I avoid his gaze. "Nothing else happened."

How is he psychic like this?

He looks at me. I look at him.

"We ran into Mason. But that's not a something."

"Mason?"

"AshLynn's fiancé."

"Oh, the one you want to bone you."

I roll my eyes. "I don't want him—"

"Don't lie. How did he look?"

"When I say we ran into him, well, I mean literally. I almost knocked myself over chasing after P-Tink."

"She got loose?"

"Yes, and went straight for him."

"Did you know he was there?"

"No, how could I?"

He shrugs.

I sigh. "He didn't have his shirt on when it happened."

"Oooh, and . . ."

"Not your type. Beautiful. But too little body hair for you to get excited about."

"He was shirtless when you ran into him? Was he sweaty?" Zach smiles big. "Did he get his sweat on you?"

I blush and groan. "Yes."

"I like it. And then what?"

"And then we walked back through the trail and I came home."

"Liar!"

"We talked."

"About?"

"I don't know. Favorite way to spend an evening, ice cream, movies, I don't know, stuff."

"He's trying to find out what you like."

I wish.

"No, he's not."

"Trust me. Men do not ask women about their favorite anything unless they want to know for a reason."

"He was just making conversation."

Zach waves his hand in the air, dismissing my statement.

"He's engaged to AshLynn," I argue.

"They've been engaged for a hot minute. It will never last," Zach counters.

A girl can only hope.

"Don't be that way, Zach. It's not nice."

"Nice? Have you met your half sister? I'm a realist, baby."

"I don't know, I think she's really into him."

"Puh-lease." He rolls his eyes.

I look at him, pleading with him to see my side of things. Otherwise he'll just get my hopes up and then I'll be disappointed. And I really hate being disappointed.

"Fine," he says. "I will give you my assessment after breakfast once I've seen them interact in person."

"I'm going to take a shower."

"Yes, please, stinky exercise girl."

"Ohmigod, do I smell bad?" If I do and Mason smelled me, I will never recover. Not ever. I raise my arm to sniff my pit. It's not bad. Not great either though. It was that damn run after P-Tink. Mason was running, how come he didn't stink?

Because he's perfect.

"Not funny, Zach," I tell him.

"Hurry along anyway, I'll be here planning all the ways you can make it up to me when I'm right about Mason being into you."

I wave my hand over my head and disappear into the house.

Brain, you have been overruled and are instructed to disregard that last statement as it does not apply.

Right?

13

MASON

AshLynn is still asleep when I return to the hotel. I take pleasure in *accidentally* slamming the bathroom door as I head in to take a shower. Then I use the wireless speakers to play music while I'm in there. Both of which should ensure she wakes up. I know its petty, but I'm mad at her.

Still.

And I slept in a chair.

I make sure the door is locked, then pull up my blues playlist and turn up the volume. Kenny Wayne Shepherd comes on and I sing along as I step under the stream of hot water. Less than a minute later, AshLynn pounds on the door asking me to turn it down.

"Will do, sorry about that," I yell back without changing the volume. I think back to this morning with Willow as I'm soaping up. I liked her hands on my chest when she ran into me. I also liked the way she checked me out since my shirt was off. It makes me wonder if I will be able to redeem myself once she finds out this entire stupid engagement is a complete farce.

I hope AshLynn plans to come clean soon. I can't imagine that it's easy or fun for her to continue the charade, she doesn't benefit from it. If anything, the longer she carries on, the worse it will be when she finally admits it was all made up.

Though, maybe it won't bother Willow at all and she will agree to go on a date with me. She kind of agreed to go to a ball game in a roundabout way. I don't care what we do. I'll do whatever she wants. As long as she'll spend time with me. I just want to get to know her better.

What would life be like with her in it? Falling asleep with her in my arms, waking up to that beautiful face. Taking her in the shower, she faces the wall with that gorgeous butt thrust back at me while I pound into her from behind. Pushing her to her knees in front of me, big green eyes blinking up right before she takes my cock into her mouth.

I groan.

My dick gets hard. I pull on it roughly, envisioning it's Willow sucking me off. Her red hair wet and slicked back, luscious lips wrapped around me, one hand at the base of my cock to trail her mouth, the other tugging lightly on my balls. Grabbing her cheeks and fucking her face, watching my jizz hit her chest before the water from the shower washes it away.

Oh god.

Her long, lean body pressed tight against mine. Her creamy thighs wrapped around my waist. I've got her pinned against the wall, fucking her slowly as she moans my name. Feeling her muscles spasm around me as she finds her release.

So hot.

Before I realize it, I'm the one moaning *her* name as I pump out everything I have, my cock jerking in my grip. I lean one hand against the wall to support myself, breathing heavily. The shower feels uncomfortably hot all of a sudden. I turn the water to cold and let it shock me out of my fantasy and back to reality.

AshLynn pounds on the door again. "Hurry up or I won't have time to get ready."

I finish up and step out of the shower, grabbing a towel and wrapping it around my waist before stepping out of the bathroom. Steam floods into hotel room.

"Finally, jeez. What were you doing in there?"

"Jerking off," I tell her.

"What. Ever," she says rolling her eyes. AshLynn locks herself in the bathroom and I hear the shower start anew.

Judging from the coffee set-up on the table, I see she ordered from room service not bothering to ask me if I wanted anything. I pick up the coffee carafe, happy to discover there is still coffee in it, then grab an unused mug and pour myself some. The coffee smells good and fresh, without that burnt smell that seems so popular lately.

I pull on a fresh pair of boxer shorts under the towel, then use it to dry my hair, and toss it in the corner. I'm not entirely sure what to wear, but I figure the club can't be too formal at brunch during the week. Most of my clothes are with me since I did a little traveling before heading to my buddy's party. Of course, my wardrobe consists of a pair of dress slacks, khakis, a few pairs of jeans, assorted tees, a few nice long- and short-sleeve shirts, workout clothes, and a few different pairs of shoes and boots. I find a mostly clean pair of khakis and a short-sleeve button-down Tommy Bahama style shirt with some soft leather loafers.

When you have so few articles of clothing, it's easy to travel with all of them. I have other stuff packed in boxes at my mom's. But for now, I don't need it. I comb my hair into submission and belatedly realize as I see my reflection in the mirror, that I should have taken the time to shave. I splash on a little aftershave regardless, ready to roll.

When I check the time, we still have two hours before we are meeting the rest of her family for brunch. I look around the room for something to do, having already finished the book I had with me. It's either the hotel activity guide, or the television. Deciding, I flip on the TV and settle back on the bed to channel surf for a while. It's going to take AshLynn at least two hours to get ready anyway.

Speaking of, if she doesn't tell the truth today, you need to.

I'm unsure if my inner self is right with that directive, but it seems like a smart move to make it happen sooner rather than later.

And not something you have to think about now.

I find an episode of Magnum P.I. on one of those channels that broadcasts all the *old* shows, and get sucked in. It's not until it's over that I realize AshLynn hasn't come out of the bathroom yet.

"Hey, AshLynn, you okay?" I yell out.

Nothing.

"AshLynn?"

When she doesn't respond again, I get up and head to the bathroom, knocking loudly on the door.

"What?!" she screeches like an angry monkey.

"You didn't answer, I just wanted to make sure you were okay."

"Of course I am. I didn't answer because I didn't feel the need to talk to you."

Why did I expect any different?

"Okay, well it's just under an hour before we need to meet them, I'm going to take a drive around the island. Want me to swing back by to get you?"

"No. I'm riding with my parents."

"Okay. Well, I'll see you there then."

"Yep."

"Good talk," I mutter to myself.

I take a stroll around the hotel grounds before heading to the valet station for my car. The weather is clear and in the high 70s. In other words, perfect. The valet station is not busy, which I find surprising given it should be about checkout time, and he has my car to me in minutes. I tip him a twenty and put the top down on the convertible before heading out.

The day calls for classic rock. I find a playlist and put it on shuffle mode and head out. "Highway to Hell" by AC/DC cycles on first. I turn it up, happy that I splurged for the upgraded stereo system with this rental, because some guitar riffs call for loud with bass.

The sun is shining and peeking through the trees at random intervals, everything is green, and the rain from last night makes it smell clean. This is my favorite part about Washington State, just after the rain when the air feels pure, the sky is the lightest blue, and it feels like nothing can go wrong with a day that begins like this.

"Feel Like Making Love" by Bad Company plays next. I sing along with the chorus and think of Willow. A flash fantasy runs through my mind with me singing this song to her. Her wrapping her arms around my neck and pressing her body against mine, gyrating her hips, my hands on her ass squeezing those delectable globes.

I've made it about a third of the way around the island when my phone rings. I answer it through the Bluetooth connection in the car. It's my buddy Jake whose party I was just at in Leavenworth.

"Yo," I answer.

"Dude," he replies. "Where the hell are you?"

"Bainbridge. Why?"

"Wanted to make sure that girl you gave a ride to wasn't a serial killer."

"Ha, funny."

"I thought so."

"Not a serial killer, no. But you won't believe what's happened." I proceed to tell him the entire story as I'm driving. Not surprisingly, he laughs at most of it. Especially the part where I'm on my way to have brunch with her parents at *the club.*

"It's not funny," I say laughing. Because even I know it's kind of funny. "I have no idea how the fuck I got myself in this situation."

"The sister, the one you like, she's going to be at brunch too?"

"Yeah, man. What are the chances she'll want to go out with me after she finds out this was all a lie?"

"I'm going to say slim, but I can ask Lisa if you want a female opinion," he says of his wife.

"No, don't tell her. She'll give me shit about this for the rest of my life."

"Too late, man. I tell that woman everything."

"You're a dick."

"'Preciate it."

"That wasn't a compliment."

"Could've fooled me," he says.

"I'll let you know how the brunch goes," I tell him.

"Good luck, man."

"Thanks, I'm going to need it."

I disconnect the call and try to come up with a plan for how all this is going to go down today.

14

———

WILLOW

Zach and I arrive at the club for brunch a few minutes early. I'm surprised to see Mason is already there.

"Where's AshLynn?" I ask. Before I do something stupid like tell him he's beautiful. Or that he smells so good I want to bathe in his scent.

"She decided to ride with your parents," Mason says.

Zach elbows me, none too gently.

"Do I sense trouble in paradise?" Zach asks.

"They're fighting," I whisper-yell.

"How would you know?" Zach asks.

"He had to sleep in a chair," I say.

"Oh, that's not good," Zach says.

"I'm right here," Mason says, then offers Zach his hand. "Mason Cartwright."

"Yes, you are," Zach says looking him up and down. Then shakes his hand. "Zachary Thornton, bestie with testies, queen extraordinaire."

Mason chuckles. "What's a bestie with testies?"

"You know, testies," Zach says. "Testicles. Because we are men." Zach lowers his voice on the last word and does a modified shoulder check on Mason.

I smile at Mason and touch his arm to get his attention. "Zach is my best friend. We used to have a third best friend, Marlie, but she died our senior year of high school. Brain aneurysm. One minute she was there, and . . . well, I miss her every day."

Zach elbows me in the middle. "We," he says.

I look at him, then realize what I said. "Sorry, *we* miss her every day."

"Thank you." Zach nods for me to continue.

"Anyway, we were all best friends from grade school. Zach wanted his own special title. He's such a queen. So, he became the bestie with testies for both of us. And, with Marlie gone, just for me. I don't know what I'd do without him to be honest."

Zach turns to me. "If we're being honest, we both know it wouldn't be pretty." He turns to Mason. "She's a wreck without me." The he turns back to me. "He's yummy."

"Stop, you'll make him uncomfortable," I say, slapping him lightly on the arm.

Zach turns back to Mason. "When you're ready for the meat instead of the muff, you let me know." He winks, then turns to offer me his arm. "Shall we go inside?"

"We shall."

The hostess seats us at a table large enough for ten people instead of just six. It will make my father and Cassandra happy. Bigger is always better.

Zach orders a round of mimosas. "Because we are celebrating," he says without acknowledging what the occasion is.

My family arrives a short time later, unfortunately *before* the mimosas arrive. They take their time getting situated at the table.

My dad clears his throat to get our attention. "First of all, good morning. Zachary, I wasn't expecting you, but it's nice to see you."

"And you, Mister Brooks. You look very well this morning." Zach tries to hold my dad's gaze, but Dad looks away. Zach turns to Cassandra. "Missus Brooks, may I say that both you and AshLynn look especially lovely today."

Cassandra bats her eyelashes and AshLynn nods. Neither say anything in return nor thank him for the compliment.

"Well," my dad begins, always one to wait until all eyes are on him to say anything. "I wasn't sure it was going to happen so easily but, Mason, I have a job lined up for you in my firm. As a VP in the marketing department. Don't get me wrong, there's a few VPs, you wouldn't be the only one. But it shouldn't be too hard. Great pay, full benefits, hefty retirement, and lots of vacation time."

"Isn't that great?" AshLynn trills.

My dad holds up his hand to indicate he's not through. "I've also taken the liberty of putting a down payment on a plot of land in a new upscale community just up the road from where Cassandra and I live. It's close to us, to the office, and to the club back home. Think of it as an early wedding gift."

AshLynn beams and bounces in her seat.

If she's not careful she'll bounce her bosoms right out of that dress.

Mason chokes. On what I'm not sure. I reach over to pat him on the back, then blush as I remember brushing off his bottom earlier today.

"With all due respect, sir, I don't need a job from you," he says to my dad.

Dad looks at him, surprised. "Oh, do you already have something lined up?" my dad asks.

"Lined up?" Mason asks.

"A job, do you already have a job lined up? Or housing."

"I already have a job. And if I need housing, I will take care of it."

"It sounds like our job here is finished, Jonathan. He doesn't want anything from us," Cassandra says, sounding offended.

"I think what Mason is trying to say is that it's very generous of you, Daddy," AshLynn says.

"I think what I'm trying to say is that we are leaving out some vital steps here," Mason says.

The server delivers the mimosas. Mason drains his immediately and asks for another.

"Shall I bring a pitcher?" the server asks.

"Yes," Mason answers without checking with anyone else. He folds his hands on the table in front of him. "Mr. Brooks, let me be clear, I'm not an office work kind of person. I'm in construction. I like construction. I don't plan to change that."

"Hmm." My dad rubs his chin, thinking. "Well, first, you must call me Jonathan. We're due to be family after all. Construction, huh. Very worthy trade to be sure. Which developer do you work for?"

"I work for myself."

"Are you a developer?" It's obvious from his tone, this impresses my dad greatly.

"No, I'm not," Mason says. My dad frowns.

The server brings the pitcher and refills Mason's glass. He drinks almost half immediately.

"So, you work for other people then?" Cassandra asks. My dad pours them each a mimosa.

"I work for myself," Mason repeats.

"I don't understand," Cassandra says, then turns to AshLynn. "What is he talking about, AshLynn?"

AshLynn shrugs like this is all new news to her too.

Mason glares at her.

They're definitely still fighting.

Zach and I both finish our mimosas and he refills our glasses from the pitcher.

"Definitely enjoying this," he murmurs to me.

"Which part are you having an issue with, Missus Brooks?" Mason asks.

"You should really call her Cassandra," AshLynn pipes in.

"Yes," Cassandra says. "We are all on a first-name basis here. After all we're soon to be family."

"I'm not sure—" Mason starts.

AshLynn interrupts. "Maybe he should call you Mom and Dad?"

"Excuse me," Mason says. They ignore him.

"I think I'd like that," Cassandra says.

"Construction, huh?" My dad thinks aloud, running his thumb and forefinger along his jaw.

"How soon will you move to Southlake?" Cassandra asks Mason.

"Can we go back to this whole mom—" Mason starts.

"I've got an idea!" my father announces, then pauses to make sure he has everyone's attention. "Mason, since you're in construction, I'm going to hire you to help Willow renovate her house. You've seen it, the house has great bones, and obviously in a fabulous location. Am I right?" He gestures in what I think might be the direction of my house —as though he's presenting the idea of renovating it to Mason as a gift—satisfied smile on his face.

"Jonathan, why do you think you need to give me a job?" Mason asks.

"Dad, I don't need you to hire someone for me," I say. "In fact, I don't want you to." He doesn't get it. He never gets it though, not really. I have to do this on my own. It is my idea, my money, and I need it to be my effort. To prove to myself that I can do it.

"Yes, Willow, I know you can afford it on your own. You have more money than you could ever hope to spend. But let me do this for you. And for AshLynn. How often can a man say that giving another man a job will benefit both his girls? Huh?"

"Actually," I explain. "I was going to say that I really wanted to do this on my own. It's not about money. It's about the work. Working with my hands. Seeing the results of my labor. That is important to me."

"Is anyone going to acknowledge that I don't want or need the job?" Mason asks.

"Why wouldn't you want that job?" AshLynn asks him. "You get an office and a secretary. It's a great opportunity." He looks at her, his neck straining forward and his eyes bulging with brow furrowed.

My dad turns to me. "Willow, honey, there will be lots of things in life that are important to you. Something else will come along. And, surely, there will be things that you just aren't equipped to do on your own. Things you can't find on YouTube or in a book. Like electrical work, for instance. You will have to hire a professional for that."

"Yes," I say. "But Mason isn't a certified electrician."

"I'm sure you have experience in electrical work, don't you Mason?" Dad turns to him, brows raised.

Mason squints his eyes at us. "What? I have experience in what?"

My dad waves his hand in the air dismissively. "If he works for himself in construction, he's bound to have worked every aspect of a home. That includes electrical work."

"Mason is great with his hands," AshLynn says. "Look at his hands, Mommy."

"I'm not an electrician," Mason says.

"They look very rough and weathered," Cassandra adds.

"So, maybe you'll have to call someone out to check your work, but isn't that what the inspectors do anyway?" Dad turns to Cassandra. "Don't be crass about his hands." Then takes a sip of his mimosa. "Ugh. I hate the cheap champagne they use in these. Who ordered this anyway?"

"I did, Mister Brooks," Zach raises his hand.

"Well, that was a nice gesture, Zachary," my dad says.

Mason buries his head in his "rough and weathered" hands and groans. "Are we finally talking about the wedding?" Cassandra asks. "Oh good. I'm thinking semi-formal. AshLynn, what do you think?"

"I love that idea," AshLynn says.

"No," my dad says. "We are talking about my hiring Mason to help Willow. If he stayed with her, then I wouldn't worry so much about her being alone on this island."

"You don't have to worry about me," I say with a small smile. "The island is civilized. Well populated, even. With running water and a police force and all sorts of modern conveniences."

"Wait, so Mason is going to stay with Willow? Like at her house?" AshLynn asks.

"Well . . ." I start, then realize I don't have anything to stay. It's a valid question. Because as much as I hate to say it, my dad has a point. Maybe Mason working with me isn't such a bad idea. I do a gut check to make sure that's my brain talking and not my dried-up lady parts that haven't had the attention of a man in months.

Hmmm. Hard to tell. Both appreciate the man.

Would he stay with me? If he did, how long would I last before he knew I was attracted to him? Will he work with his shirt off? If so, could I take pictures? What if I walk in on him in the shower? 'Cause that would for sure be picture worthy.

Stop! He's your sister's fiancé.

Half sister.

"I don't want to live in Washington," AshLynn says. "So, if Mason is living here, where am I supposed to live?"

"And I wasn't really looking for roommates," I say.

"It's not a roommate," my dad says. "It's your sister and her fiancé."

Well, damn, how do I argue with that?

I can't have Prince Hunky McDapperness from the Land of the Suave and Insanely Handsome parading around here *without* AshLynn to keep him in check. I rub the spot behind my left ear and try to think of a way out of this.

"There's no second bed at Willow's," AshLynn says. "And I don't want my fiancé sleeping with my sister."

"We'll go get a bedroom set today for the guest room," Cassandra says.

Mason closes his eyes, his nostrils flaring.

"Will you pay him as much money to help Willow as if Mason worked for Daddy instead?" AshLynn asks the question to Cassandra.

"I'm not—" Mason starts.

"Is anyone going to ask me what I want?" I interrupt.

All eyes focus in. Only the members of my family can make me feel uncomfortable like this. With anyone else I'm a fucking warrior princess doing what I want, when I want, and how I want.

"Stop!" Mason yells.

And we do.

15

———

MASON

"Could we stop? For just a minute?" My voice is close to a yell, but I don't do anything to change that. I shut my eyes and breathe deeply through my nose trying to calm myself.

These people are out of control.

When I open my eyes again, all five heads at the table are turned toward me, mouths agape, eyes wide.

"Everyone is talking at once," I say. "It's impossible to focus. Can we just go one at a time? Please."

"Of course," Jonathan says. "I should have thought of that."

"Well, naturally, I should go first since I have questions about the wedding that need immediate answers," Cassandra says.

"I'm sure I can answer all your questions, Mommy," AshLynn replies. "There's no need to involve everyone at the table."

"But surely Mason has opinions on what you do."

"I can assure you, I have zero opinions," I say. "Especially on the *wedding*." I air quote the last word for AshLynn's benefit. Because I'm still unsure as to why she's continuing on with this wedding-planning bullshit. She knows there is no wedding. I'm sure as hell not marrying her—we don't even like each other. She has nothing to gain by allowing her parents to continue to move forward with the planning, knowing it's just going to be cancelled.

Unless she doesn't care if they waste time and money on this.

Speaking of.

I signal the server for another pitcher of mimosas, as we've flown through the one she brought already.

"Mommy." AshLynn directs her statement at the entire table, even though it appears as though she's addressing her mother.

"Did I tell you that Mason is an artist," AshLynn says, placing her hand on my thigh. "And his work is fantastic."

"Oh, I'd love to see it sometime," Willow interjects. "I'm a closet art nerd." She reaches up and rubs the spot behind her ear again. I've seen her do it a few times now, but I don't think she's aware that she does. I remove AshLynn's hand from my thigh and place it in her lap. I don't know what kind of game she's playing now, but it's not going to work.

"No closet about it," AshLynn adds turning to me. "She's a straight-up nerd, the older the art, the better. All that Goth-like Renaissance stuff. Ugh." She shudders to prove her point.

"It's not Goth," Willow says.

"Whatevs," AshLynn mumbles only partially under her breath.

"Mason," Cassandra says. "How many grandchildren do you plan to give me?"

I choke on my mimosa; Willow reaches over to pat me on the back. It's the second time she's had to do that during this meal.

"He wants a lot of kids," AshLynn says.

I never said that.

"Like, six, right, Mason?" AshLynn asks.

What the fuck?

"I don't recall having that conversation, AshLynn," I grit out.

"Oh, sure you do. Remember last night, on the beach, when Willow's dog lost her ball?"

Shit.

"Oh, yeah," I say humorlessly. "Now I remember."

I was wrong before, whatever game she's playing, apparently I'm playing too.

"How many siblings do you have, Mason?" Jonathan asks.

"None. I'm an only child to a single parent."

"Oh, that's sad." Cassandra puts her hand over her heart and frowns. At least I think it's a frown. Her face doesn't move much regardless of the expression.

"AshLynn," Zach says. "You're okay with six kids?"

"Whatever Mason wants," she says.

"Do we know anyone with children to be a flower girl in the wedding?" Cassandra asks.

AshLynn and Cassandra begin suggesting names. I sit back in my chair with a huff.

"You okay?" Willow leans over and asks softly.

"As well as anyone having six kids can be," I mumble.

"Do you really want six?" Willow asks with a smile, her voice low enough so only I can hear.

Not with AshLynn.

Maybe with you.

I look at her. Her big green eyes peek over the rim of the champagne flute as she takes another drink. Hers is almost empty, so I refill it with the pitcher once she returns it to the table. I can't quite read the expression in her eyes.

I try to be as honest as I can. "I wasn't aware AshLynn would say I wanted six kids."

"Does that mean you do or don't?" Willow presses on.

"I don't think AshLynn or I are ready for six kids."

"Pfft," Willow says. "Ain't that the truth."

I raise my flute and cheers the air in agreement.

Zach leans toward me behind Willow. "What are we cheering to?"

"Not having six kids," Willow says out of the corner of her mouth.

"I second that motion." Zach raises his own glass and we cheers again.

Willow stands. "I don't know about you all, but I'm getting breakfast before all this champagne goes to my head."

"Oh my goodness," Cassandra says. "I almost forgot why we were here."

"Not me." Jonathan pulls out her chair for her and helps her to stand. "I've been eyeing that buffet table since we arrived."

We file toward the food; I hang back a bit to be last in line. The spread they have is incredible. Fresh fruit, bagels with cream cheese and lox, omelets, ham, bacon, crepes, waffles, as many toppings as you can possibly imagine for all the above. I return to the table with my plate piled high.

AshLynn looks at it. "You know you can go back for more, right?"

"Just getting started, dear," I tell her.

"You'll want to watch that in later years," Cassandra leans to AshLynn and says, as though I'm not sitting across the table from her. "His metabolism will slow down and he'll get a paunch." She looks pointedly at Jonathan. Who does not have a paunch. And who is starting his day with oatmeal.

Forty-five dollars apiece for a champagne brunch and he chooses oatmeal.

Cassandra has fruit, as does AshLynn, but both Willow's and Zach's plates are similar to mine with Willow's at maybe half the size.

AshLynn touches my arm. I look at her. She sets her fork down and clears her throat. "I guess if we're to be staying with Willow, I'm going to need to get a bedroom set for Mason and me to sleep on. Then we can get started on those six grandkids for you, Mommy."

Fuck me.

What the hell have I gotten myself into?

16

WILLOW

My dad looks to me when AshLynn mentions buying a bed to stay at my house.

"I gotta say, Wills, I wasn't sure you would really go through with it, but I am impressed that you are. And, AshLynn, you are finally settling down and taking something seriously. First getting engaged, and now talking about buying furniture. I gotta say, it makes your old man proud."

I see the look in my dad's eyes. A cross between pride and contentment. Maybe even some happiness. I remember a time when I thought he'd never be happy again.

"Uh . . . I'd like final say on the furniture choice since it will be staying at my house," I say.

"That's fair," my dad says.

We finish our brunch mostly in silence. Or at least I do. And Mason and Zach as well. Cassandra and AshLynn continue to bounce ideas back and forth about the wedding with my dad chiming in every so often to joke about the cost. I wonder why Mason doesn't care about the wedding details. I've heard that's how men are, but it still surprises me a bit.

As we are all leaving, my dad turns to me and says, "Okay, well, are you and Mason ready to get started?"

Does he mean on the house?

Today?

I look to Mason.

"Do you mean work on the house? That was fast," Mason says.

"It's a big house," my dad says. "No sense in wasting time." He claps his hands together. "Okay, problem solved. And, if nobody needs me, I'm going to head to the pro shop down the way, see if I can get a membership and some clubs then get nine holes in." He pulls out his phone and starts typing as he walks away.

Cassandra turns to AshLynn. "Should we go find you a bed?"

"Yes!" AshLynn is obviously excited to be furniture shopping. I would rather poke my eye out. She turns to Mason and asks, "You don't mind if I pick it out, do you? Since you have to work and all?"

"Knock yourself out," Mason says, but AshLynn is already turned and is walking away with Cassandra.

"Send me pictures before you buy anything," I call out. Neither responds.

"So," I say, looking around the empty house.

Mason nods. "How . . ." He grimaces and looks off toward the view of the water. "Never mind. You want to show me around and let me know what you're thinking about doing?"

"Sure." Both he and P-Tink follow me into the house. I go through the things I envision happening, then show him examples from Pinterest.

"I don't even know if half the stuff I want to do is possible," I say. "I was kind of just planning on poking around with this for a year or two."

"Well, what's your end goal?" He pulls a notepad out of his pocket along with a small pencil.

"You just have that stuff in your pocket?" I ask.

He shrugs. "You never know when you might want to draw something or write something down, leave a note for someone."

"Just use your phone or send a text."

"I like paper," he says.

"Ohmigod, are you one of those people who still insists on reading an actual newspaper and a real paper book instead of using a tablet or e-reader?"

He smiles and looks down, saying, "Guilty," then back up at me. "But, in my defense, my mom owns a used bookstore, so it's in my blood."

"Wow," I say. "That's got to be tough in today's economy. Where's it at?"

"Downtown Seattle. Where I'm from. She gets a lot of tourist traffic, and much of her inventory is donated. Plus, she deals with tracking down rare editions, so she does okay."

"I'll say. Downtown Seattle must be pricey to rent in."

"The building owner likes her, gives her a really good deal."

"Oh, that's so sweet! Maybe he'll sweep her off her feet and marry her. I'm a sucker for a good happily ever after," I tell him.

He chuckles. "I think she's going to have a strong lifelong relationship with him."

"I love that."

"She's amazing. I would like to see her happy with someone, but it won't be the building owner. At least not romantically."

"Why?"

He laughs. "Let's just say he's otherwise engaged."

"Oh, that's too bad," I say. "I love the idea of romance."

"The idea of it?"

"Yes, the reality is way too messy. I could never do what you and AshLynn are doing. Meet someone and just decide to get married."

But you can meet someone and lust after him.

"Well, it's not—"

I shush my inner critic and interrupt Mason to keep talking. "I've been in two *serious* relationships." I air quote the word serious. "It's not like I was engaged or anything, but I lived with one of them for almost a year."

"What happened?"

"He cheated. They both did. The one I was living with? That one hurt a lot more. I thought he was it, you know? Anyway, that's why I don't have any furniture. I packed my clothes and left. He got to keep everything even though I paid for it all. He'd had sex on most of it anyway, and not with me. So, it's not like I wanted to keep it. That was over a year ago. I've lived in random hotels and furnished short-term rentals since. Until now at least. Which is why the reality of romance: totally not worth it."

I never should have kept talking. I just verbal vomited all over him.

He just looks at me.

Because you are looney tunes.

"I can't believe someone would cheat on you," he says.

"Oh, that's nice of you to say."

"You're smart, funny, pretty, ambitious."

I scoff. "Clearly I've got you fooled. Mission accomplished. Woot!" I raise a fist in the air in victory. Like the true geek that I am.

Just stop, Willow. Please stop.

We've gotten way off track here. Time to turn this thing around. "Okay, so what's first?"

He pauses, as if waiting to see if I'll say more. I stay quiet. Which is not easy. Because, really, I could keep going for hours. I could tell him my entire life story.

Literally.

Like from my earliest memories at age three until now.

"Well," he starts. "Most of what you've shown me in your pictures is cosmetic. Do you want to remove or add any other walls? Change anything major structurally?"

"I don't think so. Just these ones in the living room here to open up the space." I knock on the wall that partially blocks the kitchen from the living room.

"Create an open concept, I like it. We'll need to see if it's a load-bearing wall first?"

"Load-bearing?"

"One that holds up the house."

"Oh, jeez. Yeah, let's definitely do that."

He laughs.

I list off some of the other things I'd like to do that are more structural in nature.

"Yeah, it would be easy to extend the master bathroom, take up part of the room next to it. You could even add another guest bathroom behind it since the plumbing will already be there. Wait, I need to ask, what's your budget?"

"I don't really have one," I tell him, embarrassed. "I mean, I know you heard what my dad said. My grandmother left me money. A lot of it. For now, this is what I'm doing while I figure my life out."

"Okay, let's start with the room you need the least."

"I'm partial to them all," I say.

He laughs. "If we start with the master bathroom, can you and AshLynn share the guest bath and the powder room?"

"I can only answer for one of us," I say. "But yes."

He looks at me. "Okay then. Let's clear out that bathroom, we can get started on taking that wall down. Got a sledge hammer? Wheelbarrow?"

"A . . . no, I don't."

"What tools do you have?"

I show him my cute purple toolbox set that came with all purple-handled tools. He laughs.

"Okay, get your credit card ready, darlin'. We're going to need some tools. Real tools. Man tools." He growls the last few words, making me giggle.

I ignore the flip in my belly when he calls me darlin'.

17

MASON

WE SPEND SOME SERIOUS CASH ON TOOLS AND ESSENTIALS AT the hardware store. A few we are able to take with us in my small rental car, the rest they will deliver later today so we can start work tomorrow. I feel terrible about how much money it is, but she keeps saying that it's fine, so I go along with it. By the time we finish its mid-afternoon and I'm starving. She's in the passenger seat glued to her phone, typing away furiously.

"Everything okay?" I ask.

"AshLynn," she says rolling her eyes. "Look at this atrocity." She holds her phone out to me, then immediately pulls it back. "Sorry, I forgot for a minute she's your fiancée and not just my sister. Well, half sister. Anyway, for all I know, you'll like this and then I'll feel bad for hurting your feelings by already hating it. And that's a terrible way to start out our new sister/brother-in-law relationship."

The thought of being Willow's brother-in-law makes me queasy. I like her. She's fun to be around, smart and an easy conversationalist, plus she has a dry sense of humor that is rare in women and makes me belly laugh.

I can't help it. She's gorgeous. And you don't notice it at first. She's not overtly beautiful the way that AshLynn is, it's subtler with Willow. And it really shines through when she smiles. And not to continue to compare the two sisters, but when I combine that with how this has all gone down and how pissed I am about it. It's really easy to favor Willow over AshLynn right now.

Like it would ever be hard.

I can't believe her dad tried to get me a job. Who does that? The corporate job, not the one working on Willow's house. I'll totally take the one on the house. Not because I need the money, but because of the house. The architecture is stunning, and Willow wants to restore a lot of it to its original glory while bringing in certain modernity. I've not done that before with a house like this and I'd like to be a part of it. I'm sure spending every day with that amazing view won't hurt either.

The view of the sound not Willow.

I think.

"Just show me the picture," I tell her. She holds her phone back out to me. I laugh. Hard.

"Thank god," she says, laughing with me. "I mean, who puts a zebra print headboard in a beach house?"

"Who puts a zebra-print headboard in anything?" I ask.

"Well, we are from Texas," Willow says. "Animal prints have their place." She smiles. Seeing it makes me feel warm inside. I smile back as my stomach growls.

"You hungry?" I ask.

"Starving," she says. "Oh my god. There's a great Mexican place about two blocks over." She points to her right; I turn at the corner. "Wait, you do like Mexican, don't you? Of course you do. Who doesn't? Wait, you do, right?"

"Is the salsa spicy?"

She nods.

"Is the beer cold? Are the margaritas big?"

"They sure are, sir." Her smile grows bigger.

"Count me in."

We pull into a place called *Tacos Amigos*. The server tells us to seat ourselves, we agree on a booth in the back. We order drinks and entrees, her a margarita and me a beer; I eat half a basket of chips, Willow the other half.

"Oh god, I'm already full and we haven't even gotten our food. I can't knock down a wall after this. I won't be able to move." She rubs her stomach and lets out a small burp. "Excuse me. Oh, P-Tink isn't here to catch it."

"You know she's a really cool dog, right?"

She sighs. "Yeah, she's the best. I lucked out."

"You're also lucking out because we don't knock down walls after we've been drinking."

"Oh, thank god." She laughs. "Not that I don't want to do it, just after this morning, and all this stuff with AshLynn, no offense—"

"None taken. This morning was a new kind of exhausting."

"I just want to spend the rest of the day playing in the sand with Princess Tinkerbell."

"That sounds amazing," I say.

"It does, doesn't it?" She looks down at her phone. "Oh, ready for another furniture debacle?" She looks at it closer. "Actually, I think I kind of like this one." She holds the phone out to me.

"I like that," I say of the set. The frame is reminiscent of driftwood, and the dresser is a decent size without being too obtrusive. "Remind me which room this will go in."

"Well," she says rubbing the spot behind her left ear—the habit I kind of like about her—before continuing, "at first I was thinking the room with the little private patio, but that's too close to my room and I do not need to hear y'all having sex." She blushes and takes a long sip of her margarita.

"I . . ." I start. Not knowing what I intend to say. But it doesn't matter because she keeps talking.

"So, now I'm thinking the one at the far end of the hall with a view of the beach."

I clear my throat, and stupidly blurt, "We don't have sex. I mean, we haven't." I feel my face heat. How ironic that I'm now the one blushing.

She looks at me, head tilted. "You're engaged and you haven't had sex?"

"Uh, yeah," I say, the second word ending on an upswing, making me sound moronic.

Why did I say that? It's totally inappropriate and none of her business.

She continues talking, "How do you stay in the same room, the same bed even, and not have sex?"

"I—"

"I'm so sorry," she says. "That is absolutely none of my business."

I clear my throat. Again.

"Just forget this whole part of the conversation. Let's go back to the guest room. Oh wait, that's how this all got started. Well, pretend it's a guest room you won't be staying in."

Oh thank god. I've said enough for one day.

I laugh, but it's an uneasy laugh, and sounds unnatural. "Well, if you want the guest room to have a patio, you could always add one if you want."

"I don't want y'all staying *that* long." She laughs. "Can't make it too nice. You've gotta get back to Southlake sometime."

"Southlake? As in Texas?"

"Yeah. Where we're from? Where AshLynn lives."

"I'm not living in Southlake," I tell her.

"AshLynn agreed to move?"

"Well . . . no. I mean, we haven't talked about it," I say. "But Texas is a non-starter for me."

"Huh," Willow says. "Y'all haven't really talked about much, have you?"

Our food arrives saving us from further conversation on the point. Willow eats half her food before pushing the plate away. "I can't. I'm so done. I never want to see food again."

The server comes by to check on us. "Another round?" she asks.

Willow looks at me, then decides for herself. "I have no walls to knock down thanks to margarita number one, so, yes, please to number two."

"What the hell, me too," I say, then pull Willow's plate over to my side of the table. "May I?"

"Of course. It's so good, I just can't. I've got a food baby as it is. Who knows how long it will take for that to birth. Or digest. Go through me, or whatever. Actually, that's gross. Forget I said that." She leans her head back against the chair top and closes her eyes.

I dig in to her food, she's right, it is good. I finish her meal as well as mine, plus more chips. It's not until I'm finishing my second beer that I feel full.

"Wow, you can really pack it away," Willow says. "Where does it go?" She peeks under the table as a joke. I laugh.

"You kidding?" I say. "It takes a lot to fuel this machine." I lean back and stick my stomach out, gesturing to myself. This time she laughs. I like making her laugh. It makes me feel good.

We drive back to her place shortly after. The others aren't back yet, so we head out to the beach with Princess Tinkerbell. She chases the ball for a while, but soon seems content to just dig in various places.

"Watch this," Willow says. She piles a bunch of sand up and pats on the top, then says, "Oh, look, a sand castle."

P-Tink's ears perk up and she comes rushing over to where Willow sits, stopping right before she steamrolls the castle. She picks up her paw and taps it on the top just like Willow did. "Good job, P-Tink," Willow coos. The dog yelps in response, then turns and sits on the castle, flattening the entire thing.

Willow laughs. P-Tink yelps some more and runs in circles in the sand.

"Will she do that with me?" I ask.

"Try it," Willow says.

So, I do. P-Tink does not disappoint. Soon Willow and I are sitting next to one another rapidly piling sand together and laughing uncontrollably as the dog pats it then takes it down. Willow stops to catch her breath and lies back in the sand, covering her eyes with her forearm. I do the same, our shoulders and arms touching. I think about touching her hand with mine.

But I don't because that would be inappropriate since I'm pretending to be ENGAGED TO HER SISTER.

What is wrong with me??

So, so much.

"Oh man, I haven't laughed like that in a while," she says.

"Me neither," I agree.

"It's funny." Willow turns her head to look at me. "I only laugh like that anymore with Zach. I mean, I like to think I'm a pretty frickin' happy person, but full-on belly laughs don't happen all the time, you know?"

"I don't think I've laughed like that with anyone," I tell her honestly. "Not in a really long time."

"Not even AshLynn?" Willow asks.

I turn my head to look at her, our noses inches apart. "No."

She looks sad for a moment. Like she's sad for me. It hits me, hard, I don't want her to be sad. Ever.

I open my mouth to say something when I'm interrupted.

"What are y'all doing out here in the sand?" AshLynn calls from above us. "Didn't you hear me calling you?" I didn't even hear her approach, let alone call our names.

"AshLynn, you gotta see this," Willow says bounding up. She sets up the sandcastle for P-Tink and we both giggle while the dog does her thing.

"Cute," AshLynn says without much emotion. "The furniture should be here in a couple hours. Mommy and I stopped for lunch, but we brought back some burgers for you in case you're hungry." She turns and heads back to the house.

"We had—" I say at the same time Willow calls after her, "That's so nice of you, thank you! I'll be right in."

"Are you going to eat a burger?" I ask, shocked.

"I'm sure going to try. We can't have them know we went to lunch. AshLynn would get jealous and Cassandra would get the wrong idea." She stands and brushes the sand of her clothes and legs.

"What's the right idea?" I ask, despite myself.

"That we're . . . friends?"

She ends on an up note, but I know she's not actually asking a question. Even though I know it's not smart, it makes me happy to know that she questions the nature of our relationship, because maybe I do just a little bit too.

18

WILLOW

MY ALARM GOES OFF AT SIX O'CLOCK IN THE MORNING. My second morning of dealing with my family in town. And first morning with Hottie McHunksterpants staying in my house. So far, I think I'm handling it okay. At least today I get to burn off lots of excess energy. The tools and equipment arrived late yesterday, so today is the day that Mason and I start demo on the bathroom wall. I need time to walk with P-Tink before we start. From the sounds of it, P-Tink is not happy about waking this early. If it's even possible for a dog, she drags her feet as she follows me down the hall.

I start a pot of coffee then open the back door to let P-Tink do her thing. She yelps and jumps on one of the recliners. I duck behind the counter then peek over it to try to see if someone is out there.

A bad guy?

Would she be jumping on and licking a bad guy, though?

Probably not.

A head full of brunet hair pops up from behind the back of the chair.

Mason?

What's he doing out there?

"Mason? Is that you?" I call out the doorway.

I get a muffled response in return, but I'm fairly certain it's because P-Tink is giving him a doggy facial via her tongue and slobber. I go outside and confirm that Mason is the one on the double lounger and my dog is happily sucking up as much attention as she can from him.

"What are you doing up this early?" I ask.

"I wasn't exactly up." His voice is froggy.

"Oh no, did P-Tink wake you up?"

"Yeah." He clears his throat. "It's okay. It was time for me to get up anyway."

"Wait, did you sleep out here?"

"Yeah." He runs his hand over his face a few times then back through his hair. I notice there is only one pillow, but I ask anyway.

"Where's AshLynn?"

"She . . . uh, well, we got into a bit of a fight and I slept out here."

"Again? Oh no!" I laugh and immediately cover my mouth to stifle it. I don't mean to laugh at people's misfortune. It's just that many times I find it funny. You know, as an outsider looking in. Cassandra has told me plenty of times it is highly inappropriate. That has yet to stop me.

"I'm so sorry," I snicker.

"It's not funny," he growls.

"I know, you're right, it's not. I laugh at all the wrong times." I laugh harder. He gives a half smile then laughs with me.

"I guess it is kind of funny," he agrees. "Of all times for you to have no other furniture, huh?"

"Maybe I should go get a couch?"

He shakes his head in response, then says, "Do I smell coffee?"

"Yep, just made a fresh pot. Want some?"

"Desperately. I'll come in. I need to visit the restroom anyway."

I go inside to get a cup of coffee, and set out another mug for Mason, then head back out to the deck to watch P-Tink run around in the sand and watch for her doggie deposits so I can pick them up after her. Mason folded up the blanket and set the pillow neatly on top of it before he went inside.

That was nice of him.

He comes back out a brief time later with his own cup of coffee and sits next to me at the edge of the deck to watch the dog and the shoreline. The area of Bainbridge that I'm in has a small beach between the houses and the water. It's mostly grasses, but a small strip of about twenty feet is sand. I like it. So does Princess Tinkerbell.

"Do you think I need a dock?" I ask Mason.

"Do you have a boat?"

"No. But I'm thinking that maybe I should get one. Most of my neighbors have boats." I gesture to each side, up and down the sound.

"Do you know how to sail?"

"No, but I think I'd get one with a motor. Then you just steer it, right?"

"I think it's a bit more difficult than that, but sure, go with that." He chuckles.

"Maybe I'll start with a kayak," I say.

"Have you kayaked before?"

"No."

"Have you done any water sport before?"

"Swimming. A little water skiing. Tubing."

He nods and sips his coffee.

I like this companionable silence we've slipped into.

It's comfortable.

Too comfortable.

Time to end it.

"Are we knocking down a wall today?" I ask, standing.

"We are. Better carb-load, keep your strength up."

"Aye aye, Captain."

I head inside to grab some leftover donuts from the fridge and almost run into AshLynn who is rubbing her eyes, blindly walking through the kitchen.

"Hey, there's coffee if you want it," I tell her.

She grunts at me in return then asks, "He leave?"

"If by *he* you mean Mason, then no. He's out on the deck."

"Hmmph." She fills a cup with coffee then adds a lot of sugar and creamer.

"You kicked him out last night?"

"He told you that?"

"Well, kind of. I mean, I caught him sleeping on the lounger outside. He didn't really have a choice. He said you guys argued. I can stay scarce if you want to talk to him."

"He knows where to find me if he wants to talk."

"Okay, but if you're the one who kicked him out, maybe you should make the first step toward apologizing."

AshLynn takes a large gulp of coffee. "I am *not* apologizing. I didn't do anything wrong."

"Well, still, it's going to be awkward if you two are fighting, don't you think?"

"I don't care. He's in the wrong. He's always in the wrong."

"What happened?"

"He won't agree to work for Daddy and I want my inheritance."

"What does one have to do with the other?" I ask.

"Mommy won't let me have it unless I'm married and he takes the job with Daddy."

"Wow. That's pretty—"

"I know," she interrupts. "Mason is being really lame. I'd be set if he'd just do this one little thing."

"I was going to say that's pretty controlling of Cassandra."

"Controlling? Not even. She's going to give me the money—all he has to do is agree to take the job and go to work every day."

"And what do you do while he does that?" I ask.

"Same as I do now."

"So, let me get this straight. Mason takes the job with Daddy and goes to work every day?"

"Yep."

"And as long as he does that, Cassandra gives you access to your trust."

"Exactly."

"But Mason doesn't want to do that."

"No." She sighs. "And he doesn't want to move to Southlake. The whole thing is so ridiculous."

"I'm surprised you want to stay in Texas."

"Wills, in Southlake I'm amazing. People know us, they know Daddy, they do things for me, I'm important. In Texas, we are rich. And let's face it, most people adore me."

I scoff at her (lack of) humility.

"But in Washington, no one knows me. I have no friends. There's no fan club. I'm not the society princess with Mommy as queen. And if you look at some of the houses around here, not yours of course, you can tell you have to be way richer than we are to be rich here. And I still want to be rich."

"So, it's about money?" I ask.

"Of course it's about money. It's always about money."

"You're willing to give up the man you love just for money?"

"Who said anything about love?"

I shake my head. Certain I didn't hear her correctly.

"You're getting married," I hiss.

"And?"

"So, of course you love him."

She shrugs.

I look at her. Mouth agape, eyes wide.

"Don't look at me like that."

"Then why the hell are you getting married?"

"I want my inheritance."

Poor Mason. He has no idea what he's getting himself into.

"AshLynn, getting married is a big deal! You can't treat it so lightly."

"I can treat it however I want to."

She's got me there. This is a freaking disaster.

"You need to fix this. It's not fair to Mason. You go to him and you apologize right now," I demand.

"Why do you care?" she asks.

"It's not that I care so much as it is common courtesy, AshLynn. You can't just manipulate people like this."

She reminds me of—

"Daddy does," she says.

Exactly.

"Just do it." I push her toward the patio door.

"Stay out of it, Willow! And quit talking to my fiancé. Stay out of my relationship and stay out of my life!"

"AsHLYNN SAYS she doesn't love him," I tell Zach via video chat.

"Then why is she marrying him?"

"That's what I asked!"

"And what did she say?"

"Nothing much, that it didn't matter."

"Clearly a match made in heaven."

"Right?"

"So, let's break them up and then we can share him."

"No. I'm not going to do that to my sister."

"You're so nice."

"You say that like it's a bad thing."

"Hey, if you feel it then you should own it. Besides, you're the one who made me move to this god-forsaken place and now you won't even entertain me with breaking up AshLynn's faux relationship?"

"I made you do nothing. You were more than ready to leave Southlake with me. And it's not a faux relationship. Plus, you love your condominium. Right in downtown, close to everything, a view of the Space Needle, not to mention your dating pool quadrupled."

"Fine. Whatevs. No operation relationship annihilation. What now?"

"They are going to be staying with me."

"What? Why on earth would you agree to let them stay with you?"

"I don't know!"

"OHMIGOD, you want him to stay with you!"

"No, I don't."

"Oh, but you do."

"Well," I hedge. "He has interesting ideas about the house."

"You little trollop!"

"I know! What do I do?"

"I'm coming over. I'll take the water taxi, be there in less than an hour."

"One of us needs a boat—"

"We'll discuss it when I get there."

"Thank you!"

"On my way. Don't do anything salacious without me."

I'll do my best.

19

MASON

Willow is taping paint sample papers on the wall in the living room. She's dressed like a handyman's wet dream— red, plaid flannel shirt tied at the waist over a white tank, jeans shorts, and Timberlands with knee socks pushed down to the ankles.

"We're a ways away from painting," I tell her.

"Ack!" She jumps as she screams, paper paint samples go flying. "Jeez, Mason. You scared me half to death." She turns to pick up the paint samples that she dropped.

I move to help her. "Sorry."

"I know, painting is like last," she says as we both straighten. I hand the papers to her and my fingers brush against hers. I feel a jolt through my system. She looks up at me, likes she's surprised. I meet her eyes, knowing I should look away. Knowing I should pull my hand away. Somehow not able to do either.

She takes the papers and turns away before she continues, "But I just wanted to get used to seeing some of these on the wall for a few days. Plus, Zach is coming over and he has a great eye for color."

I miss her touch.

"The bestie with testies?" I ask.

"You remembered." She beams.

As cheesy as it is, I feel warmed by her smile. So I return the gesture.

You're being an idiot, Mason.

"Okay, so what are we doing first? Knocking down a wall?" she asks.

"Yep. Grab a sledgehammer and some safety goggles and follow me."

We face off with the wall. "Ready?" I ask her.

She nods, the look on her face serious. I gesture for her to go first. She picks up her sledgehammer and gauges the weight in her hands, then raises her arms above her head.

"Whoa, wait a minute." I grab the hammer out of her hands, and she turns to look at me, eyebrows raised. "You're going to hurt yourself that way. When you are first starting out, take it from the side, like this." I show her how to come at the wall from an angle. "Make sense?"

She nods and takes the hammer back. "Like this?" She replicates my earlier motion.

"Good," I encourage. "Now have at it."

She stretches her arms back and curves her torso, almost like a golfer would, then swings with a grunt. The hammerhead hits the wall, making a small hole in the sheetrock under the paint.

"Wow!" she exclaims. "I kind of like that. It's very satisfying to hit the wall."

"It will get better when you start taking chunks out of it." I swing my hammer taking a large slab of drywall away with me.

"How come you get to raise it over your head?" she asks.

"One, because I'm stronger. Two, because I'm experienced."

She looks from my hammer to my arms and back again. I resist the urge to flex them.

Willow swings again, harder this time, and pulls away a decent-size chunk of wall with her.

"Nice job!" I say.

"This is fantastic!" She swings a few more times, each with more gusto than the one before. I swing alongside her and soon we have half the drywall pulled away from the framing.

"Do you guys have to make so much noise?" AshLynn appears at the door with a smirk on her face. I can't tell if she's joking or not.

"Want to help?" Willow asks her.

AshLynn wrinkles her nose. "No. That is all you. Mommy is coming to get me, and we are going shopping."

"For what?" Willow asks. I scoff thinking the same thing.

"Clothes. The weather is totally different here."

"Not this time of year. If you are cold, just layer," Willow says.

"No, thanks," AshLynn says.

"What's this I hear about shopping?" I hear a male voice from the doorway and turn to look.

"Zachy!" AshLynn cries, jumping into his arms like she didn't just see him yesterday.

"Lil' Brooks, how goes it." Zach hugs AshLynn and sets her down quickly.

"They don't think I need new clothes." She pouts and pats her hair to make sure it's still in place and pulls some forward over her shoulder.

Zach frowns. "Nonsense. There is never a time where a girl doesn't need new clothes. Trust me, I know."

"That's because you're a shopping whore." Willow smiles, removing her safety goggles and setting her hammer down.

"Takes one to know one," Zach says as he approaches Willow and kisses her on each cheek. "And, my goodness, aren't you a straight man's wet dream in this getup." Mirroring my thoughts from earlier. I drink her in while the attention is on her.

"What?" Willow asks looking down, wiping dust from her clothing.

"Mm hmm." Zach looks her up and down then turns to AshLynn. "Lil' Brooks, you sure you want to leave your man with the likes of Willow today?" He gestures to

Willow's legs. Which, as I've noticed, look incredible in the cut-offs.

AshLynn waves her hand dismissively and looks down at her phone. "Oh, gotta go. Bye."

Zach turns to me. "Where are the paint swatches, darling?"

"Living room," she says to him, then turns to me and says, "Be right back."

I take a deep breath when they leave. I find much of the charade to be exhausting, mostly the energy it takes to deal with AshLynn right now.

I start swinging, harder now that no one else is in the room. By the time they return, I've got over half the drywall and framing down.

"Zach is a genius. We are going with *Dorian Gray* for the living room." Willow comes back in the room with Zach trailing behind her. "Hey, wow, you made a lot of progress. How long were we gone?" She laughs as she puts her safety glasses back on and picks up her hammer.

"Pity there's only two hammers. I'll just be over here," Zach says. "Watching."

"Do you want music?" she asks me.

"Anything upbeat is fine," I say, swinging again. Willow's eyes bulge just a bit, then she turns to Zach.

"Z—will you find us some music to listen to?"

Zach looks up from his phone and takes Willow's from her, then disappears from the room. He comes back a short time later with a wireless speaker, from where I have no idea, and starts playing old-school Journey. When he sings along, he sounds eerily like Steve Perry.

"He's a really good singer," Willow says to me. "We kill it at karaoke."

"I'll bet."

She starts swinging, and then singing. Unlike Zach, Willow does not have a good singing voice. It's off-key and screechy. Which makes P-Tink start to howl along. At that point I figure all I can do is join in as well. As loud as possible to help drown Willow out. I look over at her, but she's oblivious to how bad she sounds and seems happy just to be singing, swinging, and working.

Zach leaves the room, for what I'm not sure. I get in a zone and just keep taking down the wall and clearing away debris. Willow and I have the entire thing down in a short amount of time. I know Willow took a couple breaks to talk to Zach and to get us all some water, but I have yet to stop. Staying active helps calm my mind. My mind that can't stop thinking about AshLynn and just how bad this whole situation is. I don't know what kind of game she is playing, but I do know she's not going to like it when I don't play back.

I load as much debris as I can into the wheelbarrow and take it out to the front. Then repeat until I have the room cleaned out. We rented a half-ton bag at the hardware store that they will come and dump each time we fill it.

"Hey, you want lunch?" she asks. I nod even though it seems like we just had breakfast. My stomach growls loudly, obviously not agreeing with me about breakfast. I check the time surprised to see that it's been almost four hours since we started.

"Zach is going to go pick something up. Feel like deli sandwiches?"

"Sounds good. Did he already leave?"

"No, he's outside writing."

"Oh, is he a writer? What does he write?"

"Children's books."

"No shit?" That surprises me. Only because he doesn't look like the kid book type. Though if I think about it, I'm not sure what that type looks like.

"He writes under a pen name, TJ Lane, about a gay superhero named Captain Cupcake who travels around the world teaching anti-bullying tactics and helping children and pre-teens accept themselves as they are regardless of sexuality."

"That is really cool." I find myself developing a newfound sense of respect and awe for the man I previously thought of as the frivolous gay sidekick. Then I feel ashamed of myself for having those thoughts in the first place.

"He's had a tough time of it. His parents abandoned him when he was young, he spent some time in the foster system before he was adopted by a family who is very well off financially, but very closed off emotionally. And not accepting of him when he came out."

"That's tough."

"Yeah, he's always been a pretty boy which didn't help matters when he was young. He's the most important person in my life. I would do anything for him."

"I admire that," I say honestly.

"You don't have a friend like that?"

"Maybe my buddy Jake whose party I was at the night I met AshLynn. But that'd be about it."

"You only need one."

"True."

She fiddles with her phone a moment then hands it to me. "Okay, here's the menu, let me know what you want."

I'm reading what they have to offer when she gets a text. I realize from the preview that it was definitely not meant for my eyes.

ZACH: Me hungry. Stop drooling over Lil B's hot AF fiancé—he's off-lim . . .

Hot as fuck?

Is she drooling over me?

I peek over at Willow, she's studying the space where the wall used to be, lips scrunched, with one finger rubbing the space behind her ear, thinking about something.

Me, maybe?

It would never work between Willow and me. I'm pretend engaged to her sister. Who is blackmailing me for perving on Willow through her window.

Wow. I'm an asshole.

Willow looks up at me and catches me watching her. "I'm so sorry," she says. "Did you say something? I was totally lost in my own world there."

I shake my head. "No. I uh, I'll go with the Italian, extra pepperoncini. And, you got a text."

She takes the phone and looks at it. Her face turns a deep shade of red. "I'll . . . ah . . . okay, extra . . . yep." She leaves to give Zach our orders. I run a hand over my face and sigh. Questioning, once again, just how the fuck I got myself into this situation, and how I'll ever get out of it.

20

WILLOW

"Kill. Me. Now." I sink down next to Zach in a patio chair.

"What happened?" he asks, looking up from his tablet where he's currently sketching illustration ideas for his book.

"He saw your text," I whisper in case Mason comes out here while we are talking.

"Which one?" Zach whispers back.

"Which one? The one you *just* sent!"

"What was he doing with your phone?"

"I was showing him the menu for the sandwich place. And your text popped up."

"Oh. You should really have the text preview turned off."

"You think? Not that it helps me now. Must you be so graphic in your texts?"

"Don't blame this on me. Besides, you were the only one who was supposed to see it, so it didn't matter."

"Ugh." I bury my head in my arms.

"I hear you're going to get sandwiches. Can you grab me a couple sodas too?" I hear Mason's voice from behind me.

"Of course, I can. And put your money away. As long as you are working, we will make sure you are fed." Zach stands and closes his tablet.

"Thanks, man," Mason says.

"Ta-ta for now," Zach says, and I hear his footsteps retreat. The chair next to me squeaks and a shadow falls over me. I'm assuming Mason has sat down, but I refuse to look up to see.

"Hey," he says softly.

I put one hand up and wiggle my fingers slightly in return. I'm not going to lift my head. Not ever again. I'm going to stay here like this until Mason is through with waiting for me and decides to leave and go back to where it is he comes from.

"Can you look up?" he asks.

"No."

We sit there for a moment before he says, "Okay, so I saw the text. It's no big deal. So, you have a little crush."

"It wasn't about you," I lie.

"Oh," he says. "Who was it about?"

"Someone else's fiancé."

He chuckles. "Doesn't Zach call AshLynn Lil' B?"

"No."

"Oh."

"He calls her Lil' Brooks."

"Right." He draws the word out slightly as he says it.

"And anyway, we were talking about her other fiancé. You aren't the only one, you know. She has many. So don't go feeling all special."

"Got it," he says.

I really want to look up now. If for no other reason than to convince him that it's not true and I'm not drooling over him.

"I'm sure the fiancé you were referring to is flattered."

"Flattered is like the worst word in all word history."

"Why?"

I turn my head to the side, so I can see him a little bit. "Because it's like a backward compliment. Or something where you think you're letting the other person down gently but really you're just rejecting them in a condescending manner."

"How is being flattered condescending?"

"It's like this," I say straightening to look at him. "You say you're flattered, right? What that means is *oh, what you're saying is so cute. I can't possibly be bothered to reciprocate, but it's nice of you anyway, you poor little deluded dear.*"

"You get all of that from one word?"

"Yep." I add a pop sound to the "P."

"What if I said if things were different, I'd feel the same way. Is that condescending?"

Shit! Now we are getting into dangerous territory. Abort. Abort.

"Um . . . I don't think that would be condescending. No—"

His phone buzzes and he looks down at it.

Thank god for the interruption.

He frowns as he reads whatever it says.

"Everything okay?" I ask.

"I don't know. AshLynn's just . . . I mean, no offense, but what's with her hang-up about money? Are you all that way?"

I take a deep breath not sure how I want to answer that. I mean, I think AshLynn is always manipulative and immature, but I don't know if that's what he means by *this* so I don't want to taint his view of her.

Or do you?

"I'm not. But in truth that's probably only because I have it. You have to understand the way they think. My father changed after my mom died. Actually, that doesn't really matter because AshLynn wasn't even born yet. Or maybe it does because then it shows how she was raised." I think on it for a minute, then glance over at him. He's watching me intently. Waiting for me to give him all the answers.

Could be waiting a long ass-time for that, buddy.

"My mom came from money. A lot of money. But my grand-mother had primary control over it. My dad is an idea guy. But not all his ideas are good. My mom believed in him and would fund any and every business proposition he had. He made a lot of money, but he lost a lot more than he made. So, my grandmother put a stop to it. She felt he was reckless. It hurt my parents' feelings when she did that, but my dad was making money at the time, so they didn't worry about it."

It makes me uncomfortable to speak ill of my father or my sister. But at the same time, I want Mason to know why they are the way they are. Maybe it will help him to be more lenient and understanding with their behavior.

"Then his luck changed, and over the next year he lost a lot of money."

"How much is a lot?"

"About five million."

"Holy shit!"

"Yeah. And I only know this because I heard my mom and my grandma talking about it. It was only a few months later that my mom was killed. He was the sole beneficiary on her life insurance, the main heir in her will, and the trustee over my inheritance. That's what he spent first."

"How? Aren't there rules against that?"

"All investments were within the trust so if he made anything it would have been added to it. And what he lost was taken away."

"How much was it?"

"All total? Thirty-five million."

His mouth drops. "Who *are* you people?"

"I know. Problem is he's been extremely lavish with Cassandra and AshLynn. They have never wanted for anything. But he overleverages, so eventually his luck will run out—it's starting to lately. And Cassandra and AshLynn have been put on a budget. They don't like that. AshLynn has an inheritance that my dad started for her when she was born, but she doesn't have access to it yet. So, yeah, everyone's thoughts lately are primarily about money."

"Did he spend all of the money from your mom?"

"No, I don't think so. But I'm sure what's left is too little for comfort. And then my Granny Violet passed and left me everything—"

"I don't want to know how much."

I laugh. "I wasn't going to tell you. But I think it made them all a little bitter."

"She was your mom's mom?"

"Yep, so no relation to any of them, but my dad and Cassandra still felt like Grandma Brooks should have at least left AshLynn money."

"Wait, how is your dad's last name Brooks?"

"He took my mom's name. The Brooks name is important in the business world and especially in our hometown of Southlake. It's helped him considerably in his dealings."

"I'm baaack!" Zach comes through the back door with two large bags filled with sandwiches and sodas, essentially ending my conversation with Mason.

I get up to help him bring everything to the table, happy for the disruption, then go inside to get paper plates and napkins. I take a moment to fan my face with the paper plates, still feeling warm from Mason seeing Zach's text and our conversation after, then join the boys outside. The weather is perfect—seventy degrees and clear.

Mason asks Zach about his books. Zach preens as he discusses his favorite topic: himself. I eat my sandwich in silence and listen to the boys talk. I've done enough talking for today. They switch to discussing other people's books and who their favorite authors are.

I already know Zach's faves are Fitzgerald and Hemingway. But I'm interested to hear who Mason likes. I'm anticipating the typical answers of Robert Ludlum, Lee Child, or David Baldacci. But he surprises me when he answers with Raymond Chandler. And they go on to discuss *Double Indemnity*, which even I've heard of. I'm not a big reader like Zach is, and when I do read, it's always something romantic with a happy ending. It drives Zach crazy.

I'm surprised to find that Mason is a big reader as well. Knowing Zach can go on and on about books, and happy for the break in hard manual labor, I recline my chair and close my eyes. Shade covers me and I open one eye to see Mason has moved an umbrella to cover me. I smile in thanks and close my eyes again.

I know I don't fall asleep because I can hear their voices rising and falling along with the occasional laughter. I like that I've given them each a friend. Or at least that they are getting along and have things to talk about. P-Tink climbs up next to me on the lounger, circles four times, and flops down with her head resting on my thigh.

The next thing I know, Zach is sticking his wet finger in my ear. Not a fun way to wake up.

"What the—"

"Wakey, wakey, time to help the beefcakey."

I glance around to make sure Mason didn't hear him say that. The last thing I need is another embarrassing scenario with him. I slap Zach on the arm.

"Shut up, he'll hear you."

"He won't. He's all the way in the back vacuuming the dust and stuff with that big orange thing you're afraid of."

"Do you ever wonder why so many hardware things are orange?" I ask.

"No."

"What'd you guys talk about?"

"Books and shit."

"What does he need my help with?"

"I don't think he does; it was just time for you to wake up. Mason didn't want to disturb you, thought you looked too peaceful. I, on the other hand, don't give a fuck. So now you can entertain me."

"How long was I asleep?"

"Not long, maybe forty-five minutes."

"Wow, I don't even remember falling asleep."

"That's usually how it happens," Zach says drily.

"Ha ha."

P-Tink wanders into the house, I hear her barking at the wet/dry vac a brief time later. And I realize this might be her first experience with a vacuum and decide to get up and videotape it. Because, yes, I'm one of those people who videotapes everything the dog does. Or is it just video since there aren't tapes any longer? Anyway, I video and take pictures. I head in the house through the back door and run into AshLynn before my eyes have a chance to adjust.

"Hello to you too," she says. "My god, what is all that racket?"

"That's the wet/dry vac," I say.

"I mean the dog barking," she says.

"Well . . . that's the dog."

"I don't know how you put up with that. Ugh."

"She's barking at the shop vac. I think it's cute."

"You would."

"Where's Cassandra? Did she come back with you?"

"No, she and Daddy were meeting at the golf course for cocktails."

"Did he golf again today?"

"Yes. But we are having dinner with them this evening, command performance and there's a dress code."

"You and Mason have a command performance with your parents?"

"No, all of us."

"Us meaning me?"

"That's what us means, isn't it? Me, you, Mason, Mommy, Daddy, and Zachy since he's here."

"What's this about us? I heard my name, what's happening?" Mason walks in with Zach trailing behind him.

"We're having dinner in a couple hours with Mommy and Daddy," AshLynn says.

"We?" Mason asks.

"All of us," AshLynn says.

I turn to Zach. "Sorry to say, she included you in her list. That means you're coming too, mister."

"Well, fuck," Zach says.

21

MASON

Dumbest thing I've done this week? Agreeing to stay at Willow's instead of getting a hotel room or a vacation rental. Shit, even staying at my mom's would have been smarter. Instead I'm spending the bulk of my time in a place that's not remotely mine, trying to make AshLynn—who I can't stand—happy. And avoid my feelings for Willow which are growing stronger every day.

Now dinner with a dress code? It's not a special occasion or holiday. Why do we have to dress up? AshLynn, of course, bought a new outfit for tonight, and she started getting ready almost an hour ago. We still have an hour before we have to leave to meet them.

My mom is naturally pretty and low-maintenance with her beauty routine, so it wasn't until I started dating that I realized just how long a woman can take with her pre-outing rituals. I used to find it fascinating, now I find it annoying.

I reach over to pet P-Tink, who's sitting next to me on the edge of the deck. I've got a beer, P-Tink has a chew toy, and

I'd say we are both pretty damn content. This has got to be one of the greatest locations for a house, ever. The serenity of the water, with the views of the city in the distance, trees all around for privacy, and just the edge of the beach connecting you to anyone else.

I've thought about buying another place near my mom and staying in one place for a while. But there are still so many things I want to do, so many places I want to see. A place like this though, I could stay in a place like this. For a first-time renovator, Willow has a lot of really good ideas for what she wants to do with the house. It will be amazing when she's through. Correction, when *we* are through. She credits social media for most of her ideas, but she's talented. She has an instinct for how to best maximize space and take advantage of the natural elements already surrounding the home.

Speak of the devil.

"Hey, I just wanted to make sure you were good with tonight. You know clothing-wise." Willow stands over me, concerned look on her face.

"Thanks, I appreciate it. I've got something I think will work, just black slacks and a button-down, but they're wrinkled. Do you have anything to help with that?"

"I have a steamer you can use."

"Is that like an iron?"

She laughs. "Yes, only easier. I'll show you how to use it."

I stand to go into the house, P-Tink in tow.

"She really likes you," Willow says of her dog and me.

"I think you have that backward," I say. "I really like her."

She smiles, almost like she's grateful that someone likes her dog. "It's just surprising is all. I mean, I know I haven't had her for long, but usually she's glued to my side when other people are around. And with you she's different."

I like knowing that.

I follow Willow inside the house and she shows me how to use the steamer so that I can get the wrinkles out of my clothes. I find it funny that she has a clothes steamer, but no furniture. Although, I totally get her wanting to wait and see how the house turns out before selecting furnishings.

I clean up and dress in the other spare bathroom, the one without a shower. So I make do with soap, a washcloth, and some cologne. I exit the bathroom on one side of the house, buttoning my cuffs. At the same time Willow exits the other bathroom on the opposite end of the house.

In a towel.

I watch her dart down the hall: hair pinned up, damp skin, and amazing legs. Not that I haven't seen her legs before—I have in shorts. But something about being in a towel, fresh out of the shower, makes a girl look really fucking sexy. I don't look away.

"I see you," a voice says behind me. I turn spotting Zach waving a finger in my direction as though scolding me.

"I wasn't . . . I was just . . ."

His eyebrows rise.

"Yeah, all right, but I was just looking. And it was a quick glance."

He nods. "Hurt her, and I kill you. And by I, I mean nasty, rotten people that I hire to do my dirty work for me."

"How will I . . . I'm—you know—engaged to her sister."

"Right." He draws the word out as he brushes past me, then turns. "You want to talk about that?"

Before I can answer we hear, "Mas-ey!" trill down the hall. I give Zach a chin nod and head to the room I'm supposedly sharing with AshLynn.

I knock lightly and open the door. AshLynn is standing there in a lacy bra and thong, staring at the bed. Three dresses laid out before her. Each still with the tags on.

"Jesus Christ, AshLynn, what the hell?" I say, turning my back to her and covering my eyes.

"It's nothing you haven't seen before."

"I've never seen you without any clothes on."

"I mean a woman. Unless you've never seen a woman in her underwear."

"What do you want?"

"Tell me which dress to wear."

"I'm sure all three look good." I shrug.

"You barely saw them. They are all totally different," she says.

"Okay, the black one."

"Really? You don't think the neck is too high on that one?"

"Then the red one."

"I'm just not sure that's the right shade of red for me, and I've already done my makeup so I can't compensate."

"Well, then why did you buy it?"

"Not helping!"

"Okay, fine, the white one."

"It's not too . . ."

"Too what?"

"I don't know, virginal."

"It's hard when I haven't seen them on you. And I barely got a glimpse of them on the bed. What look are you going for here?"

"I want to look nice for dinner."

"AshLynn, it's just dinner. Is there a special reason I don't know about?"

"No."

"Then go with the black one."

"Okay. Thank you. You can go now."

"Before I do," I say with my back still to her. "How much longer are we going through with this? I have a life to get back to and we are two days past the favor I was originally doing you."

"Well, I don't know, Mason. How much longer would you like to stay out of jail? I mean, for all you know, I have a picture of you looking through Willow's window."

"Do you?" I grit out.

"Hard to say. Now be a good boy and run along. We are celebrating our engagement at dinner tonight."

I leave the room with a sigh.

I need a drink.

Zach is lounging on a couch in the living room with his feet up on an ottoman. I take a seat in the armchair next to him.

Wait a minute.

"Hey, there's furniture in here."

Zach shrugs.

"How did it get here? Whose is it?"

"He bought it online without telling me. From one of those same-day delivery places. Who, for the first time ever, got here with the stuff within the delivery timeframe window." Willow steps in the room, still fastening an earring in her ear. "I was going to kill him, but I decided I kind of like it."

Holy shit.

My body heats, and my heart starts to race. Its response to Willow is quick and visceral.

"Vintage Audrey Hepburn," Zach says. "You can't go wrong with a classic. And your hair is perfect. Pose for me then do a spin."

Willow giggles and stops in the middle of the room, arms straight, hands pointed out, and does a twirl. Her heels making clicking noises on the floor. I don't know what a vintage Audrey Hepburn is, but her dress is navy blue, tight on top and loose past the waist, reaching down to just below her knees. The neck is high and the straps on the shoulders are thin. It's modest in design but still sexy as hell.

"Nice A-line skirt, beautiful color. What is that, silk?" Zach asks.

"I don't think so," Willow says. "I got it from that vintage shop on Third downtown. Here, feel it." She comes over to where Zach and I are sitting. I can smell her perfume. A light woodsy smell with a touch of sweetness. Maybe sandalwood?

Whatever it is, it's perfect on her.

Zach feels the skirt material between his fingers and sighs. "Polyester. Shame. But still beautiful on you. And we match. Perfect for wheels five and six, respectively."

"Thanks." She smiles at him and plops into the chair next to me. "I ordered an Uber for five forty-five, so it should be here soon." She turns to me. "Where's AshLynn?"

"She's getting dressed."

"I hate waiting," Willow says.

Me too! Especially since this is the second time in as many days AshLynn has kept me waiting.

"Want to shoot some beer and burp at P-Tink?" Zach asks.

"God, yes," Willow says. "I don't have any beer though."

"I bought some at lunch." He smiles, looking proud of himself.

"This is why you're my bestie," she says, blowing him a kiss.

Zach goes into the kitchen and brings back three bottles of beer in short order, popping off the tops as he goes.

"Sorry," Willow says. "Zach and I mostly drink hefeweizens, so that's what this is."

"All beer is good beer," I say tilting the bottle to my lips.

"No drinking yet," Zach says.

I look at him.

"The rules are we start at the same time—winner is whoever finishes first."

"What do I get if I win?" I ask.

"The title of being the winner," Zach says with flourish.

"He usually wins, just to warn you," Willow grumbles.

Zach looks at me, smirk on his face. "It's because I can open my throat. Wide."

If I'd taken a sip, I would have choked on it. As it is, I choke on nothing.

Willow laughs. Zach counts down. We drink.

P-Tink sits between us, tail swishing on the floor behind her, waiting to devour any burp that may escape. Sure enough, Zach finishes first. But what surprises me is that Willow finishes second.

I lose.

A beer drinking contest.

That never happens.

Zach burps three times in succession. The dog jumps after all three. Willow burps next, loud and long. P-Tink jumps at the start of it. Then yelps as it continues. Which leaves me. Except I can't get it to come. I can feel the air bubbles in my chest, wanting to break free. The three of them look at me, waiting.

"I can't get it to come," I say.

"Try bouncing in your seat a little bit," Willow says. So, I do.

Nothing.

"Here," Zach says sitting on the arm of my chair to pat me on the back.

Nothing.

"Well, how are we going to do best two out of three if McHunkster over here can't burp?" Zach asks.

McHunkster?

That makes me laugh. Which in turn makes me burp. Long and loud. Right as AshLynn comes into the room.

"God, you guys are disgusting. Don't you have anything better to do?"

We look at each other, then P-Tink, then back at AshLynn and all say at the same time, "Nope."

22

WILLOW

AshLynn looks incredible, as usual. It's no wonder Mason wants to marry her. Her dress is short, low-cut, white, and tight, showing all of her assets to their best advantage.

"Wow, Ash, you look great," I tell her.

"Yeah?" She looks down and smooths the nonexistent wrinkles from her skirt. "Thanks."

"I thought you were going to wear the black one?" Mason asks.

AshLynn shrugs. "I changed my mind. What? You don't like this one?"

"It's great," Mason says.

"Great?" AshLynn squints her eyes and looks at him. I know that look, he should be careful about what he says next.

"You look lovely," Mason amends.

"Thank you." She smiles.

Zach moves over so that AshLynn can sit down. She waves him off.

"It's fine. The car should be here soon anyway."

"About one minute to be exact," I say looking at my phone.

"How do you know?" AshLynn asks.

"Because I ordered it."

"Daddy didn't order it?"

"What car are you talking about?"

"The town car that Daddy is sending. What car are you talking about?"

"The Uber that I ordered."

"Oh, well, why go in an Uber when we can have a town car, right?"

A car honk sounds from outside.

AshLynn looks through the window. "Who drives a blue Camry?"

"Oh, that's our Uber," I say. "Good."

"You didn't cancel it?" AshLynn asks.

"No," I scoff. "When? In the last four seconds before he got here? Just let Daddy know that we got our own ride."

"I wanted a town car." AshLynn pouts.

"Well, you're welcome to wait for it," I tell her, "but I'm taking the Uber that is here now."

I give P-Tink a chew toy, say goodbye, and head out the door. Zach gets up to follow me.

We both get in to the back seat and Mason calls out that they're coming. I scoot to the middle so that AshLynn has room to get in, leaving the passenger seat for Mason, since he's the largest of all of us.

But instead, Mason opens the passenger door for AshLynn, waits until she's in, then shuts it after her.

"We were leaving the front for you since you're largest," I tell him when he squeezes in next to me.

"You know I get car sick, Willow," AshLynn says from the front seat. "I have to sit in the front seat."

"No, I didn't know that," I say.

"Well, I do."

She doesn't sit in the front seat in a town car. But I refrain from bringing that up for now.

The driver confirms the address and we are on our way. Only instead of heading to dinner, I feel like we are on our way to a firing squad and I'm up first.

I try to make myself as small as possible between the two men flanking me. Zach is nowhere near as big as Mason, but he's still a big guy. I squeeze closer to Zach in an attempt to not touch Mason. It doesn't work. As soon as I free up a little bit of room, Mason takes it. I scoot my legs to the other side of the hump in the back seat and he spreads his legs a bit more. I lean to the side, he's able to straighten his shoulders. His upper arm presses against mine, our thighs fuse together, all I feel is heat everywhere his body touches mine.

My face warms even though there's nothing touching it. I can't get enough air to my lungs and I'm fairly certain my heart is going to beat out of my chest. I place one hand to my throat, hoping the coolness of my fingers will temper the boiling under my skin.

His cologne makes me dizzy. I indulge in a quick fantasy where I climb all over him and roll in his scent, he smells that good. I don't know what kind of cologne he wears, but it's light and spicy at the same time. Maybe with a bit of sage or sandalwood? He hasn't worn it before when we've been working.

Tonight is the first time I've smelled it on him. Which makes it seem as though I go around smelling him, and I don't. If I pass by him I might take a whiff. And it's possible I smelled his shirt once when I accidentally put it in with my laundry.

Accidentally on purpose.

To be a nice host who caters to his needs.

I'll show you how to cater to his needs.

I bury my laugh in my hand and go back to my less lecherous thoughts. Like how I almost tripped over myself when I first walked into the living room earlier tonight and saw him sitting there with Zach laughing over something that was said. To say he cleans up well is an understatement. Dirty, sweaty Mason is delicious. But dressed-up Mason is like the cherry on top of the delicious.

He's dressed in all black. Black slacks, black button-down shirt, black shoes and socks. Which is not an easy look to pull off. I know from experience. There are way too many variables in shades of black. But Mason makes it work.

Zach scolded me earlier for my crush. But in the same breath admitted that he has one on him too. Only his crush is allowed because "Lil' Brooks is not his sister."

I wish I could pinpoint what it is about Mason that makes him so desirable. He's good looking, but so are a ton of other guys. My dog loves him and vice versa, but she loves Zach too. He's good with his hands, but construction workers are a dime-a-dozen in the Seattle area due to all the expansion work. His smile makes my heart swell. And, well, yeah, no one has ever done that before.

Sigh.

Mason is out of the car quickly when we arrive at the club. He helps me out first, then turns to open AshLynn's door. I like the feel of his callouses against the palm of my hand. Which makes me wonder how they would feel on the rest of my body. Which makes me pinch myself so I can snap out of this senseless train of thought.

It's just a crush.

You're testosterone starved.

Zach chooses that moment to put his arm around me, and I lean into him. Sadly, he doesn't count as testosterone. I mean, he does, but not the kind I need.

We've arrived five minutes before we are supposed to meet my parents and are told they are having a pre-dinner cocktail.

That sounds good to me.

We file through the bar area in a single line following the hostess, with AshLynn taking the lead and Mason bringing up the rear. I love this time of day, when the sun is setting behind the water and the entire bar is cast in its pinkish glow.

"Oh look, Willimena, it's so romantic," Zach murmurs in my ear from behind.

"Dork." I laugh.

We reach their table, which only seats two, forcing us to stand there in a half circle in front of them.

Ready for inspection, sir.

Not one to disappoint, Cassandra gives us all a once-over, subtly nodding her approval.

"Well, Zachary, you are looking good. I didn't expect to see you here this evening as well." My dad stands and shakes Zach's hand.

"What can I say, Mister Brooks. I missed you," Zach says.

My dad stopped giving Zach hugs once he found out Zach preferred men. Zach in turn flirts with my dad and stares at him with dreamy eyes, often batting his eyelashes. I love Zach for that. Well, I love Zach for a lot of things, but especially that.

Dad turns to shake Mason's hand, then holds his hand out to Cassandra so he can help her stand. The hostess shows us to our table, large and in the middle of the room. Just the way Dad and Cassandra like it. AshLynn whispers something in Cassandra's ear that I don't catch, Cassandra turns to look at me then whispers something back.

I really hate them sometimes.

"Careful, Regina George is in the house," Zach whispers in my ear, referencing our favorite character to hate in the movie *Mean Girls.*

I end up seated between Mason and Zach at the dinner table and across from my dad. Which is fine by me, I wanted to be near Zach and had no desire to sit next to Cassandra or AshLynn. Having Mason on my other side is just a bonus.

I do feel like I've known him longer than just a few days. It's always amazing to me when that happens. That's how it was with Zach and my friend Marlie before him. Maybe Mason and I will be friends. That would be nice.

Sure, yeah, watch him go through life with your sister. That does sound nice.

I open my mouth, *this* close to voicing my thoughts aloud back to my sarcastic thoughts in my head, then snap it shut.

Would you get it together, woman!

The table goes quiet.

I look up. Five pairs of eyes stare back at me.

"What?"

"Were you going to say something?" my dad asks.

"No. Nope. No." I shake my head.

The server comes to take our drink order. I ask for a vodka martini, extra dirty.

I have a feeling I'm going to like the extra emotional buffer the vodka will add to the evening.

AshLynn waits until after the server leaves, then leans forward, "Mason, Daddy has a surprise for us."

She claps her hands and smiles big. Mason tenses beside me. It's subtle, but I catch it. Zach relaxes back in his chair and whispers, "This ought to be good," out of the side of his mouth.

Mason clasps his hands on the table in front of him. Obviously bracing for what comes next. He may not have known this family long, but he knows enough.

I wish the cocktails were here.

"I was able to secure the main ballroom at our club back home for the wedding. There was another wedding schedule there already, but I promised at least three hundred in attendance, so they are moving the other party to a smaller room."

"Tell him the best part, Daddy," AshLynn squeals.

"We can do it in two weeks," Cassandra interrupts, clapping her hands.

"Here we go," the server says as she sets our drinks in front of us. I'm always surprised when they remember who ordered which drink when they didn't write it down.

Mason downs his whiskey in one gulp before she's finished setting all the drinks down. He hands the glass back to the server. "I'll have another, please."

She does a double take, similar to the server with the mimosas at brunch the other day. My family just has that effect on people.

He takes a deep breath. "Did you plan this?" The question directed at AshLynn.

She doesn't answer, instead looking at my dad for the answer, who stays oddly quiet. Mason looks back and forth between Cassandra, my dad, and AshLynn. I can feel anger radiating off him from my seat.

"Can I speak to you, please?" Mason stands and pulls AshLynn's chair out for her. "Excuse us a moment." He grabs her upper arm and leads her toward the nearest exit door.

"Ruh roh," Zach whispers.

"Well, that reaction does not seem very grateful of him." Cassandra's lips are pinched into her judgey face. She takes a sip of her wine. White. Probably Pinot Grigio or something equally boring and pretentious.

"You just sprung this on him, catching him totally off guard. How do you expect him to react?"

"Nonsense," Cassandra says. "He and AshLynn have discussed it. He knew this was happening."

"Um," I say. "I'm pretty sure he didn't."

"You've been talking to him about his relationship with AshLynn?" Cassandra asks. "Why would you do that?"

"Not just Willow," Zach interjects.

Thank you, Zach!

"It came up in conversation, very casually," Zach continues. "We were both there, Willow and I. It was over lunch. He mentioned wanting a long engagement."

"He told you that?" my dad asks.

"Not in those exact words," I add. "But yes, basically."

Zach and I are both lying, of course. No such conversation happened. We are both just hoping to redeem him in Cassandra's eyes. I hope they are able to work this out. For everyone's sake.

And I'm hardly even lying when I think it.

Hardly.

23

MASON

I drag AshLynn through the restaurant and out the side door to the patio. Luckily there aren't many people out here, so our conversation won't be overheard.

"You want to tell me why you are continuing with all of this fake wedding bullshit? And in a few weeks?"

"Look, first Daddy got you a job and you totally snubbed him. Now you can't even be excited for the wedding?"

"AshLynn, we aren't really engaged! This isn't real!"

"I know." She crosses her arms over her chest and pouts.

"Spill it. What is the real reason behind all this?"

"Fine. I'll tell you. I get my inheritance when I get married."

"And you can't find some poor sucker to actually marry you?"

"Not that they will be happy with. You're older and you have your shit together. They love that."

"You do see the flaw in your plan, right?"

"What?" she asks.

"We aren't really together, AshLynn. We aren't actually engaged, we aren't in a relationship, and we are definitely not getting married."

"I know all that." She rolls her eyes like an annoyed teenager. "I figured we would pretend, I would get my inheritance, and then we could break up."

"This ends today, AshLynn. I'm not continuing on with this façade any longer."

"Then I will report you to the police for being a Peeping Tom."

"Fine, go ahead. I'll deal with it."

"Why are you being so stubborn?"

"Why are you being so unrealistic?" I wait for her to say something. Anything really. But she remains quiet. "You aren't even keeping a foot in reality with this, AshLynn. There is no relationship here."

"I know that."

"So, what's your endgame?"

"What do you mean?"

"How are you getting us out of this? How is this playing out?"

"I just need a few more days," she says.

"You have until tonight. I don't care if you do call the police, it's your word against mine. And I need my life back. I've done you more than enough favors. I've been patient and done everything you asked of me. We aren't even friends, AshLynn. We don't know one another. I've done all this as a stranger. Just to be nice. But I'm done."

"Fine. I'll figure it out."

"Tonight."

"Yes, tonight. Jeez. Can we go eat now?"

I nod.

All four sets of eyes bore into us as we approach the table.

"Is everything okay?" Cassandra asks.

"We're good." I pull out AshLynn's chair for her and return to my seat.

"I was speaking to AshLynn," Cassandra says.

"We're good," AshLynn parrots.

I scoff in response to my thoughts and take a sip of my whiskey. The first one went down nice. This one should just be the icing on the cake.

"Well, shall we continue our wedding-planning conversation?" Jonathan asks.

"If it's all the same to you, sir, AshLynn and I have decided to table that discussion for a bit."

"Whatever does that mean?" my dad asks.

"How long is a bit?" Cassandra asks.

I look back and forth between the two, wondering who to answer first. "Jonathan, in answer to your question, it means we aren't getting married in two weeks. And, Cassandra, in answer to your question, I'm not sure how long. At least until we figure a few things out." I look to AshLynn for confirmation, but she's looking down at her lap.

The table is quiet. I look down and take a sip of my drink.

Of course AshLynn stays quiet. She only speaks up when it bene-fits her.

I look up. Everyone is staring at me. I catch AshLynn's eye, she makes an *I don't know* face back at me.

"I'm sorry, my mind must have drifted. What did I miss?" I ask.

Cassandra rolls her eyes.

Literally.

A grown woman rolls her eyes when I ask a question. *Seri-ously, lady?*

Willow leans toward me. "They asked about the wedding expenses if you aren't getting married in two weeks," she whispers.

"What wedding expenses?" I ask.

"There's the deposit on the venue, the deposit for the caterer, the cost of the invitations, and the house lot down payment."

"Excuse me?"

"We only had two weeks," Cassandra says. As if that answers the question.

I sigh. "Okay, so, what exactly is it that you are saying?"

"If you and AshLynn are *tabling things* and not getting married in two weeks, then we'd like to know how you plan to reimburse us." Cassandra's tone is matter of fact. Like this is an everyday occurrence. I look at AshLynn, she averts her eyes.

"I didn't . . ." I start. "AshLynn, you want to take this one?"

She remains silent and does not look up at me. Don't know why I thought she'd actually say something.

"I'm asking you, Mason," Cassandra says.

Reimburse them for a pretend wedding after a fake engagement. Jesus Christ.

"How much are we talking about?"

"Twenty-seven thousand three hundred forty-two dollars," she says coolly.

"*Excuse* me? How much?" Because surely she didn't just say—

"Twenty-seven thousand three hundred forty-two dollars," Cassandra repeats.

Holy fuck.

"What is this? Some kind of fucking con your family pulls?" I'm pissed. "Your daughter grabs some unsuspecting guy, plans a quick wedding, then sticks him with the bill?"

"Don't insult us," Jonathan says.

"Don't insult me. I didn't agree to any of those things. I can't even imagine what you could have already spent twenty-seven thousand dollars on."

"Ten thousand is for the lot that you turned down," Cassandra says. "The remaining seventeen thousand is for the nonrefundable deposits —eight thousand for the venue, three thousand for the catering, and the other six thousand paid for the invitations."

"Six thousand dollars for invitations? Are you kidding me?"

"No. I'm not. Hand-addressed was a must, and it was important they go out immediately because the wedding was planned to happen in a couple weeks. I had to pay a rush fee."

"You couldn't just send an email?" I feel like an ass for asking. But I'm an ass with twenty-seven thousand on the line, so I'm going with it.

The server brings our food.

I push my plate away once she leaves. "I'm no longer hungry. In fact, if you'll excuse me—"

"Please stay," AshLynn says.

I look at her. Her eyes pleading.

It's one dinner. Suck it up.

I nod at AshLynn and scoot my chair back in at the table. No one says a word. I slice into my perfectly cooked steak and take a bite. It may as well be cardboard for how much I am enjoying it. We eat in silence for several minutes until AshLynn finally speaks.

"It's not Mason's fault."

I look at her, surprised that she's speaking up at last.

"I lied when I said he was willing to move to Texas. You never would have put money down on the property or the wedding otherwise. I thought I could convince him to move, but the truth is I'm not sure I want to get married. And I don't think he wants to either. I'm sorry, Daddy." She looks sorry, eyes downcast, expression somber.

The table stays silent until Jonathan finally speaks. "I'm extremely disappointed in you, AshLynn. But it is very mature of you to admit the truth."

AshLynn nods in return.

"Surely you aren't going to ask him to reimburse you, right?" Willow asks.

Cassandra looks at her, eyes narrowed and lips pressed into a thin line.

"It has nothing to do with him," she continues.

I don't need her fighting my battles for me. Shit, I don't need anyone fighting my battles for me.

"It's okay," I say. "I understand the frustration with this entire scenario. And while I don't believe that I owe you anything in return for money that was spent unbeknownst to me, I don't want this to get any more uncomfortable than it already is. So, what I will do is compromise and pay back one-third of the total."

If for no other reason, then to stay out of jail.

"You mean one-half?" Cassandra says.

"No, I mean one-third. Apparently, there are three parties in this planning process. You and Jonathan, AshLynn, and me. So I will take responsibility for my part."

"This is ridiculous," Willow says.

"It's okay," I say to her, placing my fingertips on her thigh to get her attention. I ignore the flutter in my chest when I touch her.

"So stupid," Willow mumbles under her breath. I'm pretty sure I'm the only one who heard her. This has obviously made her angry. I can feel the tension in her body from here in the next chair. I know she takes it personally when her family does things that she doesn't agree with, so I will try to find a way to convince her that it's okay.

I return my attention to my now cold steak. The table around me is quiet. Everyone's mood somber. We finish dinner in silence and don't stay for dessert, after-dinner cocktails, or dancing in the lounge. Jonathan and Cassandra give us a ride to Willow's in the town car, which is really a limo. I find it incredibly ostentatious that this is the way they choose to travel but keep my thoughts to myself. I've said enough about my feelings toward them tonight. No need to exacerbate the situation further.

The limo pulls to a stop in the curve of the driveway in front of Willow's house and I'm the first one out. I poke my head back in to address Jonathan. "I'll leave a check with Willow. Unless you're worried it won't clear."

"That will be fine," he replies, not quite meeting my gaze.

I wait on the front porch for Willow to unlock the door. I can hear P-Tink sniffing around the door and letting out the occasional Husky howl since she somehow knows it's Willow. Sadly, I'll probably miss the dog the most. Maybe second only to seeing this house come into its full glory. I won't begin to rank where Willow lies on the list of things

I'll miss. I step aside to let her through to the door, Zach follows behind her.

"AshLynn is going to stay with her parents tonight," he says to me. I nod in response. It doesn't matter, I'm not staying. I'll go to a hotel or my mom's. There's no reason for me to be here any longer and I'm not about to take advantage of Willow's hospitality. "So," he continues. "Looks like you'll have the guest room all to yourself finally."

"Oh, I'm not staying," I say.

Willow turns. "Why not?"

"I don't want to impose."

"Don't be silly," she says. "You staying in the guest room does not impact me in the slightest. Given everything that's happened tonight, I would really appreciate it if you'd stay."

"Okay," I say. "Thank you." Making a new plan to be gone before the sun comes up anyway.

"I don't know about you guys, but that was exhausting. Mason, I'm so sorry for the way my family has handled this. I feel embarrassed to even call them family right now."

"It's okay," I say. "It has nothing to do with you. Shit happens. This is just one of those things, you know?"

She nods. "Okay, well, regardless, sleep well. I'll see you in the morning." She leans in and gives me a tentative hug. I return it just as hesitantly. Zach shakes my hand, and the two retreat to Willow's bedroom while I head for the guest room.

Three hours later I'm still not asleep. I toss and turn, not sure what would make me feel better at this point. My brain won't turn off and my body feels blitzed. I get up to use the restroom, then decide to head out to the deck to watch the water for a while. Someone has already beat me to it.

Willow is bundled in sweats, Ugg boots, and a puffy coat. She is turned to the side, her features illuminated by the light of the moon. I want to sketch her this way. She looks beautiful. I commit the image to memory, knowing that after tonight I'll never have a chance to see it again.

24

WILLOW

I'VE NEVER BEEN A GOOD SLEEPER. ONE OF MY FAVORITE things about living here is sitting on the deck at night when I can't sleep and watching the sound.

I hear someone behind me. I can tell it's Mason over Zach by the way he moves in my periphery. "Couldn't sleep either, huh?"

"No. I don't always sleep well anyway, but tonight is unusually bad."

"I have some melatonin pills if you want to try it."

"Maybe in a bit. Is it okay if I join you?"

"Sure. And just so you know, the melatonin did not help me tonight, so take the offer accordingly."

"Will do." He takes a seat next to me on the edge of the deck. P-Tink sighs and moves to place a paw on his foot, which I think is adorable. Her head and other front paw are resting on my feet.

"Crazy couple of weeks, huh?" I ask him.

"Definitely. And totally out of character for me."

"It's AshLynn." I sigh, hating to admit the truth. "She does that to men. They lose their mind over her."

"I didn't—" He starts to deny it but stops. Because I'm guessing that's exactly what happened. That like most men, he stopped thinking rationally when she was around and pretty much lost his mind.

He laughs and confirms my theory. "I guess so, huh?"

"Don't feel bad, you aren't the first," I say. "My dad takes the prize for that. Just in a different way." I scoff. "He'd do just about anything for her. It's remarkable to witness at times."

"He'd do the same for you," he says. Which I find funny since he has no way of knowing that and is obviously just trying to make me feel better. It's sweet, but unnecessary.

"Maybe before my mom died, but definitely not after," I say. "Her death changed him. And not for the better. He wasn't *good* again until AshLynn came along, and maybe even a little while longer after that."

"I'm sorry you went through that," he says.

"It's okay. I've dealt with it."

"Therapy?"

I wave my hand dismissively. "Therapy, alcohol, travel, you name it, I've done it to help me cope with both parents leaving me. Even though my dad didn't die, he disappeared mentally and emotionally right after my mom did, and never really came back."

"That's got to be hard."

"Eh, I mean, you never had a dad, so really what's worse?"

"Probably having one and losing him, over never knowing one at all."

"Maybe," I say, then change the subject because I don't want to talk about my dad any longer. Especially after tonight, when the disappointment that I feel in him is so monumental it's hard to breathe.

"So, what's next for you?" I ask.

"I'm not sure," he says. "I've been traveling a bit and ended this last jaunt at my buddy Jake's party in Leavenworth where I met AshLynn, so I'll probably go visit my mom for a bit. Take it day by day."

"Why do you think you've never done things the normal way, if you don't mind me asking. You know, like get a job, find a house, stay in one place, etc."

"Good question. I think it has to do with never leaving or going anywhere as a kid. My mom was poor, so we never went anywhere. We rented a tiny house, and nothing ever changed about it. The owner was old as dirt, and he preferred everything be the same. Even if an appliance broke down, it was replaced with something just as old, but in working order. She worked multiple jobs my entire childhood, so I spent a lot of time in that shitty little house.

"Don't get me wrong, she made the inside of the house as pleasing as she could, but there wasn't a lot of time or money for that. No yard to speak of, and what was there was dirt. Neither of us knew how to tend a yard or fix anything. It wasn't until I was in fifth grade that I started tinkering with fixing shit, growing grass, landscaping. I went to the library and read as many home improvement, gardening, and fix-it books that I could find. Experimenting on the house kept me out of trouble, and I learned a valuable trade."

"Like my big orange book," I say with a laugh.

"Yeah. But, in answer to your question, I think being sedentary for so long awakened something in me. I knew after that I didn't want to be stuck in the same place again. And if I were, it would have to be someplace incredible." He sighs. "You have a place like that here, you know."

"Thanks. I was lucky to find it."

"You going to hire people to finish it?"

"What? No. The whole point is to do this myself. Good or bad."

"Your family seems to think you won't do it."

"Yeah, well. Don't get me started on them. I don't need to sour your opinion on my family even more."

He chuckles, but it's hollow sounding.

"No," I continue, "I need to prove to myself that I can do something hard and time-consuming. That I have stick-to-itiveness. Though, to be honest, I'm not entirely sure why. I mean I know I'm trying to figure my life out. What it means, how I want to live it, what I want to do with it, but at the end of that journey I want to have something quantifiable that I produced. Does that make sense?"

"More than you know. I think I know exactly what you mean," he says softly.

I look up slightly from where I'd been studying the sand in front of us. He's staring at me. He reaches out and tucks my hair behind my ear. His touch makes me shiver.

"Cold?" he asks.

I shake my head. It's hard to be cold in the proximity of someone who radiates so much heat. I wonder for a quick second if he's going to kiss me. And by wonder, I mean hope. But instead he drops his hand and stands.

"I think I'm going to try sleeping again. You okay out here on your own?"

"Yeah, but I'm going to go in too." I follow him inside with P-Tink padding softly behind me. We say goodnight in the living room and each head in separate directions to our rooms.

I crawl into bed next to Zach. P-Tink acts as buffer between us, usually on her back with all four legs in the air displaying her belly for anyone who may want to scratch it in the middle of the night. I lie there, waiting for sleep to claim me. Which doesn't happen for another hour, but when it does, my dreams are filled with my family chasing off all my suitors, then mailing them bills for the expenses.

I WAKE to P-Tink's nose touching mine. She has no concept of personal space when sleeping. Sometimes it's cute, and sometimes I wake to us touching noses. Zach is still sleeping soundly, so I gently get out of bed, and coax P-Tink to follow. I want to make coffee before Mason leaves.

But as soon as I'm in the hallway I can tell that he's already gone. Still I double-check the driveway and the guest room to be sure. I feel heavy inside. Weighted down by regret and disappointment. I can't believe he's gone. Without even saying goodbye.

What would you have said differently this morning that you couldn't have said last night?

I ignore my rational thought process and go on feeling sad. P-Tink whimpers and rushes through the living room and kitchen to find him.

"I know, girly. He's gone. But that doesn't mean we can't still have coffee and enjoy our day, right?"

She looks at me like I'm stupid.

I often feel like she's smarter than she lets on. She lies down in the middle of the kitchen floor in a huff, her head resting on her front paws. She actually looks sad.

That's puppy dog eyes, dork.

I scoff at myself and move to make coffee. A note is propped against the maker, with a check underneath it. Made out to my father in the amount of nine thousand one hundred fourteen dollars. My family is a bunch of assholes. And Mason is a really good guy. He didn't deserve any of this. Maybe I can figure out a way to pay him back without him knowing.

I pick up the note, recognizing the paper from Mason's little pad he keeps in his pocket and am thankful for his *antiquated* habit of pen and paper.

Willow,

Thank you for your hospitality. I appreciate everything that you've done. I want you to know I enjoyed our talks. I'm sorry I won't be here to help you finish the house, but I just know it's going to be spectacular. I may not have known you long, but I know for certain that you are stronger than you think. You've got this. Truly. I'm a better person for having met you. Give P-Tink a belly rub for me.

-Mason

PS—I stole a travel coffee mug, but I will make sure it's returned.

PSS—Hopefully waking up to coffee helps take the sting out of the missing mug.

He's right about that. Waking up to coffee is my favorite thing in the entire world. I know I could just set a timer and make it the night before, but I never know for certain when I will wake in the morning. I know, how sad for me that I have no schedule for when I must be awake. It actually is inconvenient at times.

That's a lie. It pretty much rocks.

Regardless, it's just easier to make it fresh each day. So having it ready and still steaming hot, is truly a treat. I fix a cup and head out to the deck. P-Tink follows me but doesn't romp in the sand like normal. We watch the ferries traverse the sound while we slowly wake up. The slight chill in the air has me grabbing a blanket and wrapping it around me.

Zach joins us a short time later, with his own blanket and coffee.

"He gone?" he asks.

I nod.

"Sorry."

"It's okay. It's just a crush. Plus nothing was ever going to come of it anyway."

"You never know."

"Of course I know. He was engaged to AshLynn. I'd be sloppy seconds. No way could I ever compete with her."

"Oh stop," he snaps.

"Stop nothing," I say. "She's the male species Achilles heel, taking men to their knees since puberty. She's fun and spontaneous, beautiful and sexy. Hell, she was going to get married to someone she just met. And he was so taken with her, he agreed."

"She wasn't going to marry him," Zach says.

"Yes, she was. Where have you been for the last couples of days?"

"Come on, Willicent, think about it. When has AshLynn ever committed to anything?"

I shrug.

"Plus, this is exactly like something she would do just to get a rise out of your father and Cassandra."

"No. She acts out, but she doesn't involve other people in it."

"Really? South Padre Island? Disneyland? Spring break her sophomore year?" He names three instances where she did something outrageous for attention and it affected my life too.

"Okay, fine. So what if you are right? That changes nothing."

"He didn't love her."

"So?"

"I'm just saying, it's not much skin off his back to be out of this is all."

"Except that he left a check for over nine thousand dollars for my dad."

"I gotta say, Willie, that was the most ballsy thing I've ever seen. And I see a lot of balls if you know what I mean."

"Cassandra asking for money?"

"Yeah. Cassandra asking Mason for money. That was straight-up outrageous. Made the whole insufferable dinner worth it just to see that in person. Because if you had just told me about it later, I guarantee I never would have believed you."

"I wouldn't lie to you about something like that."

"I know. It has nothing to do with you. It's a suspension of belief that you've witnessed something so completely extraordinary that your brain almost can't comprehend. Like, remember when little Mikey Lawson got the compound fracture in soccer practice and we saw the bone sticking out of the skin, but you couldn't believe it was actually bone you were seeing?"

I shudder at the memory. "Yes. Ugh."

"It's like that."

I laugh. "You're such a drama queen."

"Takes one to know one."

"Fine." I finish my coffee and go get another cup.

"My point being," he says when I return, "is that there would be nothing odd about you and Mason getting together."

"Except—"

"Nothing odd about it," he interrupts.

I keep my mouth shut and think about it. Maybe he's right. I mean, it happened in that movie *The Family Stone* with Sarah Jessica Parker's character.

"It's not like it would ever happen anyway. I don't even have his phone number."

"I do."

My heart leaps into my throat.

You are not *going to call him.*

"Well, if I ever need it, I will let you know."

He nods and drops the subject. We finish our coffee then take P-Tink with us to breakfast before he catches the water taxi back to Seattle. And I'm left on my own in my house once more.

25

MASON

I KNOCK LIGHTLY ON MY MOM'S DOOR. WORRIED THAT MAYBE she won't be awake yet. If that's the case, I'll just go grab coffee and come back later. The door swings open a moment later. Her face registers surprise when she realizes it's me.

"Mason! What are you doing here? What a wonderful surprise. I wasn't expecting you. Are you okay?" She rattles off questions faster than I can answer them.

"I'm good. Just wanted to see if I could take you to breakfast."

"I just had some toast, but I could eat something light," she says.

We walk to the Biscuit Bitch on First Ave. Not exactly light fare, but damn good.

Once we've ordered and found a seat, she begins with her questions.

"So, what's going on, Mason?"

"Nothing. Why?"

"Because you have that look about you. You want to talk about something, but you don't know how to start, and you're afraid I'm going to be disappointed once you do."

"How do you do that?"

"It's a mother's gift. Now spill it."

I sigh. "I met a girl in Leavenworth."

"At the party?"

"No, but at the same hotel."

"She must be some girl if you're telling me about her."

"She is, but not in the way you're thinking. I don't want you getting all excited until you hear the entire story, because it's not going in the direction you're visualizing."

She nods. "Okay."

I tell her about meeting AshLynn in the hotel bar, and about the crazy days that follow. More about Willow's house than she probably found interesting, and finally the dinner at the club. I leave nothing out.

I pause as our food arrives and take a break to dig in. I ordered a Hot Mess Bitch which mirrors my life right about now. It does not disappoint. My mom ordered a Buttered-Up Bitch, which just has butter and jam. We finish at the same time even though mine is close to three times bigger than hers.

"So, you're wondering how to see Willow again?" she asks.

"Willow is the sister," I say for no good reason, knowing that she knows that.

"Let's walk."

We walk back toward her condo, but she waits a block or so to continue talking.

"It's obvious Willow is the one you're attracted to."

"How is that obvious?"

"By the way your voice changes when you say her name. The words you choose when describing her. The way she dominated the story even though it wasn't about her."

"Will I get this same crazy intuitive talent if I'm ever a father?"

"I can only say for certain with mothers." She smiles.

"Well, I can't do anything about it, anyway."

"Why not?"

"Ma, I was pretend engaged to her sister."

"I know."

"Chicks don't get over that stuff."

"She doesn't sound like that type."

"Well, I can't stand her family."

"I concur. But it doesn't sound like she's happy with them either right now."

"She doesn't believe in relationships."

"Show her she's wrong."

"I don't believe in relationships."

"That's not true."

"I don't believe in them for me."

"You just haven't had a good one yet."

"Okay, well, how about this, I don't think the timing is right."

"If not now, when?"

"You sound like an inspirational poster."

She laughs.

"Enough about me," I say. "You opening the store today?"

"No, the girls are. I actually have plans today."

"Plans? Really? With who?"

"The nice gentleman who owns the coffee cart out front."

"And what are you two doing?"

"Lunch and a movie."

I continue to tease her and ask questions about her date the entire way back to her condo. We part with plans to have dinner this week. And then I find myself alone. Alone with my thoughts and with nowhere to go. Usually I plan ahead for what happens after I finish a house or a trip, but I didn't this time. I got all mixed up in the Brooks family and failed to look out for number one.

I get my motorcycle out of the garage area in my mom's building. Then head out to a motel I've stayed in a few times before when I was between jobs. Maybe I should decide on a forever home, or at least a "for right now" home, to have a home base to come back to. I have plenty of money in the bank, if I buy something, I won't have a mortgage. I could take my time with the renovations and make it exactly the way I want.

I settle in at the hotel and hook up to the Wi-Fi, then take a look at a few of my favorite real estate sites. Nothing showing as "available" on the market grabs my eye, so I send emails to a few of the guys I know to see if any pocket listings are coming up. Listings that aren't yet advertised but can still be purchased.

I look at the clock. It's only been forty-five minutes since I checked in to my room. My god, how is it that time is dragging so much? What is wrong with me that I can't find something to occupy my time?

I need a project.

I need to get laid.

I need to put the Brooks family out of my mind. I grab my wallet and head out to a pub down the street.

THE PUB WAS BORING. I'm not sure what I expected for two o'clock in the afternoon. But it wasn't that. None of the people were interesting to talk to. I didn't see any girls I might want to fuck. And the bottomless mimosas ensured that everyone was drunker than me and I wouldn't be able to catch up.

I walk around downtown for a bit, then head over to a lookout near the ferry terminal to watch them for a while. I take out my notepad and start a small sketch of the *Sealth*, one of the ferries running today. Not that they don't all look similar. I finish the *Sealth* and start sketching one of the islands, Vashon, I think. I wouldn't mind living on Vashon Island.

If Bainbridge Island didn't already have the perfect house.

I need something that will take my mind off everything. Times like this I wish I did drugs. Deciding on a plan to work out, I head back to the hotel, change, and hit the boxing gym. Because when all else fails, getting the shit beat out of you while trying to do the same to someone else, is a surefire way to numb your brain for a while.

Mom's bookstore isn't exactly on my way back to the hotel, but I go that route anyway so I can grab a few books to read. I see the coffee/juice cart in front of the shop that my mom mentioned, along with a couple of small tables for people to sit at. It wasn't there the last time I was here, which was only a few weeks ago. But makes for a nice addition, I'm surprised no one thought of it sooner.

I had my fill of water at the gym, so I order a *rejuvenating orange-pineapple fusion* from the kid working the cart and head in to the store. Amy, a young graduate student who hopes to be a writer, is working the counter in front while Meghan, a single mom with teenagers who likes to pass the time while they are busy, is at the help desk in the back. Both are nice and work hard. Mom trusts them, so I do too.

"Hey, Amy, how's it going?"

"Oh, hey, Mason. I didn't know you were coming in today."

"Neither did I. Just want to grab a couple books if you don't mind."

"Help yourself."

I peruse the *Noir* section, like usual, and grab a Dashiell Hammett and a Dennis Lehane before also snagging a copy of *The Postman Always Rings Twice*, which I haven't read in a couple years. Then I move over to literature and grab a copy of *A Moveable Feast*, which Zach recommended. I sit in the lounge and start that one first.

Thinking of Zach reminds me of Willow. And thinking of Willow reminds me of the shit-storm that is AshLynn. And thinking about *that* makes me want to bury my head in a hole in shame.

Nine thousand dollars.

Better than jail, buddy.

What in the actual fuck was I thinking writing a check for over nine thousand dollars? I must be the world's biggest idiot to pay for a fake wedding that wasn't even my idea in the first place. My mom said it was chivalrous for me to do that. Chivalrous and generous. It was neither of those. It was stupid and moronic. Like I let them lead me by the balls to the bank of ideocracy where I opened the vault for them to take whatever they wanted.

I grab my phone and send a text to my buddy who was looking for help with a house in Santa Barbara a couple weeks ago, letting him know that I'm available. Then I settle in with my orange-fusion-rejuvenation-whatever drink and tune out everything else so I can read.

I finish a good chunk of the book before the girls are ready to close up shop, so I leave a note with what I took with me and head back to the hotel. By the time I get there my buddy has texted me back. He could definitely use my help if I have a few months to spare. And I do.

I text him back to let him know I'll be there in a few days and start making plans to disappear for a while. The work will do my brain and my body some good. By the time I come back, I'll have a plan for what comes next, I won't be all tangled up in thoughts of girls with tree names, and I'll have some extra money in my pocket to try and recoup the nine thousand that I burned.

26

WILLOW

I show the kitchen guy at the hardware store my rough idea for the new kitchen. I may have wanted to do this house on my own, but no way in hell am I going to try and hang cupboards by myself. There are some things I need to leave to a pro. I did, however, lay the tile on the kitchen floor by myself and I plan to do part of the backsplash on my own. The floor is a little uneven, in part due to the tile I chose, and in part due to my tile cuts and mud laying. But I can look at it knowing that I, P-Tink, and a book handled it on our own.

The kitchen space is large, especially after taking down the wall between the dining room and kitchen, and then the one between the kitchen and living room. I will have enough space around the kitchen island to seat four and the dining room table I have my eye on seats four but expands to six. So if I ever decide to have friends over other than just Zach, I will have a place for them to sit when I entertain.

Ha! Entertain.

I have spent so much time alone with P-Tink over the past few months, that I think we communicate telepathically now.

"Okay, so riddle me this," I say to the man. "Can I do a walk-in pantry in this corner, a wall of cabinets here, and then counter space with cabinets above and below, here, here, and here?" I point to all the places I would like them to go and he shows me the styles I can use and how many I can fit given the dimensions. I bought an app for my iPad that lets me rearrange my kitchen as many times as I would like.

"I have a thirty-six-inch Wolf range I'd like to put here," I point to my diagram and the picture of the stove. "And then oven over here."

"Okay," he says. "But remember your gas inlet is over here."

"That's fine," I say.

"You need to have your range near the gas inlet."

"Oh, well then, where do I put these countertops?"

"You'll have to flip them like this." He moves some things around. I don't like it.

"What would you do if this were your kitchen?"

"Well," he says. "I'd want counter space on either side of all appliances, except for maybe this side of the fridge. And this over here." He continues to move things around in my app. I tune out his voice and just watch his hands. They are big and rough looking. The man himself is not attractive, but his hands are. I remind myself that fantasizing about the kitchen guy's hands is not a smart idea.

But they look like Mason's hands.

Shut up, inner self. We aren't thinking about him any longer. He is persona non grata to the nth degree.

The kitchen guy sits back in his chair and pushes my iPad toward me. I look at what he's done.

Oh, that's good.

"Wow, you really know your stuff, huh?" I ask.

"It's kind of what I do for a living," he says.

I laugh.

He doesn't.

"Can I put a bigger fridge here?" I ask, knowing already that my fridge is larger than what he has there but not wanting him to rearrange everything again.

"Yes," he says. "These just shift this way." He shows me how the cupboards and counters shift a bit to one side. Which just lengthens a half wall a bit. My island stays the same, and he even adds a faucet over the stovetop.

"Is that for putting out fires?" I joke.

"It's for filling pots. It's a pot-filler faucet."

"I know. Never mind." I'm embarrassed now. I place my order with pretty much everything that he has suggested and get the quote. It's a lot higher than I thought it was going to be. Let's face it, everything has cost a lot more than I thought it would.

"It's a bit higher than I thought it would be," I tell him.

"You went with the custom cabinet option. Your original quote was all premade cabinets."

"Oh."

"But, with custom, you get exactly every size you want, as well as the special finish."

"Okay."

He helps me order the tile for the backsplash, and pick out the marble for the counters, reminding me the installers need to measure everything after the cabinets are in before ordering the marble. I'd already gone a little crazy at the Sub-Zero, Wolf, and Cove showroom in Seattle for all of my appliances and a wine fridge. And I have a guy coming out next week to talk to me about outdoor grills. I don't grill. But I figure I can learn. Because, heck, look what I've figured out so far.

The kitchen is the last room to be done. I finished the master bathroom in about a month. That was true trial and error. Painting took over three weeks. I didn't do a whole lot to the other bedrooms outside of painting and adding or replacing windows. I put French doors on the guest room with no patio, as well as a patio. And French doors instead of a slider leading from the master bedroom to the deck, all of which took over a month. A heck of a long time to refinish the wood floors, and then another month for each of the guest baths. But, now it's almost time to pick furniture. Which, oddly, I'm looking forward to even though shopping isn't really my thing.

It took me some time to regroup after the whole AshLynn and Mason debacle. Mostly because I hadn't really thought through what I wanted when we tore down the bathroom wall. I mean, I had. But it was also partly getting to work with Mason and I wanted to get going. Even so, I love how it turned out. I've got a claw-foot tub in a corner, with a huge glass shower adjacent. Separate water closet, and his-n-her vanities, and plenty of storage. Plus, two skylights for natural light and a great big window that faces the water. It's perfect.

I finish with the kitchen guy and check my phone. I have a little time before I'm meeting Zach for lunch, so I head over to the garden department to check out flowers. I still want to plant annuals and perennials in the front, and maybe get some smaller potted plants for the back deck.

Oh! An herb garden would be cool.

I start to fill my cart, then realize they won't all fit in my car. I grab a couple now, and decide to come back for more later, then head out to meet Zach.

We'd arranged to meet at a place on Sixth Avenue. It's a gorgeous day and only about a fifteen-minute walk from where I am now. I take my time enjoying the sites and checking out all the stores in the area that I may want to come back to. Like this little bookstore.

Ohmigod.

Bookstore.

I wonder if this is Mason's mom's shop. I peek through the window, but don't see much outside my own reflection.

"They're open," I hear a voice say and I turn. The guy at the coffee cart gestures to the store. "They're open if you want to go in."

"Oh . . . no . . . I just . . ." I clear my throat. "I'm late for a meeting. Thank you, though."

He tips an imaginary hat at me and I scurry on my way. And now I'm late meeting Zach. We are eating at a sushi place we've been to before and love. The entire front opens up, like al fresco dining, weather permitting of course. And today the weather permits.

"Hey, sorry I'm late." I find him at a table already, near the front where we can people watch while we eat.

"No worries, I've been soaking up the atmosphere." He angles his head toward a table to his right where three incredibly attractive men are lunching.

"Oh my," I say. "That is some atmosphere."

"Right? So"—he leans forward, elbows on the table—"tell me, what sort of happy homemaker projects have you accomplished today?"

"Kitchen cabinets and countertops!" I say it like I'm excited, because I am excited. I saved the best for last. The best being the kitchen. I'm not much of a chef, but I plan to learn.

"Fascinating," he says drily.

"It's going to be amazing. And you're going to be jealous that you don't have a kitchen like mine."

"I don't cook."

"I know, me neither, but this is going to be the kitchen of all kitchens. Like the kitchen to inspire those who don't cook, to cook."

The server comes to take our drink orders, we both go with a Japanese beer each and a sake to share, plus edamame and a seaweed salad to start.

I decide to play this next part casual.

"Oh, hey, I passed a bookstore on the way here that you might like."

"A bookstore, huh?"

"Yeah, it was a cute little used bookstore. There's a coffee cart in front and I think I saw a lounge in the back where you can read."

"Really?"

"Yes." He's acting weird.

Why is he acting weird?

"Why are you acting weird?"

"Me? I'm not acting weird. You're acting weird."

I look at him, eyes narrowed.

He looks at me, eyes wide.

"What?" I ask.

"Well," he says cagily. "It just occurred to me that we know someone who owns a used bookstore."

Is he on to me? Does he know that I think it might be Mason's mom's store?

"Oh?" Now my eyes are wide. On purpose. "Who might that be?"

"Missus Cartwright."

"I'm sorry, who?" I ask, trying to appear as innocent as possible.

"You remember, like maybe six months ago or so, AshLynn was engaged for a hot minute?"

"Of course I remember."

"The guy she was engaged to, Mason? Well, his mom is Missus Cartwright."

"Oh, of course, how silly of me to have forgotten that." I'm almost believable when I say it. We haven't talked about Mason in almost a month. The fact that I know how long it's been speaks volumes. He looks at me as though he doesn't believe me, though. I don't blame him.

"Fine." I sigh. "That was the first thing I thought too, that maybe it was his mom's."

"Did you go inside?"

"God, no."

"Why not?"

"Zach!"

"Willicent!"

"What if his mom was there?"

"Why? Because you've met her? Because you think she knows about you?"

"No. And no. But what if Mason had been there?"

"You would have said hi. And that you hated to run, but you were late for a luncheon."

"Guys have it so easy."

"You think we don't get nervous?"

"Clearly."

"Pashaw! I totally get nervous. Remember how I was with Brandon?"

"Yes. Fine. I guess."

"Good. Now, since you brought it up, let's talk about Mason."

"I didn't bring it up and there's nothing to talk about."

"Well, let's see. You saw a bookstore and immediately thought of him. You were afraid to go in which means there are still feelings surrounding it. And you are pretending it doesn't bother you when it does."

"Fine."

I pour myself some sake and drink it in one gulp. Then I do another for good measure.

"You're right. I still think about him. But I'll be honest. Sometimes I forget what he even looks like."

"Oh, honey. You need a refresher? You let me know, I have an image of that man burned into both my brains."

I laugh. "In my defense, I haven't met or even talked to any other guys since him, so it would be hard to have someone else in my head anyway."

"Do you want someone else in your head?"

"I don't want anyone in my head. I want to figure my life out and decorate my house."

"Okay, nuff said."

"Okay."

Our food comes and eating keeps us quiet. I'm a little annoyed that he's not pushing the Mason thing. But I don't know how I'd want him to do that or what I'd want him to say. Or even why I'd want him to say anything. The Mason point needs to be moot. And it needs to stay that way.

27

MASON

I plan to surprise my mom at the bookstore today. I'm ninety-nine percent sure she's working. I haven't seen her in person in about six months, since I've been in Santa Barbara, though we talked on the phone often. She knew it was an escape for me, I knew it was an escape for me, but we both ignored the obvious and pretended it was a regular work trip. Now I'm hoping we can continue pretending there wasn't a reason for said escape.

I nod a hello to the guy running the coffee cart in front of the store. I doubt he's the guy Mom has been dating because he looks about thirty years too young for her. Shit, he'd better not be the guy, he's younger than I am. I find my mom in the back of the store logging in new arrivals before they are shelved.

I sneak up behind her and cover her eyes.

"Guess who?"

"Mason, is that you?" She turns and gives me a hug. "I'm so happy to see you! How was Santa Barbara? When did you get back?"

"Me too, Mom. Santa Barbara was great, I actually just got back this morning and I came to see you first. Wanted to see if you'd like to grab lunch or coffee or something?

"That sounds lovely. I would love lunch. There's a sushi place down the way I've been dying to try."

"I was hoping for something a little more substantial."

"More than rice and fish?"

"I haven't eaten since yesterday. What do you say we compromise and do fish-n-chips?"

"Whatever you would like." She dusts her hands on her jeans and fluffs her hair.

"Hey, Mom, that guy out there at the cart, he's not the one you're seeing, right?"

"I don't think so. Abe has the day off today. Why?"

"No reason. Just like to see who my mom is spending time with."

28

WILLOW

Zach and I go to the bookstore that might be owned by Mason's mom after lunch under the guise that he's a writer and needs to know about all the local bookstores. Luckily it's two young girls working, so obviously neither are his mother, which results in equal feelings of relief and disappointment on my part.

"I know we said we weren't going to talk about it again," Zach says. "But just out of curiosity, what would you do for real if you saw Mason again. I mean, Seattle is big, but it's not huge."

"Well, it doesn't really matter since we agreed we aren't talking about it, right?"

"Yes, we did. But humor me. Just pretend."

"Fine." He and I are sitting in the lounge part of the bookstore. It's in the back of the store and has huge cushy furniture, perfect for grabbing a book and losing yourself for a few hours. Which I would be doing now except Zach has started up a conversation and who am I to deny him if he wants to talk. Never mind that it's about Mason. That has nothing to do with it.

"Um," I continue, "Well, it depends. In this scenario of yours, was he previously engaged to AshLynn or am I just meeting him randomly?"

"This fictitious scenario is based on reality. So, previously engaged."

"Okay." Not that I'll admit it to Zach, but I've thought about this a lot. More than is probably healthy. Because the main question, always, is whether I could *be* with someone who was *with* my sister before. Even if they didn't have sex, which he only briefly hinted at once, and I've not been able to come up with a satisfactory answer to that. I mean, the reality is they were barely together a few weeks. The fact that they rushed an engagement doesn't really factor in that heavily. All parties involved ultimately admitted it was rushed and too fast. They weren't even in love. So, what's the harm? Right?

But then there's another part of me that would always wonder if I was as sexy as AshLynn? As good a kisser? Is my body as alluring as hers? Am I as spontaneous? As pretty? As funny? Even though she's so much younger than me, I feel as though I've lived in AshLynn's shadow her entire life. She came out of the womb perfect and beautiful. She never had one of those awkward phases as a tween, her teeth were naturally straight, her hair naturally blond, and eyes piercing blue. Her body proportions are every man's dream —big boobs, small waist, narrow hips with just enough curve to entice. And she's short. That perfect five feet three inches.

Meanwhile, I'm weighing in at five feet nine inches, close to six feet in heels. And my body is fairly straight up and down. I'm slender, I know that. But I have no curves. My boobs are small, my waist is normal, my hips are narrow. In fact, my waist and hips are almost the same. I have the build of a tall slender boy. It's why I favor A-line skirts and dresses. I can fake hips. And a million other items help me fake boobs. I am the epitome of false body advertising.

Not that a lot of men have stayed interested enough to get past the false part of the advertising. Whereas AshLynn falls in love multiple times a week it seems, I played it close to the vest, with my two past relationships. So, here's me a too-tall woman in her early thirties with an unnatural attachment to her dog, her dead best friend, and her gay best friend: no real interests to speak of, no hobbies, no job.

My god, I'm boring.

"Am I boring?" I ask Zach.

"Are we changing the subject already?" he asks.

"No. Maybe. I'm not sure."

"I vote no. Tell me what you would say. Would you make me proud and go balls to the wall? Or would you puss out and run away?"

"I'm sure I'd puss out and run away."

He sighs. "Let's say you went balls to the wall. What would you say?"

Think big balls.

Big balls to the wall.

"What about—I know you were engaged to my sister, but it was clear that match was doomed from the start. I think you and I have got something and I want to give it a shot. What do you say?"

"I like it. Straightforward, simple, perfect."

"Thanks," I preen.

Zach and I both know I'm not that person. But wouldn't it be fun if I was? I'm more the person that would clam up, turn red, stammer a lot, and look at my feet. But I always want to be that cool collected gal who doesn't blush, has all the right words, and stands tall and proud, maintaining direct eye contact.

One of the many things that I love about Zach is that he challenges me like this sometimes. To prepare me for real-life situations. Obviously seeing Mason is not something that would happen, but it does help me to feel a little badass regardless when he puts me through these scenarios.

"I'm going to get another coffee from that cart out front. Do you want anything?" Zach asks.

"Um, sure. Maybe just an iced tea."

"Cool. Be right back."

We are the only people back here in the lounge section, and it's nice. Almost like our own private living room, except there is a humongous assortment of books to choose from. Zach has a crazy impressive library at his house, but I think even he gets bookstore envy when we visit them. And this one has such a great vibe, it makes me feel kind of cool just hanging out here.

My phone beeps.

ZACH: Hey, do you remember if there was a copy of *Strangers on a Train* in the Noir section?

ME: Not sure. Want me to check?

ZACH: If you don't mind. Highsmith is the author.

ME: Smart to tell me. Thanks!

I place books in our seats to save them, just in case someone else comes back here. I think it's funny that Zach has started reading Noir since having a few book conversations with Mason. I head to the section and find the Hs. There's a guy kneeling in the aisle looking at the bottom shelf. Kind of scruffy looking, wearing dirty shorts, a flannel shirt with maybe another shirt under it, and a grungy baseball cap. A semi-full, uneven beard covers his face. When I get closer to him, I realize he's right in front of the Hs.

Figures.

I lean back on the adjacent shelving and wait for him to finish. He finds the book he's looking for and straightens. He's tall. He's got almost half a foot on me. I wish I read more. I could strike up a conversation with this guy, who is obviously a reader, and maybe we'd fall in love and live happily ever after. And I could wake up each day thinking, Mason who?

He turns.

I feel faint.

Unless I'm mistaken . . . oh holy hells balls!

29

MASON

"Willow?" I can't believe my eyes. Of all the bookstores in all of Seattle.

Holy shit.

"Mason! Uh, hey." She catches my eye fleetingly then looks down and shuffles her feet slightly.

"Wow. What are you doing here?"

"I, uh, I'm looking for a copy of *Strangers on a Train*."

No fucking way.

"That's the book I was looking for," I say. "I think I got the last copy." I hold up the book so she can see it. It's one of my favorites. I can't believe she was looking for the same one. I didn't think she was much of a reader. Which was disappointing in a way. But apparently she's picked up the habit in recent months. And she's going for the same one that I love. What are the chances?

"Oh no." She looks disappointed.

"You can have mine." I hand her the book. She takes it, her hand shaking slightly. "That's crazy that we were going for the same book. It's one of my favorites. My mom and I were just talking about it. I've read it quite a few times, so take it, please. It's worth the read, you won't regret it."

"Oh, it's not for me," she says.

My stomach falls. I want to ask who it's for, but I can't. It's none of my business.

"Oh," I say.

"Yeah, Zach wanted a copy. Apparently, he's become quite the fan of Noir since you two discussed it."

Great, Zach is my book soul mate.

"That's great. I'm glad he's enjoying it."

We look at each other, then both look away.

This is the definition of awkward at its finest.

I take my cap off and run my hands through my hair. "So, how have you been?"

"Me? Good. I've been good. You?"

"Oh, yeah, good as well. I just got back from a big job in Santa Barbara, helping a buddy with a huge estate in Montecito. Hey, how's the house?"

"Ohmigod! It's so amazing. It's almost finished. I just ordered kitchen cabinets and picked out countertops this morning. That was the last thing outside of landscaping. I'm going to need a lot of flowers and plants, I think."

"That sounds awesome! I can't believe you've practically finished it. What an accomplishment. How does it feel?"

"It feels good. Surreal, but good. I've put so much time and energy into it for so long, for it to be almost finished, I'm not sure what I'm going to do with my time."

"I know what you mean," I say. "I thought that by the time I was done with this job with my buddy, I would have my next gig all set up. But I don't. So now I'm kind of flailing on what to do next."

"Well, you could always help me plant flowers." She laughs but it sounds unnatural.

I pounce on it anyway. "Really? I'd be happy to."

"Oh. Um. Yeah, definitely. Do you know much about annuals and perennials?"

"Not a thing."

She laughs again. This one sounding genuine. Like music to my pathetic starving ears. "Good thing I have a book."

"Of course you do. You must have a library of DIY books by now."

"Close. They are about the only books I read."

"Do you read Zach's books?"

"I read the first couple, but not really since, no."

"I bought a few of them for my buddy's kids. They love them."

"Oh, that's awesome. You'll have to tell him, He's here, he just went out to get coffee."

"Great, I'd love to see him again."

As if right on cue, Zach appears holding a coffee and an iced tea. "Well, Mason Cartwright. As I live and breathe. What on earth are you doing here?"

"This is my mom's shop."

"Really? Every time I think it's a big world, something like this happens to remind me just how small it actually is."

"Yeah, that's for sure. Hey, you guys want to meet my mom? She's around here somewhere."

"I would love to," Zach says. Willow just nods.

"Wait here, I'll go find her. Or, go back to your seats. Or, wherever you're comfortable. I'll find you. Okay? Cool."

I can't believe what an idiot I sound like. I should have been expecting something like this to happen. That I would run into Willow or Zach, or both at some point. It's the law of averages, right? I find my mom up front talking to her assistant, Amy.

"Hey, Mom, got a sec?"

"Sure, honey." She comes over to where I'm waiting.

"Some friends of mine are here, I want you to meet them," I say in a normal voice, smiling in Amy's direction. Then as we walk between the book stacks toward the back, I whisper, "It's Willow and her friend Zach."

"Willow? *The* Willow."

"Yes—"

"The one you ran away to Santa Barbara to avoid your feelings for?"

I guess we aren't ignoring that any longer.

"Yes, Mom, listen. Just be cool, okay. Don't say anything about anything. Please."

"I will do my best. I can't make any promises. I forget things all the time in my old age."

"Mom!"

She laughs. "I'm just kidding. I won't embarrass you."

"Thank you," I mumble out of the side of my mouth as we get to the lounge area where Willow and Zach are hanging out. "Willow, Zach, this is my mom, Caroline. Mom, Willow and Zach."

"It's lovely to meet you, Missus Cartwright," Willow says taking my mom's hand in both of hers and clasping them.

"Oh please, call me Caroline," Mom says. "I've heard so much about your family I feel like we know one another already."

I groan softly and hang my head. Mom may not think what she said is embarrassing— actually she probably knows and just doesn't care. Her way of pushing me in what she believes is the right direction.

"That doesn't bode well for me," Willow says. Her unnatural laugh is back.

Zach moves in and hugs my mom thanking her for producing such an *easy on the eyes, strapping young man.*

Making us all laugh and taking the attention off Willow, which I'm sure is his intent.

"All good things, dear. I assure you." My mom smiles at Willow. "What brought you two here today?"

"Oh . . . uh," Willow starts.

"I'm a writer," Zach interjects. "So I consider it to be my civic duty to patronize all local bookstores. I've already found so many books I want to buy."

"Well, you just keep right on looking then," Mom half jokes.

"We should probably get going soon, unfortunately," Willow says. My stomach bottoms out. I don't want her to go. Not yet. Though if she's leaving it probably means she wants nothing to do with me.

"Why?" Zach asks.

"I thought you had to go," Willow says, bugging her eyes at him.

"I don't have anywhere to be. We can spend the entire afternoon here as far as I'm concerned."

Willow turns red. I hate that she wants so little to do with me that she'd make up excuses for leaving.

Think about it. You were engaged to her sister, then you dumped her sister, bailed without saying goodbye, and took off for six months.

I'm probably right. She wants nothing to do with me and I can't say that I blame her.

30

WILLOW

WE MAKE SMALL TALK WITH MASON AND HIS MOM FOR A FEW minutes, then she says, "Please excuse me, I need to finish my inventory in the back. But don't leave without saying goodbye. Promise?"

"Of course," Zach assures her.

"Be right back." Mason holds up his finger and turns to follow his mom to the back of the store.

"What the hell was that, Zach?" I'm angry at him. I'm sure he can tell. Especially after I backhand him in the chest.

"What the hell was what?" His voice is nonchalant and he's thumbing through a novel as he responds.

"You know what," I say.

He looks up at me. "I *don't* know, or I wouldn't ask."

"I made a perfectly good excuse to leave, and you threw me under the bus."

"Tomato tomahto."

"What are you talking about? That doesn't apply here. What does that even mean?"

"You say I threw you under the bus. I say I saved the day and am giving you the perfect opportunity to reconnect with lover boy."

"There is no need to connect, let alone reconnect. No way can I date someone AshLynn already dated."

"Yes way, you can. He's your guy. You two have so much chemistry I can blanket myself in it."

"No, we don't." My first instinct is to deny whatever he says. What I can't deny is the flicker of hope I feel at Zach saying we have chemistry. Mason seems so awkward with me; I can't imagine he feels anything but annoyed and is just trying to be polite.

What if he's not? What if he does like you? What if it could work out regardless of AshLynn?

"You think we have chemistry?" I ask before I can stop myself.

Zach looks at me. Brow furrowed, lips scrunched, eyes narrowed.

"Okay, fine, I can answer that for myself," I mumble. "Let's say that I decide not to care that AshLynn had him first. Or that my dad and Cassandra will lose their minds. What do I do about it?"

"That's my girl! Okay, first, what did he say when you ran into each other?"

"I don't know, it was awkward. We said hi and stuff like that, talked about the book you wanted me to grab and about the house. Oh, he offered to help me with the gardening at my house."

"Well, there you go. Take him up on it."

"I'm sure he wasn't serious."

"He was, trust me."

"How would you know?"

"Because I saw how he was looking at you just now."

"And how was that?"

"Like he wanted to eat you alive. And by eat, I mean—"

"I know what you mean." I hold up my hand to stop him. "Fine. When he comes back, I'll ask him."

"Promise?"

"Yes." I roll my eyes.

"Good. Here's your chance." He tilts his head to the side where I see Mason approaching us. My heart skips a beat. Like literally skips a freaking beat. Traitorous heart trying to cause trouble here.

Really, what's the big deal?

He was engaged to my sister.

Half sister.

As in getting married.

It wasn't serious.

Marriage is always serious.

Says who?

AshLynn is all thirty-two flavors. I'm plain vanilla.

So, your vanilla will shake things up a bit.

The only time vanilla shakes is at Dairy Queen.

Whose side are you on?

Yours. Maybe his. Hard to tell.

Mason sits on the couch next to me. "It's a great place, huh?" He gestures to the store.

"I love it," I say. And I do. For a bookstore, it's still got a real homey feel to it. Books line shelves in offset rows throughout the store, as well as shelves on the walls. And there are chairs and small benches scattered about, but my favorite spot is back here in the reading lounge. I didn't just call it that, there's a sign on the wall that says: **Reading Lounge: You can lounge as long as you want, you'd just better be reading while you do it.**

Mason's mom has it set up like a large living room. A colorful rug with a tree motif on the floor, surrounded by couches and chairs. Two large brown leather couches flank the rug and three red leather chairs are interspersed between, with large beanbag-type chairs in neutral colors scattered about as well. Side tables and foot stools finish off the room. I could stay here forever.

"I may write my next book here." Zach smiles. He looks satisfied as he watches Mason and me. If he embarrasses me, I will kill him.

"I'm so glad I ran into you guys," Mason says.

"Yeah?" Zach asks.

"I guess, you know, I want to make sure there aren't any weird feelings between us after what happened." He looks to me.

I shake my head, even though I have tons of weird feelings about it. It's just most of those feelings have to do with how I feel about him, and not necessarily about what happened with AshLynn.

He continues talking. "I like you guys. I'm hoping we can all be friends. Especially since we live in the same city."

I give Zach my best "I told you so" look when Mason says *friends*.

Mason turns. "I also want to do something for you, Willow."

"For me?" I swallow hard. Not sure how comfortable I am with this new development. By that I mean trying not to get my hopes up about it. I glance at him, then back down at my lap.

"I left you high and dry with a knocked-down wall and a huge renovation I was supposed to help with and I'm sorry for that. Maybe I could buy you dinner to make up for it."

Don't look at him. If you look at him, you'll cave. If you cave, AshLynn will hate you. If AshLynn hates you, all future family gatherings will be awkward.

I look at him.

Gah! Those big brown eyes. That scruffy jawline. Why does he have to be so good looking!?

"I would love that," I say. At least I think it was me. My lips moved and words came out, but surely, I couldn't have betrayed myself like that.

"Great." He looks relieved. "How's tonight?"

"Tonight?"

"Too soon?"

"No. Tonight is great. That works." And there I go again.

"Pick you up at seven?"

"Yeah. Okay. Sure."

"Awesome." His smile widens. "Okay, I'll see you tonight. And, Zach, I'm sure I'll see you soon. I have to go. Okay, see you tonight." And with that, he's gone.

My head might be spinning just a bit.

"Go ahead, say it," Zach says.

"Say what?"

"I'm waiting for a '*you are right, Zach, I'm so sorry I doubted you*' kind of statement to come from your lips."

"No way. This is an apology dinner. You heard him."

"When did you get so stupid?"

"Thanks a lot, jerk."

"I'm serious. You are being so lame about this guy it's like I don't even know you."

"He's my sister's ex—"

"Blah, blah, sister, blah blah—"

"—fiancé."

"How long will that be your excuse?"

"It's not an excuse, it's a reason."

"Tomato tomahto."

"You are so frustrating. *Shut up!* If you weren't my best friend I think I'd hate you."

"Ditto." He studies his nails, a bland look on his face. Zach is much better at being a bitch than I am.

"Fine," I say.

"Fine."

We sit there a moment. Me glaring at him, and him ignoring me.

"Fine," I say. "What do I wear?"

"Now you're talking. You up for some shopping?"

I roll my eyes and shake my head. "Sure, what the hell." I'm not that annoyed though. Let's face it. Regardless of the reason why it happened, I'm going out with Mason Cartwright tonight. I'm pretty sure I've been dreaming about this for months. AshLynn be damned. I like this guy. It's possible he likes me. I'm going to roll with it.

I'm gonna make this date my bitch.

I am woman hear me roar.

I HATE SHOPPING. So very much. But Zach? He loves it. He freaking lives for it. Lives. For. It. He had to turn the smallest bedroom of his condo into a closet. He has so many clothes, shoes, and hats. Conversely, I was able to turn half of my closet into a bathroom.

I'm through with shopping by the time I've tried on my fourth dress.

"Just one more, please. Look at how cute this one is?" He holds up a dress that is a light kind of flimsy material, but most of it is lined, so it's not see-through. It's white with black polka dots, cinched in at the waist, short sleeves, V-neck, and looks to be knee-length. The lining stops about an inch before the bottom hem and the ends of the sleeves which gives them a ruffle-type look. It's flirty and fun without looking like it tries too hard.

I love it.

"Fine." I sigh. "I'll try it on. But this is the last one." Because I can't ever let Zach know that I like something he's picked, I'll never hear the end of it.

I slip it over my head and settle it past my hips before daring to look.

Wow.

The girl in the mirror doesn't even look like me. She looks like someone who has a curvy figure and isn't too tall and gangly.

Someone like AshLynn or Cassandra?

Get that out of your head. They aren't a part of this.

I open the door to the dressing room. Zach looks me up and down and back up again, then bites the heel of his hand.

He grunts. "Oh, that is so good. *So good*. I've outdone myself. You look perfect. Beyond that even."

I smile. "Thanks, Zach. I like it too," I say, so overcome by his reaction I forget that I wasn't going to tell him that.

"Now shoes!"

We find shoes quickly. Luckily. Like the dress, they aren't something I would normally pick for myself but that I somehow feel comfortable in. Red, shiny, platform base with high heels. They give another four inches to my already five-foot-nine-inch height. But instead of feeling awkward, I feel invincible. And attractive. I want to feel like this every day. No wonder women are always buying new things if this is the result.

I change back into my jeans and T-shirt, we buy my things, and head out.

"That wasn't so bad, was it?" Zach asks throwing his arm around my shoulders.

"No, it wasn't. I don't want to make a habit of it, but it wasn't so bad."

"Okay, now for tonight, keep your hair down and curl it. Pull some up on the sides but keep it all kind of loose overall."

"Loose, got it."

"And light makeup."

"When do I ever do heavy makeup?"

"True. But go red with your lipstick."

"Red?"

"Yeah, you know that one you got for my third book release party? The one where we vamped you up a bit and you pretended to be my girlfriend?"

"I remember." I smile.

"That one. Trust me."

"If you say so." I don't doubt him even though I may sound like I do. If there's one thing that Zach knows, it's people and attraction. And he knows just as much about what attracts a man to a woman as he does a man to a man. He's a good friend to have at times like this, for sure.

"You're going to blow his mind, you know that, right?"

"Is that a good thing?"

"Hell yes, that's a good thing. Anytime you can blow anything on a man, take full advantage." He wiggles his eyebrows at me. I laugh. I wish I had his confidence.

Tonight, you will.

This date is your bitch.

Tonight, you roar.

31

MASON

I bought a Jeep. I didn't plan it, it just happened. I was on my way back to the motel on my motorcycle and I passed a used car lot. There right in front was a Wrangler, low mileage, only a couple years old, and for a great price. Brought my motorcycle back to my mom's garage, jogged back to the lot, paid cash, drove my new baby home.

It occurred to me, as I was passing the lot, that I didn't have a car to take Willow out in. I didn't know how she would feel about a motorcycle. The forecast calls for rain anyway, so, here I am.

Now you just need a house with a picket fence so you can pump out babies, you soft pussy motherfucker.

Being courteous does not make me a soft pussy motherfucker.

Buying a car just for a date does. Two words. Beyond courteous.

I needed one anyway.

Yeah, just keep telling yourself that.

By the time I'm back at the motel with the Jeep, I've got about two hours before I'm due to pick up Willow. I grab a shower, shave, and find some clean slacks and a not-so-wrinkled button-down shirt. Splash of aftershave, and I'm ready to go.

It's only been twenty-five minutes.

If I leave now, I'll arrive way too early to get her. So I head out to my mom's to show her my car.

It's a short drive, all surface streets. I can hear the big tread of the tires on the asphalt. She lives in the center of downtown, an area where foot traffic is at an all-time high. My inner environmentalist loves that I live in a place that promotes public transit, bicycling, and walking.

I laugh that I think of that on the same day that I bought a car I didn't absolutely need. Sidewalks filled with people, sidestreets filled with cars, buildings of all shapes and sizes. I'm lucky my mom has enough allotted space in the underground garage for both an extra car and my bike.

I'm also lucky we bought it when we did. It was expensive at the time, but the value has almost tripled since then, Mom could almost retire on what it's worth now. I call her as I approach the building to let her know I'm coming. She's waiting in the garage when I park.

"I can't believe you bought a Jeep," my mom says. "Who are you and what have you done with my perpetually nomadic son?"

"It was time. Plus, it's useful for hauling tools to jobsites."

"And not much else. It's sort of small."

"Bigger than the bike."

"True, and I do like that you won't be riding the bike in the rain."

"I didn't say that." I smile. She sighs.

"Maybe you'll find a place to settle down in next," she says.

"Don't get ahead of yourself, Mom. It's just a car."

"I won't. Do you want to stay for dinner? I've got a pot roast cooking."

"I would but I have a date."

"That's why you're all dressed up, I was wondering."

I blush a tiny bit at that. "It's just pants and a shirt, Mom."

"Is this a new girl you're taking out?"

"Uh, no. Err, yes?"

She laughs. "Which is it?"

"I'm taking Willow to dinner."

Her face softens. "I'm proud of you."

"It's just dinner, Ma."

"It's not just dinner and you know it."

"It is. And I gotta go, or I'll be late."

"Tell Willow hello. Have fun. Love you."

"Love you too, Mom."

I lied. I'm not going to be late. I just didn't want to get in another conversation with her about Willow. We already did that to death at lunch today and I don't need a repeat.

Tonight, with Willow, this *is* just dinner. That I can't get this girl out of my head, after multiple months when I've never even touched or kissed her, is a whole other story.

<hr>

I TRY to decide where to take her while I'm waiting for the ferry to Bainbridge. I don't want it to be too romantic, but I don't want loud and rowdy where we can't talk either. Of course, the place with the best reviews online is quaint, small, and pricey. But I choose it anyway. From the pictures, it looks as though the tables are spaced relatively far apart, they have a big beer and wine selection. Their menu features a lot of locally sourced ingredients, fresh fish, and a clam/oyster bar. They don't take reservations but tell me that it's usually a short wait and they feature a full bar to wait in.

By the time the ferry reaches Bainbridge, I still have fifteen minutes before I pick up Willow, and a four-minute drive to her house even if I drive really slowly. I pull over to the side of the ferry parking lot to kill time and check my appearance in the visor mirror, smooth my newly trimmed beard and eyebrows with my fingers. I switch the radio station, drum my fingers on the dash, look around the lot at the cars driving by, which all together kills about another thirty-seven seconds.

Fuck it. Just go. Sitting here will only make you stress out.

The streets become narrower and more tree-lined the closer I get to her house. I like the feeling of privacy—almost exclusivity—that it gives. No sidewalks or signs of suburbia, just trees with random driveways and mailboxes on either side. Trees that blanket everything, allowing sporadic bursts of sunlight to shine through. It's the time of year where the sun won't even start to go down until after nine o'clock at night. So, while the sun isn't exactly shining, it's still light out.

I get to Willow's seven minutes early. Why I'm so concerned about every single minute that is passing is beyond me. The fence is open, so I drive straight up to the front. Then I have no choice but to go to the door since Princess Tinkerbell heard me drive up and is at the window barking incessantly. She stops when she sees it's me and starts to wag her tail, doing a little Husky howl. Willow's head pops up behind her in the window. She smiles and moves in the direction of the door.

She looks amazing. Actually, amazing isn't an adequate description. Her hair is down and curled slightly, and she's wearing a short, white dress with black polka dots, paired with red high heels that make her legs look three miles long. My body warms, a smile grows on my face despite attempts to rein it in, my heart beats faster.

"Hi," she says.

"Hi." I lean in and kiss her on the cheek. "You look beautiful."

She smiles in response. "You too. Good, I mean. You look good. Aw heck, you look beautiful too."

I laugh. She does too.

She smells good, like vanilla and something woodsy. The same scent that I remember from so long ago. P-Tink inserts herself between us and nudges my hand. I scratch her behind the ears and kneel to say hello. She licks my face in return.

"Do you want to come in for a minute while I give her a bone and grab my purse?"

"Yes, I'm dying to see the house, too."

"You'll have to wait until the kitchen is finished for the big reveal, but you can kind of get an idea based on the tape markings I've laid out."

I follow her inside, her ass sways under her skirt. I want to grab it, pull her against me and press my hardening cock against the fullness of her butt cheeks. I want to do all sorts of things that I should be discouraging since I don't know how she feels about me.

Then I see the house. "Wow, Willow, this is incredible." The space has been transformed between knocking out walls, adding skylights, enlarging window openings, and she took it one step further—the entire west wall is now comprised of La Cantina doors.

"I can't believe what a difference you've made," I say. "This is absolutely incredible."

"Thank you. I can't take credit for a lot of it since I had to hire an architect and a contractor so the house didn't fall down. But I've done as much of the grunt work as I can."

She's used tape to plot out cabinets and a large kitchen island on the floor. Mock-ups of the appliances and cupboards are taped to the walls in their assigned places. I move in to take a closer look: antique white cabinetry, marble countertops, and bold stainless-steel appliances. They will play beautifully off the dark floors.

"You pick all this out yourself?" I ask.

"Yeah, do you like it?"

"Like it? I love it. It is truly awe-inspiring. I can't wait to see it when the kitchen is completed."

"I figured I'd have a housewarming party when it's all finished," she says. "If you come, there will be three of us here." She scoffs.

"I wouldn't miss it."

Her stomach growls.

I laugh. "I guess that's our cue to go."

She blushes. "It seems as though I am hungry." She grabs a chew bone for her dog, P-Tink takes it gently and trots to her dog bed, where she turns four times before settling.

I move to open the door for Willow. "After you." I gesture.

"Thank you." I watch her ass again, making a promise to myself to walk behind her as many times as possible this evening.

"I just realized I don't know what kind of car you actually drive. The one you had before was a rental, right?"

"Yeah. I drive a motorcycle normally." I open the passenger door for her and help her in.

"This is nice, I like it. Oh wow, it's so clean."

I get in the driver's side and start the motor. "I have a confession to make. I just bought it today."

"You did?"

"Yeah. I wasn't sure how you'd feel about a bike."

"You bought a car for our date?" she asks.

"No." I laugh.

"Oh good." She sounds relieved.

"I bought a Jeep."

"Ohmigod, Mason. We could have taken my car. Or an Uber or something."

"It's okay. It was time, anyway. I've needed something for a while."

"All right. I feel bad. How about I pay for dinner?"

"How would it be an apology dinner if you paid?"

She shrugs and blushes slightly. "So, where are we going?"

"It's a surprise."

"I need to know how big the apology is."

I look at her, brows raised.

"You know, like the nicer the restaurant, the bigger the apology," she teases.

"I see how it is. Well, I've not been there before, but it gets great reviews online. It offers a wide variety of choices. Plus, forty beers on tap and a self-proclaimed extensive wine list."

"It sounds great!"

"Let's hope so," I say.

"You know you don't have to do this, right?"

"I know. But I want to."

"Well, thank you." She pauses, then says in a softer voice, "I'm looking forward to it."

"Me too." I take a chance and reach over to take her hand in mine and squeeze it. She returns the gesture.

So, I take her hand again as we are walking into the restaurant and she lets me then too.

Touching her, even as innocently as this, makes me feel giddy.

Like a little boy with a new toy.

A fantastic fucking feeling.

32

WILLOW

HE LETS GO OF MY HAND TO TOUCH MY LOWER BACK AND guide me into the restaurant. It's a move I've seen men make plenty of times that I love. I think it's romantic. I'm hardly over my internal hyperventilation from holding his hand and barely register the lower back touch. The warmth of his skin seeps through my dress. I want to curl into him so all of me can feel the way that one small part feels now.

The hostess seats us in the back of the restaurant, in a rounded booth roomy enough for four people. We both scoot toward the middle and end up closer to one another than I'd intended. The lighting is dim, not quite candlelight, but still low enough that everyone looks pretty. Except Mason, he looks rakish. And so handsome I want to capture the image and carry it around in my pocket forever.

He's trimmed his beard short and is wearing a white button-down shirt with the sleeves rolled up and the first few buttons undone, dark slacks and shoes. And he smells good, as usual. One day I'll ask him what it is. That is if I make it past tonight. This proximity to him may kill me first.

Breathe.

"Do you want a drink?" Mason hands me the drink menu. He was right, there is a huge selection of both beer and wine, plus a full bar.

"We could be here a year and never try all of these." I laugh.

"We'll have to come back," he says.

My face heats.

Tonight, you roar.

"I'd like that." I smile.

Mason orders a local lager and I experiment with a craft cocktail, called Alabama Shakes It Up, their twist on the classic Manhattan.

I take a sip. It's good but strong. Good thing I like whiskey. I didn't eat a ton at lunch, and this is going to go down smooth and hit hard.

"Have you had fun working on the house?" he asks.

"I have. More than I thought I would. I mean, it's hard work for sure. And I haven't even really done the hard stuff. But the results are so visible every step of the way. I really like that about it."

"I am sorry I wasn't there."

"It's okay. Truly. There is nothing about it that was ever your responsibility and the whole idea, well, it was just ridiculous. My dad thinking he could . . . anyway, it doesn't matter. Let's move past it."

"Consider it done," he says.

"What do you think you'll order?" I ask.

I've got to get past this small talk stage. I'm supposed to be roaring. This is not roaring. This is barely a whisper.

We talk about the menu anyway and decide to start with an assortment of fresh oysters and clams. Both of which I have to coat in sauce and chase with Mason's beer. If I chase with my drink, I'll be drunk before the entrees are served.

"Oh my god, those are so good," I say.

He laughs. "How could you tell with all the sauce?"

"That's what makes them so good! It's always all about the sauce."

He orders another beer and we decide on what to order for our meals. I pick something I'm least likely to spill on myself, the cedar plank salmon, and Mason orders some sort of steak. Despite also drinking some of his beer, I'm already on my second cocktail before we get our entrees.

Each cocktail gets you closer to roar.

I giggle at my thoughts.

We talk about my favorite movies and his favorite books and which are crossovers, and soon we've slipped into that same familiarity that we had months ago. Laughing and sharing, teasing and flirting. It's the flirting that will be my downfall. Because he is so freaking cute when he flirts. In a pantry-dropping kind of way.

I never really understood that saying until tonight. Granted, I don't have an extensive dating history by any means. I had boyfriends in high school, lost my virginity at a respectable seventeen years old on prom night, and even lived with one of my ex-boyfriends. But I never got the feeling that I have right now, where I'd follow him into the back room to have sex if he asked me to. And we haven't even kissed. I know, it's just physical attraction and my inhibitions are down because I'm drinking, but I'd do it anyway and I wouldn't regret a thing.

We finish dinner, decline dessert, and head back out to his Jeep. He opens the passenger door for me, which I adore, and then lifts me up to the seat by my waist, which freaks me out. One because I wasn't expecting it. Two because I'm not light in weight.

It doesn't faze him. My legs dangle out the side, I reach with my toe for the step to brace myself and miss, plunging forward. My hands go to Mason's shoulders to catch myself. In reality, he catches me and my hands just go naturally to his shoulders. But either way, we are here with me pressed between him and the edge of his passenger seat my hands on his shoulders, and him between my legs with his hands on my waist.

Our faces mere inches apart. He's so close I could almost kiss him.

Tonight, you roar.

I lean in and touch my lips to his. I intend for it to be a small peck as I pull away. But then I lean in again.

And again.

He groans and moves a hand up to the side of my face, holding me in place while he takes over the kiss. And. Oh. My. God. My happy place instantly floods with heat and that somersault-like feeling, my panties dampen. He steps forward and puts a foot on the step, leaning into me. His thigh works its way between my legs, and I rub myself against him shamelessly.

"Mason," I moan.

His grip on me tightens possessively. I could stay here in his arms forever and want for nothing more. Mason's tongue dances with mine as though they belong together, our lips in perfect harmony. He moves his mouth to my neck and runs gentle kisses down the side. I feel like I'm slipping into a joy coma, everything else fades away except for Mason and his kisses. All I feel is his mouth, his hands, and . . .

Oh my, is that his penis?

Oh yeah. That's his penis against my hip. I move to press my center against him.

Oh god, that feels good.

I wrap one leg around his waist to get closer, wanting to feel his hardness against me. He's the missing piece that completes my sexual puzzle. I lock my legs behind his back, grinding on him.

His breath is heavy, his moans deep. "God, Willow. I've dreamed about this. About you. Having you in my arms." He looks at me, our foreheads touching.

I'm love drunk, I can barely focus, everything in my body is raging, all I want is release.

"It's so good, Mason. How is it so good?"

"Willow, I want to make you feel good. All the time."

"Get a room," I hear someone say from behind us. I immediately drop my legs from around his waist and pull away from Mason. Embarrassed.

Beyond embarrassed even. I close my eyes and drop my head.

"I'm sorry." Mason brushes my hair from my face and tilts my face up. "I'm sorry. I didn't mean to get so carried away."

"It's my fault. I'm sorry. I'm the one who kissed you."

"Yeah, but if you hadn't, I would have kissed you, so either way it was happening. I would not have been able to help myself any longer." His eyes are like P-Tink's when she's been bad, which makes me giggle.

It's just a kiss, Willow. Lighten up and roar.

"What's so funny?"

"The look you gave me, reminded me of P-Tink when she's in trouble."

He laughs. "I hope that's a good thing."

"It is." I smile and turn my legs into the Jeep, not wanting to tempt myself any further. He shuts my door and jogs around the front to the driver's side. The ride back to my house is quick. Much faster than the ride to the restaurant. Or at least that's how it feels.

Next thing I know we are at my front door. I turn to face him. "I had a really great time tonight, thank you so much."

"Me too," he says. "Do you think we could do it again sometime?"

I nod. "Definitely."

He leans in and kisses me on the cheek. "Goodnight, Willow."

I watch him walk back to his Jeep, torn between wanting to call him back so I can give him a proper kiss, and leaving things as they are.

Roar.

"Hey, Mason," I call.

He turns, brows raised and a hopeful look in his eyes.

"Want to come in for a drink or something? Maybe give my dog some attention. I have a feeling she's dying to see you."

"Love to," he says jogging back up the path to the door.

P-Tink attacks me first when we get inside. Pushing against me and licking and yelping like I've been gone for years instead of just a few hours.

Then she sees Mason.

And she loses her poor little mind. Her tail wags so hard it moves her entire back end, and I swear she's smiling. Big. He kneels to pet her, cooing the entire time. She rolls to her back for a belly rub and he obliges. I kick off my heels, which were surprisingly comfortable, and take a seat on the couch to watch them play. I expanded my living room furniture quite a bit after Zach's first little set, and now have two couches and two chairs to fill the space, plus a raised doggie bed shaped like an armchair for P-Tink.

Mason adores my dog. God, I love that. Even if he wasn't insanely attractive and made my insides heat like lava, I would want him for how he treats my dog. It says a lot about a guy, how he treats animals. I firmly believe the gentler a man is with an animal, the gentler he'll be with his woman. I don't mean in a passive sort of way, but in how he handles and treats her. How his attitude is toward her and his temperament. With Mason I'm certainly spot on.

He looks at me. "I think she likes me."

"She freakin' adores you. I swear she went into mourning after . . ." I stop. I promised myself I wasn't going to bring up anything about AshLynn and what happened.

"It's okay. I mean we should probably talk about it anyway, right? If we're going to be seeing each other."

Does he mean seeing each other like dating? Or just because we live in the same general city?

"I had a great time tonight, Willow. And not just the kiss, but the whole evening. I want to see you again. Date you again. See where this goes."

He means dating.

I nod.

"Do you?" he asks.

"I think so," I say as honestly as I can. "I mean, I think about you, like that, a lot. But I just don't know how my family would handle it and I have to be honest, that kind of freaks me out. Plus, if I'm super honest, I'm nothing like my sister. And you liked her enough to want to marry her."

"Half sister." He smiles.

I smile back.

"Can I be honest?" he asks.

I nod.

"Brutally honest?"

"Of course."

"AshLynn and I weren'—"

"Actually, I don't want to know."

"I want to tell you."

"I don't want to know. It doesn't matter. I know myself and I'll just draw comparisons, it's not healthy for me. Let's just pretend I never asked."

"Even if knowing would make you feel better?" he asks.

"Especially then," I say.

He runs his hand over his hair, mussing it. "Uh, okay."

33

——————

MASON

"But you have to promise me one thing," I say to Willow.

"What?" she asks.

"If ever you change your mind, come to me and I will tell you everything. And ask me before you go to AshLynn. Deal?"

"Why you before AshLynn?"

"I don't trust her to tell you an accurate depiction of what happened."

"Okay," she says.

"And I just want to say this one small thing," I continue. "The way that I feel with you, Willow, the emotional connection that we have, is already a hundred times stronger than anything I ever felt with AshLynn."

Her face softens, which makes me feel good I said that. I felt as though I was taking a chance in doing so, like maybe it was too much too soon. But she obviously has some insecurity issues where her sister is concerned, which her parents exacerbate. It will be my job to help her overcome that. Especially since she thinks I was involved with AshLynn.

"It was harder being away from you for the last six months than anything I've ever done." I go for broke and lay it all on the line. "Not a day went by that I didn't think about you. Miss you."

"Where did you go?" she asks.

"Santa Barbara. A buddy of mine needed help with a huge renovation he was doing. Free room and board, plus payment. I got to do what I enjoy, and the physical labor made it easier to not think."

She nods. "I get that. I kind of did the same thing here. Probably not as physical of labor, but enough for me that I was tired at the end of the day."

"It's a great catharsis, isn't it?"

"Definitely." She looks down at her lap, then back up at me. "I missed you too," she says softly.

"Can I kiss you?" I ask.

She nods. That's all I need. I drag her to me on the couch and press my lips to hers. God, I've missed this, and it's only been a few minutes since the parking lot. I push one hand up into her hair and bury my fingers in it, holding her in place while I claim her as mine through my kiss. I move my mouth down her neck, sucking and licking and biting. She moans in my ear. Long and low.

My other hand cups her ass, and I pull her closer so she's straddling me. Her skirt rides up toward her waist and she widens her knees to connect us further. She pulls my lips back to hers, plunging her tongue inside my mouth, taking over the kiss. Her heat grinding against me.

If she comes like this, fully clothed and on top of me, my life will be complete. She buries her face in my neck and bites down.

"Fuck, I love that," I say.

God, she feels good.

I tilt her hips into mine and thrust up.

"Ohmigod, Mason. Oh god," she breathes into my ear.

Her arms and legs tighten around me as her body shudders, she muffles her cries in my neck, and grinds down, riding out her orgasm.

"Get it, baby. Take it," I tell her pulling her down against me and pumping my hips up at the same time.

"Ohmigod. Holy hell." She slumps against my chest, her head on my shoulder, face turned in, breathing heavily. "That was . . . ohmigod. How did you do that?" She sits back to push her hair away from her face, then slumps in again.

"I didn't do that, baby. You did. And it was fantastic. Do you have any idea how beautiful you are? How incredibly sexy you are? How hard you make me?"

She shakes her head.

"Feel it, Willow. Feel me. Feel what you do to me."

She leans back and reaches her hand between us and cups my balls, then moves her palm up the length of my shaft. Even through my pants her hands feel amazing.

I groan.

She giggles.

"Do you like that?" she whispers in my ear.

"Die fucking happy right now, babe."

She undoes my slacks one-handed.

Impressive.

And releases my cock. I lift my hips to push my pants down slightly and give her better access.

"It's big," she says nuzzling my ear with her nose and running her fingers up and down the sides of my dick.

"You have small hands," I say.

She laughs, which was my intent. I kiss her again; her hand moves from my dick and she rolls her hips forward. We groan in unison. The only thing separating my cock from her heat are her wet panties. She rolls her hips; the silk slides up and down my length as she does.

"Holy shit, Willow. Tell me how far to go. When to stop, baby."

She reaches down and pulls her panties to the side and drags her wet heat along my length. We are skin on skin and the feeling blows my mind. Our foreheads touch as we both watch her slide back and forth, her wetness glistening. Mouths open, lips an inch apart, breath mingling.

So. Fucking. Hot.

"Willow, what are you doing to me?" I moan into her mouth.

"I want to feel you, Mason. Please. I can't wait." She rises on her knees and takes me in her hand, placing my tip at her entrance. It's all I can do to stop myself from blowing my entire load right there.

How is this even happening? I'm not complaining, I fucking love it. But I feel like any minute I'll wake up and realize it was all a dream.

"Condom," I grit out.

"Oh god," she groans, and lifts off me. "Do you have one?"

"Back pocket. Wallet."

She reaches her hand around and pulls my wallet out of the back pocket of my slacks and hands it to me. I pull the condom out and rip the package open.

"Can I?" She holds her hand out for the condom.

"Hell, yes."

She lays it over the tip of my cock, her fingers warm against the cool of the latex and lube. She takes her time rolling it down my length.

"I like the way you feel in my hands." Her voice is low and sultry, my dick jumps in response to her words and her hands. I watch as her fingers move against me and I pump my hips into her grip making her smile.

"I like the way I feel in your hands."

"I want to make you feel good too." She pushes off me and stands. I start to protest, but she holds her hand up to stop me. I watch in fascination as she grabs the hem of her dress and pulls it up over her head, leaving her in wet panties already pulled to the side and a lacy bra.

"You are so beautiful," I breathe.

She reaches behind her back.

"Wait." This time I hold up my hand to stop her. I kick off my shoes and socks, push my slacks to the floor, and pull my shirt over my head, not even bothering to unbutton it.

I beckon her, she steps forward into my embrace so I can undo her bra; she lowers her arms and lets it fall to the floor. I watch in wonder as her breasts are revealed.

"You're perfect," I breathe. Perky and beautiful with rose-colored nipples standing at attention. I pull her panties down her legs next. She steps out of them gracefully and stands before me. My hands run up and down her hips and the sides of her thighs. I don't know where to look first, her legs, her face, her breasts, her neatly trimmed pussy. But she takes the decision away when she steps forward and straddles me again.

I take a nipple in my mouth and draw it in. She cries out. I move to the other one and her head falls back.

"Ohmigod. I can't . . . I have to." She rises and places me at her entrance then we both watch as I disappear inside of her, inch by inch. Stopping only when I hit the back of her. She moans and tilts her hips forward, taking me that much deeper.

"Oh, yeah," she says. "This is what I wanted. You feel amazing."

I was wrong before when I said my life would be complete if she came on top of me fully clothed. Now that I'm inside her, and she's naked on top of me, my life is complete. She rolls her hips and grinds against me.

"Oh, Mason."

I reach down and find her clit with my thumb and rub it as she rocks back and forth.

"Oh, feels so good," she moans against my neck. She kisses her way back to my lips and her tongue seeks out mine. I have one hand at her clit the other on her breast and I'm right on the edge. I don't want to move for fear of coming too soon. She's up and down and back and forth, my cock is buried in her warmth, her lips against mine, our tongues touching, and I never want to leave. I want this moment to last forever.

"Oh my god, I think I'm going to come again." Her head falls back as her muscles tighten around me. My control loosens. I bite my tongue. Hard. And let her ride out her orgasm. And this time, when she slumps against me, I stand and carry her into the bedroom, only disconnecting long enough to toss her onto the bed.

She gasps, and looks up at me, eyes wide and smile big. "That'll wake a girl back up."

"Good." I kneel on the bed and start to kiss my way up her right leg. "You need to be awake for what I have planned next."

34

WILLOW

I CAN'T BREATHE, MY HEART IS BEATING SO FAST. I'VE ALREADY come twice, and I think I'm about to do it again and he's barely touched me. How is this possible? How can I feel so much with another person I want to burst? Sexual tension, satisfaction, anticipation, release.

We've moved into my bedroom and he's kissing his way up my leg. He stops at my knee and begins again on my other ankle. I whimper in protest. I want Mason's mouth on me. And the closer his mouth gets, the happier I will be.

He stops at my other knee; I grab at his hair and try to pull his head back.

"What do you want, my sweet Willow?" he asks.

"I want you to lick me," I breathe, feeling very bold with my choice of words.

"Like this?" He licks the inside of my knee.

I shake my head. "Higher."

"Here?" He repeats at mid-thigh.

I shake my head. "You know where."

"Show me," he commands.

I run my fingers down my side and over my hip bones stopping once my fingers reach my center. I touch myself and moan. I'd much rather it be him. But I'll take release any way that I can right now. And my fingers know me well. I can get there fast.

"Fuck, that's hot," he says watching me.

I'm close.

He nudges my fingers to the side with his nose and breathes me in. I'm too turned on to be embarrassed or self-conscious. He can do whatever he wants wherever he wants as long as he doesn't stop. His tongue runs along the side of my clit, my hips jump in response. He repeats the same thing on the other side.

"Ohmigod, Mason."

He runs his tongue from bottom to top, right through my center.

"Oh yeah, right there," I moan, almost embarrassed by how low my voice is. Almost. "Again."

He does it again, then pushes his tongue inside me, like he's French kissing my lady parts.

"Oh god, oh god." I keep saying the same things, but I can't think of anything else to say. My mind is a blank. All my energy and focus are on Mason and what he's doing to my body and how amazing it feels.

His lips move to engulf my clit, and everything explodes. I hear my cries, but can't quite believe it's me making them. My thighs clench around his head and my hands pull at his hair. I don't care if I'm hurting him, if I'm suffocating him, I just want more. More of him, more of this. I don't want it to end.

He licks me through my orgasm. Until I'm too sensitive to touch. And all I can do is lie there, unable to move any part of my body at all.

"I think I'm dead," I tell him, my eyes still closed. "But dead in a good way."

He crawls between my legs and sits back on his knees, grabs me by the waist, and pulls me up his thighs until he's entering me again. He pounds into me, repeatedly, using my hips to hold me in place. Before I know it, I'm coming again.

This is insane. I'm going to die. I wasn't dead before, but I will be now.

He lays me back and hooks his arm under my leg, spreading me further open to him, and slams back in, grunting. He pulls out halfway and is back in again, bottoming out, growling his release. He looks primal as he comes, eyes shut, head back, mouth open, veins popping. It's rough and rugged, animalistic and hot. He drops my leg and falls to the bed beside me, pulling me into him. I hook my arm over his chest and leg over his thigh and sigh. So content, so satiated. I didn't even know sex could be like this. Could make me feel so . . . complete.

Not only that, I feel sexy and beautiful. As though I'm actually all the things he murmured to me. Mason presses a kiss to my forehead and turns. "Be right back," he says and disappears into the bathroom.

Is this when he leaves?

Would he do that, Willow? Would he just leave after that?

Maybe it wasn't *all that* for him? Maybe he always comes that hard. Maybe that's how it was with AshLynn.

Don't you dare think about AshLynn right now.

I silence my thoughts when he comes back in the room. He lies down next to me and pulls me into him.

"Just had to get rid of the condom," he murmurs into my hair. "The bathroom is incredible, by the way."

I smile. Not only because he's complimenting my bathroom, which did turn out fantastic, but also because he came back and he's holding me again.

See? Not leaving.

"Is it okay that I'm here?" It's like he reads my thoughts sometimes.

"Here like at my house? Or in my bed?"

"Here in your bed, with you. After we had sex. At your house."

"Yes." I kiss his shoulder. "Most definitely."

"Good," he says. "Because I definitely don't want to leave."

Which makes me smile.

I must fall asleep because the next thing I know I'm waking up alone in my bed. I reach over just in case, but the sheets on the other side are cold.

He's gone.

And he's been gone a while.

He got what he wanted. He's out.

I make the kissy noise to invite P-Tink up to the bed, needing the comfort of my fluffy friend suddenly. But she doesn't come.

"P-Tink?" I call.

Nothing.

Kissy noise.

Nothing.

I turn on the bedside lamp and look around. She's not in here.

Weird. She always sleeps in here with me. Maybe she got freaked out by Mason being here.

Oh god, what if he accidentally let her out when he left and now she's trapped outside? I get up, grab my robe, and set out to look for her. All sorts of horrible images running through my head. I hear voices as I near the living room and see low lights flickering.

Mason dressed in his slacks, is sitting on the couch with my dog. They are sharing a bag of chips and watching TV.

"Hey, babe, I'll have to buy you some more chips tomorrow. P-Tink and I finished off this bag. Sorry. I worked up an appetite." He winks and smiles.

He didn't leave. He stayed. And ate my chips. With my dog. And watched my TV. It feels so couple-like.

"No problem." I smile.

"I couldn't sleep," he says. "Too wired and you were zonked, so I didn't want to wake you. So, I grabbed my other girl here and I came out here to watch TV."

His other girl. Am I the first girl?

He pats the couch next to him. I curl into his chest and he puts his arm around me. "Now I have my girl and my other girl." He kisses my forehead and points to the TV. "This is one of those house rehab shows. It's ridiculous how fast they do everything, and never need permits or inspectors. Everything happens in half an hour. Drives me crazy. But I keep watching anyway." He laughs and shakes his head.

I breathe him in. He smells like a mix of cologne and sex.

Me.

My scent is on him.

I like that. A lot.

I settle in to watch his show with him. If I'm his girl, then he must be my guy.

I'm watching TV with my guy.

I smile, and close my eyes, ready to fall back asleep content and happy.

35

MASON

MY FIRST THOUGHT AS I LOOK DOWN AT WILLOW SLEEPING ON one side of me and P-Tink sleeping on the other is: I want this all the time.

But then I remember what happened when I was only pretend involved with a Brooks girl. I try not to make the comparisons, but it's hard. Even though I feel as though I've known Willow forever, I really haven't. And despite that the two girls are nothing alike, I can't help but wonder about parallels.

Wake up, man. There are none.

Reality is, tonight with Willow was unlike anything I've ever experienced. Emotionally, physically, literally. I've been with my fair share of women, even had a few semi-serious relationships, but nothing where I felt like this. Where I felt like the girl *got me.*

The show ends, the one I wasn't really watching anyway, and I turn the TV off and carry Willow back to her room. Help her take off her robe, so she's naked again, and tuck her in. I shed my slacks and crawl in behind her then pull her to me into a perfect spoon. One arm curled under my pillow, the other over her with my hand cupping her breast and her hand over mine.

Even with lingering doubts, this is the best it's ever been. I'm going to enjoy it.

While it lasts.

I'm not letting it end.

Then there's your answer.

Then there's my answer.

I fall asleep satisfied, grin on my face, my girl in my arms, her dog at our feet, and my decision made.

———

Mmmmm, that's a nice way to wake up.

I open my mouth to capture Willow's tongue with mine. She moves away. Her breath hot on my face. I smile and try again.

Hair.

Why is there hair in my mouth?

I open one eye. P-Tink is burrowing her head between Willow's and mine, licking our faces alternately. She turns to me and licks again. My mouth is still open.

Our tongues touch.

And my first morning kiss at Willow's is with the dog.

Awesome.

"Hey, girl," I whisper as I pull dog fur off my tongue. She wags her tail in response.

Willow stirs. "Morning," she mumbles sleepily.

I kiss her lightly on the lips. "Stay right here, I'm going to let P-Tink outside."

She nods in response and sighs, then is back asleep almost immediately. I ease out of bed, the dog bounds behind me to follow. I pull on my slacks and shirt and head down the hall. The house is quiet, the only sound being P-Tink's nails clicking on the floor behind me. I open the doors to let her out, then look around at the empty space soon to be the kitchen.

She has a card table set up in the corner with a coffee pot, toaster oven, and electric burner on it. Along with a five-gallon jug of water, bread, peanut butter, dog food, and a basket of fruit and veggies. A cooler on the floor completes the makeshift kitchenette. Inside I find coffee creamer, lunch meat, some condiments, hard boiled and raw eggs, turkey bacon, and a few other things.

I debate making her breakfast in bed or going back to bed and seeing if I can score with Willow instead of the dog. P-Tink comes back inside and nudges my hand toward the coffee maker.

"Coffee?" I ask her.

She wags her tail.

"Okay, coffee it is, my cute little cock-block." I prep coffee and set it to brew, then take P-Tink outside to throw the ball around a bit until it's finished. I inhale a deep breath of fresh air. The sound is still this morning and all I really hear are birds and the occasional frog. I don't recall feeling this good in a long time. Good isn't even the right word for it. It doesn't encompass all of what I'm feeling. I feel more than good. Happy? Relaxed? Content? Fulfilled? Whatever it is, I like it.

She's added some more things to the deck since the last time I was here. In addition to the badass patio furniture, she has an awning that extends out from the house and a couple of umbrellas for shade, a patio lounger for P-Tink, and some side tables. There's seating enough for ten people between the loungers, chairs, and table set.

The dog drops the ball at my feet and trots beyond me to the house.

"Are we finished?" I ask her. She doesn't turn around.

Guess so.

I grab the ball, drop it in the basket by the door, and head inside. The coffee is done so I make a cup for both Willow and me and bring hers into the bedroom. P-Tink is on the bed waking Willow up in a similar fashion as she did to me.

"Good morning." I smile.

"Hi," she says shyly. She sits up, pulling the sheet with her to cover her breasts.

I set her coffee on the nightstand, then crawl back in on the other side of the bed careful not to spill my own.

"I hope it's okay. I seem to remember you liked cream in your coffee."

"Yes, thank you." She sips at her coffee but doesn't meet my eyes.

Does she feel awkward about last night?

"You okay?" I ask.

"Yeah, why?"

"Well, for one, you won't look me in the eye."

She mumbles something I don't catch.

"What?"

"I look terrible in the morning," she says.

"Hey," I say. "Look at me." I take her chin and force her gaze up to meet mine. "You look beautiful always. But especially in the morning. With your hair tousled and the slightly confused look on your face because you aren't quite awake. A little dried drool on your chin and the crusties at the corners of your eyes."

"Shut up!" she cries, slapping her free hand at me, smiling.

"And when you're smiling, you are breathtaking." I take her hand and kiss the back of it. She leans in and kisses me. A soft kiss that last a few seconds, but still rocks my world and hardens my cock.

"Thank you."

"For what?" I ask.

"You're so nice to me. I don't know why, but I like it."

"You don't know why you like it?"

"I don't know why you're nice to me."

"I like you." I wait until her eyes meet mine before I continue. "A lot."

"I like you too," she says.

"Good."

We sip at our coffee; I return mine to the nightstand. I want to take hers from her and set it aside so that I can pin her to the bed and repeat everything we did last night and more. My cock hardens thinking about it. And then my stomach growls.

"Was that your stomach?" She laughs.

"Yeah, I guess I'm hungry."

My stomach—the second cock-block of the morning.

"Let me grab a quick shower and we can go get something to eat." She starts to take the sheet with her as a cover, then drops it at the last minute. Giving me a full view of her luscious backside as she walks into the bathroom. She stops at the doorway and turns. "You coming?"

"Hell, yes!" My clothes are completely off before I reach the bathroom. And we shower together. She turns me into an instant fan of removable showerheads and bench seating.

Especially the bench seating.

36

WILLOW

One day I'm me, taking life day by day, working on my house, playing with my dog, trying to figure out what I want to be when I grow up. The next I'm head over heels for a guy that I never expected to be in my life, finishing the house, and happier than anyone has a right to be. I'm so freaking happy, I'm giddy. And giggly. All the time. If I wasn't such a lover of happily ever after I would be disgusted by myself.

Zach keeps me grounded. Or tries to. But I'm pretty far gone over Mason. And the sex. Ohmigod, the sex. Why doesn't anyone ever talk about how great sex can be? I thought the guys I'd been with before were the norm. And maybe they are, and Mason is an anomaly. That said, I want the anomaly every day.

That's not how anomalies work.

I roll my eyes at my own thoughts and turn my attention back to Zach, who is here today to help me with the plans for the housewarming party. Mason took P-Tink with him to the hardware store to pick up a few extra shelves and some organizers for the kitchen cabinets.

Mason has helped every day with finishing the kitchen. Painting walls, hanging cupboards, centering the island, helping the counter guys with marble placement, cutting the tile and laying the backsplash, installing appliances. Well, I helped with the backsplash. I already knew about laying tile, so I had fun doing that with him. But I was more than happy to turn over the task of cutting the tile to him. Something about water with a saw has never sat well with me. I don't care if it is called a *wet saw*.

And now it's nearly finished. Most of my kitchen items are unpacked, which is why Mason decided more shelves and organizers were needed. I just need to decide on a bit of decor. Since it was the last item in my house to re-do, my house is nearly finished as well. And I'm no closer to figuring my life out than I was before. Except for the part with Mason in it.

He stayed with me that first night and has pretty much never left. Which I am more than okay with. He kept paying for his hotel and going back and forth for clothes for another two weeks before we just decided he should stay. Move his things in, give up the hotel, and call it home.

It's been three months of pure bliss. I've met a few of his friends and hit it off with their significant others, which has been a new experience for me. Not ever having had a lot of girlfriends in my life. The great thing is they accept Zach as one of the girls too. So, I miss out on nothing when I spend time with either, a seamless transition. And Mason's friends are helpful. Like, really helpful. We had a big painting party when I decided to change the color of the living room walls. And another when we refinished and stained the deck.

Mason has taken me by each of his investment properties and introduced me to the tenants, and admitted that he owns the building his mom's bookstore is in. Looking at him, I never would have known he was so successful or worth so much money. In a way, I'm glad I didn't know that going in. I wouldn't have wanted anything to influence my opinion of him. I'm not sure it would have, since in that regard I'm nothing like my family, but I'm glad I didn't find out until after we were together.

We had a small potluck last week to see how the space worked with people and it was awesome. Better than I'd ever thought it could be. Which is where the idea of the housewarming came from. Which is what Zach and I are planning now. So far, we have a guest list. Which, according to Zach is the most important thing anyway.

"You know who's not on this list?" Zach asks.

"Who?"

"Your father and Cassandra."

"They wouldn't come anyway," I say.

"Well then, what's the harm in inviting them?"

"I don't know. I feel like what they did, the last time they were here, really drew a line between us. And I'm not sure I care to cross it."

"You mean when they made Mason pay them a bunch of money for a wedding that never should have been planned?"

"That's part of it, yes."

Talking about AshLynn and Mason doesn't bother me any longer.

Much.

I still feel twinges of jealousy and insecurity, but I think that has more to do with me than with that situation. Plus, Mason leaves no doubt how important I am to him. Every day he finds some new little way to show me. Granted, he told me he loved me for the first time in the afterglow of a marathon sex session. But then he said it again later when we were clothed. So, I did too.

And it felt like I was just stating the obvious, I didn't feel nervous about saying it, or worried how he might react. He said it. I said it. My feelings intensified. Everything is good in my world.

My phone buzzes with a text. I look down, it's from Mason. A picture of P-Tink sitting in the hardware store with a barbecue brush in her mouth. I laugh and text him back an *LOL*, then show Zach. Princess Tinkerbell has been obsessed with the idea of barbecue since Mason brought home a smoker. He smoked some chicken, we gave her a bit of the skin mixed in with her kibble, and she was in love. She sticks by his side a lot anyway, but especially when she sees him get the barbecue tools out of the pantry.

MASON: I just don't know if it's a hint or a command.

ME: Command. Definitely.

MASON: Ha! For sure. Love you. Home soon.

ME: Love you!

"What's with the big shit-eating grin?" Zach asks.

I show him the text exchange.

"Oh," he teases. "Lover boy said he loved you. How adorbs."

"Shut up."

"Back to the task at hand. You sending Daddy Warbucks an invite or not?"

"They won't come, right?"

"Definitely not."

"This just shows I'm the bigger person."

"Exactly."

"Okay, what the heck. Yes, let's send them one."

He adds them to the list, and we move on to the menu. Mason will be smoking a few different meats and the girls are making salads. Mason's mom is bringing homemade cookies and brownies. Her boyfriend, Abe, is bringing an assortment of coffees in big to-go containers. It's funny, I always thought the host provided everything at a party, but these guys do things a little differently. I like their way better.

Mason decided to build an outdoor kitchen after he got the smoker and made everything look built-in. I love how he did it. Designed in a u-shape with raised bar seating on one side and food prep on the other. He decked it out with a small fridge, sink, and dishwasher. Then built a pergola over it for shade and protection from the elements. He calls it his kitchen. I have the one inside, and he has outside. And he uses it a lot. He likes to cook. Correction, grill. He likes to grill.

"I might bring someone, is that okay?" Zach asks.

"What? Of course! Who is someone and why didn't you tell me you were seeing anyone?"

"I'm kind of not. At least not yet. We've been talking online. So, I'm not sure of anything yet. But so far I really like him."

"Oh, yay! Thank you for finally telling me."

"I didn't want to rain on your little perfection parade."

"Oh stop. That wouldn't be raining, it would be adding another float."

"Oh, good one. I like it."

"Thanks."

Zach leaves a short time later. I'd asked him to stay for dinner, but he declined. He hasn't been around as much since Mason moved in. He swears there's no connection there, that he's just trying to give us some time to settle into things as a couple, so I hope that's true.

Mason gets home soon after that. And, like most nights, we sit outside for twenty minutes or so and watch the sound, talking about whatever comes to mind before going in to make dinner. It's my favorite part of the day. No distractions, just him and me talking, connecting, making sure we know everything there is to about the other. And I wouldn't have it any other way.

37

MASON

WE ARE HAVING OUR HOUSEWARMING PARTY TODAY. IT'S become a bit of a double celebration. Part the house renovations being finished and part Willow and me living together. We have about thirty people coming, so not a huge number, but not a small get-together either. Willow invited her dad and Cassandra, but they didn't respond. We've talked about it a couple times. And she's dealing with it, but it still hurts her feelings even though she was expecting it.

It was a huge step on her part to do so. The least they could have done is respond. I think Cassandra is the negative in that equation, but Willow has a harder time seeing that. And I know she really just misses her dad. I hate that he can't just man up and be here for her. Even without Cassandra. But he can't. Or he won't.

I'm in the kitchen, her kitchen not mine, where P-Tink and I are prepping meat for the smoker. And by that, I mean P-Tink waits at my feet for me to slip her small pieces of beef and chicken before I drop it in the marinade. I've got ribs, sausage, and chicken going in. Then later I'll add a bunch of veggies. Because everything tastes better cooked with fire and smoke.

"Ain't that right, P-Tink?"

The dog yelps in response. She and her mom both get me. Fucking love that.

Willow comes into the kitchen holding up regular towels and disposable towels for the bathroom. "Did we decide on disposable or real for today?"

I turn and drink her in. She's wearing cut-offs—the same pair from the day we knocked out her bathroom wall way back when—paired with a white tank under a blue flannel that's tied at her waist. White Converse on her feet, her hair curly and loose around her shoulders, cheeks still pink from the thorough fucking I gave her this morning. And goddamn if I'm not hard again.

"Come here," I say.

"Why? What's the matter?" She looks around the room, then down her front as she walks toward me. I slip off the rubber gloves I'm wearing to prep the meat, then grab her around the waist and hoist her to the counter, resting my hands on the sides of her knees.

"Have I told you lately how fucking beautiful you are?" I ask.

She giggles and rolls her eyes. "Yes, this morning and yesterday."

"You are." I run my hands up her legs and part her thighs to stand between them. "And these shorts, my god, 'Low, you give a man a coronary in these."

"You're just saying that," she says.

I press my forehead to hers. "No, babe, I'm not. You are so hot, so sexy, even when you aren't trying to be. I can't believe I get to wake up next to you in the morning and fall asleep with you in my arms at night. I'm so lucky to have you as mine. I love you so much. Thank you for giving me that."

"Aw come on!" she says. "Don't be all nice and romantic and stuff before people start arriving. I'll cry and my mascara will run, and—"

I silence her with a kiss. She moans into my mouth.

"How can I be turned on again after all the sex this morning?" she asks.

"How indeed?" I run my nose along the side of her face, breathing her in.

"You're the only one to do this to me, you know?" she says breathlessly. "Make me this crazy."

"And you me," I say nodding toward my hard cock trying to break free from my khaki shorts. I stick my hands down the back of her shorts and grip her ass. Which pulls the center seam against her clit.

"Oh, that feels good," she says, seeking my mouth. She wraps her legs around me and pulls me in closer. I grind against her seeking relief.

"Quickie?" I ask.

"God, yes."

I unbutton her shorts, and she mine, and I'm inside her in a matter of seconds. Bare. Something new we started a few weeks ago. Blows my fucking mind. I sink all the way into her. She reaches around from under my arms and grips the tops of my shoulders pulling herself closer to me. I grab a leg and loop it over my arm, opening her even further while I piston my hips.

"Oh, god, Mason. Oh god," she chants in my ear. "I love you."

"I love you so much. God, Willow, so much." I claim her lips with mine and continue pumping into her.

"So good," she moans. Her moans and cries put me right on the edge.

"I'm close, baby," I grunt.

"I'm . . . oh, Mason . . . oh yeah, right there, oh god." Her head goes back and her muscles clench around my dick, as she cries out my name. Squeezing my orgasm from me, I let go with a roar and pump everything I have into her.

God, I love this woman!

I hug her hard. She hugs back. My face buried in her neck and hers in mine. And I want to stay just like this forever.

She starts to pull back.

"Don't move," I say. "I want to hold you for just a minute."

"Mmm," she says and relaxes into me.

I nuzzle her neck, content I have everything I'll ever need here in my arms. "Thank you," I whisper in her ear.

"You're welcome," she whispers back. "Wait, for what?"

"For being perfect for me." I kiss her on her forehead, the tip of her nose, her chin, and finally her lips.

"That part's easy," she says.

I smile. She returns the gesture.

"Let's get you cleaned up," I say. I pull my shorts up, grab hers from the floor, then carry her into the main guest bathroom and use the towel to wipe me from her thighs.

"I guess we're using the disposable towels, huh?" She laughs.

"Guess so."

A crash sounds from the kitchen. I head back to see what happened. P-Tink has pulled the entire platter of meat off the counter and has finished half of the tri-tip.

"Princess Tinkerbell! No!" I yell.

She looks up and slinks back. Willow runs in, still fastening her shorts. "Oh no, P-Tink! Bad dog!"

P-Tink, knowing she's in trouble, promptly turns and throws up the first half of the tri-tip that she's already eaten. I send her outside and Willow and I try to clean it up. I wash off the other meats and start to season them again.

"We can't be mad at her," I say. "It's my fault. I left a platter full of meat there for her to drool over. That was dumb of me."

"Maybe," Willow says. "But she also knows it's not okay to counter surf. And that her food is in her bowl."

"I may have slipped her some stuff while I was trimming and seasoning," I admit.

"Mason! You can't do that. It will confuse her."

"I know, I'm sorry. She was just looking at me with those eyes." I look at Willow with my best, *please forgive me* face.

She laughs. "I hate those eyes. They get me every time," she says.

"See?"

"I was talking about you, not her." She laughs. "Okay, well what can we salvage?" She points to the meat.

"I think everything but the tri tip."

"Do we have another one?"

"No, but I can ask someone to stop."

"I'll ask Zach, he's due to be here soon anyway, maybe he can hit that little place down the street? The one with the olive bar?"

"Oh, good thinking," I say. There's a gourmet market that opened not far from us a month or so ago, and they have fresh and locally sourced everything.

She texts Zach what to get, he responds that he's just getting an Uber and will be here soon.

Willow cleans the countertop where we just had sex with antibacterial wipes. Then moves to do the same in the bathroom. She's nice like that. I probably wouldn't have thought to do it.

"I have to go change my panties, you wrecked them," she says.

I smile at her. "You could just go without."

She smiles back. "I could. But then what would you pull off me with your teeth later?"

The woman has a great point.

38

WILLOW

The party is in full swing and everyone seems to be having a great time. Mason has tasked me with enjoying myself while he handles all the food prep, serving, and party maintenance. So, I've done exactly that. One of the girls brought JELL-O shots and Zach and I are on our third each.

So. Freaking. Good.

Mason jumps up on the outdoor bar and whistles for attention.

"First, I'd just like to thank everyone for coming." A few people whistle and clap, and he lets them before continuing. "Willow put her heart and soul into this house and it shows." More clapping and whistles, a few people yell out their compliments. I blush then smile at Mason. "And," he says. "As most of you know, I've glommed onto that woman and her house and am not letting go."

"Smart man!" someone yells.

"Which is why I'd like to ask my beautiful girl to join me up here."

I roll my eyes, but head over to him anyway. He takes my hand and one of his friends helps me up on the bar, using my bottom as leverage.

"This is the only situation where touching my woman's ass will be tolerated, got it?" Mason says to him. We all laugh.

Mason takes my hands in his and turns to me, the expression on his face is serious.

My heart starts beating faster.

"Willow," he says looking me in the eye. "Never did I think I would find someone like you."

Ohmigod.

"I thank the universe every day for the completely fucked-up way you were brought into my life."

I laugh.

"And for giving me the courage to get you back and keep you in it."

My eyes begin to water. I can't believe he's going to make me cry again today.

"One thing that is increasingly clear to me," he continues, "but never more so than now, is that you're it, babe. For me. No one else. You're my one and only. I don't want anyone else."

Aw, crap. I'm totally crying now.

He kneels before me.

Ohmigod. Ohmigod. Ohmigod.

"And so, love of my life, light of my day, star of my dreams, will you do me the honor, please..."

Bawling really. That's a more accurate description. Those body-shaking sobs that render a girl tear-ugly and leave her hiccupping.

"Of becoming my wife?"

He pulls out a ring and takes my hand in his. Gasps sound through the room, combined with whistles, cheers, and the sound of women "aww"ing.

I can't speak.

All I can do is look down at him and nod. And smile. And nod some more.

I don't care if it will piss off my family. Or if it's too soon. Or if he almost married my sister. This man makes me a better me. And I make him a better him. And I want that betterment for both of us. And I don't want a day in my life where he isn't included.

He slides the ring on my finger, tears sliding down his cheeks. Then he stands and takes my face in his palms and kisses me. A kiss like no other. I don't know if it's because we're engaged, or the JELL-O shots, or the frivolity of the day. But the kiss is magical. Literally. Transporting me to another world where we are the only two people and it's perfect.

He takes the kiss a little deeper, and I wrap my arms around his neck and hang on. I vaguely hear the cheers and whistles of our friends around us, choosing instead to listen to Mason's murmurs of love between kisses.

That is until I hear someone yell, with such clarity, it stops everything. "What in the actual fuck is going on here?"

I turn and see AshLynn, Cassandra, and my dad all standing in the doorway between the house and the deck. Mason slowly lowers his hands from my face. I do the same with my arms from his neck.

What are they doing here?

I'm not sure if I think that or say it.

"I don't know," Mason says.

I also don't know if his response is because I said it aloud or because he always seems to read my mind.

Regardless, he hops down then holds his arms out to help me down then takes my hand in his and leads us to where my family stands.

"Welcome," he says.

"I didn't expect you guys to come," I say.

"Clearly," AshLynn says with pure hatred in her eyes. Which she quickly turns on Mason. "What? I didn't work out so you thought you'd try the backup sister?"

"Whoa. Wait just a minute—" Mason starts.

"Is it because she has money and I didn't?" AshLynn continues, "or because breaking one of us wasn't enough, you had to go after both? What did we ever do to you, Mason?"

"Um—" I start.

"First of all," Mason interrupts. "You know this has nothing to do with money. At least, not for me. I didn't break you, not even close, and I sure as hell don't intend to break Willow. I love her."

"Love." AshLynn rolls her eyes and scoffs.

I'm in shock. Whether it's because I'm engaged or because they're here, or both I'm not sure.

"Well, you've certainly set yourself up quite nicely," Cassandra sneers.

I can hear murmurs from the crowd wondering what's going on. While our closest friends know the details of how we met, we change it slightly for other people. And by slightly, I mean a lot. I'm not comfortable with it being public knowledge that Mason was engaged to my sister. And Mason would like to have a little more time pass before it becomes one of *those* jokes. He doesn't ever want anyone thinking I'm a rebound.

And until now, it didn't occur to me that I might be.

Or did it?

"How do you like being the rebound, Willow?" AshLynn says.

Now she reads my mind too.

"Hold the fuck up," Mason says. "Say what you will to me, but you will not speak ill of or to Willow like that. She's not a rebound, AshLynn, and you know it."

I like that he's standing up for me. It makes me want to stick my tongue out at AshLynn and Cassandra and say *told you so*. Except I'm not sure what it is that I've told them so about.

I look to my dad for support. Like usual, he's looking at the ground, not engaging in the conversation. How did he ever become CEO of one of the largest companies in Texas being so passive?

Cassandra and AshLynn are both talking at once. Mason is countering each. I'm standing here doing nothing. It's like every single insecurity I've ever had where Cassandra and AshLynn are concerned has suddenly taken hold and I'm powerless to overcome it. I look down at the ring Mason just put on my finger as though seeing it for the first time. It's beautiful. A princess cut, which he had to have found out from Zach was my favorite since Mason and I have never talked about rings. When we were younger Zach and I both decided we wanted princess cut diamond rings because of the name. A princess cut diamond must make you a princess, right?

I look to Zach. He's looking at Cassandra, his face filled with fury. I look to Mason. He's pointing to the door.

He's kicking my family out.

Wow.

I see them all turn to leave.

AshLynn, never one to let someone else get the last word, turns back one last time. "Have a nice life, gold digger."

Gold digger? Is she talking to me? To Mason?

My dad looks back at me before walking into the house, the look on his face a blend of disappointment and sadness and shakes his head.

Why would he be disappointed in me? Why is he sad?

God, what did everyone say while I just stood here, dumbly?

What is my dad thinking?

Why do I care?

Because you always care.

I need to talk to him

"Wait," I call out to him. "I'm coming with you."

39

MASON

Did that just happen?

I look at the house in shock. Then around at the party. Everyone's face there reflects what I'm feeling. Except my mom, she looks at me with sympathy.

Sympathy.

Her family crashed the party, insulted everyone here, then left.

And she went with them.

Fuck!

I have to tell her we weren't really engaged. I should have told her long ago. It was stupid not to.

Goddammit.

And now she's gone. I run into the house to stop her. But the town car is passing the bend in the drive by the time I reach the front yard.

"Willow!" I yell. The car doesn't stop. I head back into the house to get my keys so I can go after her.

Which is when I see the ring.

Right next to her cell phone.

She left the ring on a small counter in the kitchen where we keep our keys and charge our cell phones. She took it off minutes after I put it on her finger. Minutes after she said she would marry me. She took it off and left it here to follow her insufferable, fucked-up family to god knows where.

What the fuck is going on?

I sink to the floor with the ring in my hand. Looking at it as though it holds all the answers to what just happened. Is this her way of now saying no?

She nodded yes. She kissed me like she meant yes.

Kissed you back, you mean.

I can't even call her if she doesn't have her phone.

She left her ring. She doesn't want you calling her.

"Mason, are you in here?" I hear my mom, but I don't answer. She'll find me eventually. And she does. "Oh no. Oh, Mason, I'm so sorry," is what I get when she sees the ring.

"What does this mean?" I ask, looking at the ring. The fucking ring.

"I don't know, sweetheart."

"She's gone."

"I'm sorry, Mason."

"You don't seem surprised," I say. "Even out there, when everyone else was shocked as hell, you looked at me like you were sorry. What does that mean? Why did you do that?"

"I am shocked, Mason. I did not expect this at all."

"Then what is it?"

"Family dynamics are difficult. And what Willow has gone through is harder than most. She has an attachment to her family, and it's understandable. It would make sense that she would talk to them after what happened today."

"Why leave with them? Why take off the ring? Why not just do it here? With me?"

"I don't know."

"Is that the . . ." I look up, Zach is standing before me, P-Tink at his side, asking me about the ring. I nod.

"Holy fuck."

"I know," I say.

He slides his back down the wall to sit on my other side. P-Tink lays her head in my lap and licks my shirt.

"Why did she . . ." Zach starts but doesn't finish.

"If you don't know, man. I'm truly fucked. You know her better than anyone."

"Her dad has a hold on her like I've never seen. It's unreal. We've been friends forever, she and I. And Jonathan used to hug me right along with all her other friends. But when he found out I was gay, he switched to a handshake. As though a hug was something too sexual for me to handle. Or him." He scoffs.

Then continues, "That cut me. Hard. I looked to him like a father figure. I spent more time at Willow's than I did anywhere, especially my own house. And while he wasn't a super present father, he was one hundred times better than the one I had. She let him do it. Barely said a word about it. This being the same girl who walked with me every year in our hometown Gay Pride parade after I was out."

I reach over and pat his shoulder. "Sorry, man."

"You don't get it. We were the parade. It wasn't an event like you see in Seattle or San Francisco, it was her and me, sporting rainbows, walking through the middle of town. She carried this big sign that said *proud to be besties with a gay man*. Only the words *besties with* were in small letters, so unless you were up close it looked like the sign said *proud to be a gay man*. She picketed the school board when I wasn't allowed to take a boy from a neighboring town to prom. We were all still reeling from our other friend Marlie's sudden death. The one with the brain aneurysm. And there she goes, Willow championing me. To the school board. But not her dad."

I shake my head. Not sure what to think.

"What do I do?" I ask. "Is she gone?"

What have I done?

Is it because I told her family off?

I hear people start to come inside, murmuring and whispering about what's happened. "I can't deal with people right now." I wave a hand toward the deck where people are still milling about as well.

"I will take care of it." Zach stands and heads outside. I can hear him asking people to pack up some food to go and head out. He's polite about it, but that's the general gist. Willow had ordered to-go containers for people so that we wouldn't have leftovers go to waste when we couldn't finish them. How can she be both the woman who leaves her engagement ring on the counter without a word *and* the woman who buys to-go containers for guests at our party.

People leave faster than I anticipated. Soon it's just me, Zach, Mom, and her friend Abe. I can't bring myself to call him her boyfriend, even though he is. 'Cause, that's my mom. Moms don't have boyfriends.

Mom and Zach get most things cleaned up, while I sit like a zombie petting P-Tink. She left her dog. Not only did she leave me, but she left her dog. It's like she's a cult member who's been brainwashed. Leaving me, her dog, her ring, and her cell phone. All the things she cares about. Or, if I'm out of the picture already, then at least the things she *should* care about: her dog and her cell phone.

"Do you want me to stay?" Mom asks.

I shake my head. "No, you guys can go. I'm staying here in case she comes back or calls. Thank you for cleaning up, I owe you one."

My mom smiles, that bit of pity that I hate is back on her face. I hug her, shake Abe's hand, and send them on their way.

I've since moved to the living room and am sitting in my favorite chair, with P-Tink curled up on the large ottoman with my feet.

My favorite chair.

Because I live here. With Willow. Who left me.

Zach comes into the room with a bottle of tequila, limes, salt, and two shot glasses. "I don't know what you heterosexuals do when someone leaves you. I usually alternate between ice cream and chick flicks, or tequila shots and MMA. I figured you'd appreciate the latter more."

I give him a weak smile but take the shot when he offers anyway. Along with three more in quick succession after that. I feel the alcohol start to melt my insides and turn them to goo. Goo is good. Goo doesn't care if your girl returns the ring and takes off. Goo has no feelings at all.

Soon, we are half a bottle down, and yelling at the TV when it doesn't go the way we want. But we've moved on from MMA to a cooking competition show. And all our favorites keep getting eliminated.

"Fucking A," Zach says. "Lavender-infused créme brûlée kicks fucking deconstructed bananas Foster's ass every day, man. Every goddamn day. Those judges have their heads up their asses."

I raise the bottle in agreement and take another swig, then pass it to him. We moved on from glasses to swigging right out of the bottle for efficiency's sake. That and sometimes trying to pour into those tiny glasses is really hard.

"Don't take this the wrong way," Zach says during a commercial break. "But I feel like she left me too. I mean, I know I didn't just propose, or fuck her brains out this morning, or anything like that. Because gross. But she chose Daddy. Again. And I really thought she was getting past that. Especially once you guys were together. I mean, that was a hella tough fucking hurdle for her to get over. Between her insecurities about AshLynn and what her parents would think. But she did it. She chose you."

"Right, but she hadn't told them we're together. So, I think that made it easier for her."

"Good point." He nods sagely.

"But I agree about the insecurities with AshLynn stuff."

"What did you ever see in her?" Zach asks.

"In AshLynn?" I think about it for a second. "I didn't see anything in AshLynn." I scoff. "I was just giving her a ride from Leavenworth to Seattle. She blackmailed me into faking the engagement when she caught me watching Willow through her window one night."

Zach laughs. "You're a Peeping Tom."

"No, man, I was playing fetch with P-Tink, and Willow was in her room putting lotion on after a shower. I just happened to walk by. The curtains were sheer. It wasn't my fault. I think that's when I fell in love with her. Right then."

"So fucking sweet," Zach says. "But, seriously, it was all fake? All that energy and effort was pretend?"

"One hundred percent pretend. AshLynn and I were never really engaged. I'd just met her the night before we came here. Never even kissed. Couldn't stand her."

"Are you kidding me right now? Did I just hear that right? I come back after facing absolute hell with my family, mostly over stealing my sister's fiancé, and the two of you are talking about how the whole thing was faked?" I hear

Willow's voice. It gets louder as she continues talking until she ends in a scream at the word *faked*.

I turn. "Baby. Willow. Oh my god, you're home. Thank god. I was so worried." I stand and move to go to her. But when I do things get a bit woozy. Or maybe it's me that's a bit woozy. And I fall over the ottoman. Zach laughs. So I do too. Because when you're drunk and you fall and the person you are drunk with laughs at you, you laugh with them.

Which is why I don't get it at first. When Willow leans over me and says something and I have to say, "Wait a minute, baby. I'm sorry. I need to stop laughing before I can hear you." Which makes Zach laugh more. And well, you already know what happens when Zach laughs.

"GET OUT!" Willow screams. Which shuts us both up.

"What do you mean?" I ask.

"Oh, I think you're in trouble, my man," Zach says.

"I mean both of you," Willow says. Her face fierce. God, she looks beautiful when she's mad. Maybe I should tell her that.

"You're so beautiful when you're mad."

She closes her eyes and takes a deep breath, letting it out slowly, then points to the door.

Zach stands and stumbles. Not quite like I did, but enough to look dumb. It takes everything I have in me not to laugh. I might have scoffed a bit though.

He looks at me. "You can't drive."

"You can't drive," I say back.

Zach looks at Willow and shrugs. "We can't drive. Therefore, we can't leave."

"Call an Uber," she says. "Call a cab. Walk. Crawl. I don't fucking care. Just get the fuck out."

Did Willow just say fuck? She never cusses. Ever.

She's still pointing at the door. Eyes closed, face hard.

So, I go. In sweats, a T-shirt, and no shoes. I go.

Zach, dressed similarly, follows.

"She cussed," Zach says after Willow slams the front door and locks it.

"I know," I say. "I think she's really mad."

"We should call an Uber," Zach says. He pats his pockets. "Shit, my phone is inside."

I already know I don't have mine. "Mine too."

"I can't call an Uber."

"Me neither."

"It's cold out here," he says.

"I know. I think I have a blanket in my Jeep."

"Dibs!" Zach says.

"You can't call dibs on the only blanket," I say as I reach for the Jeep door handle. "It's locked."

"Unlock it."

"My keys are inside the house."

"Oh."

"Next to my phone."

We stand there for a minute, Zach hops from one foot to the other to stay warm. "I'm cold."

"Me too," I say.

"Well, shit. Only one thing left to do," he says, and he picks up a rock and huffs it through the driver's side window. The glass shatters and the car alarm goes off.

"Oh shit, we need to turn that off," he says.

"You think? What the fuck, man. You just broke my car window!"

"I wanted the blanket," he whines.

We look at each other for a moment. I'm not sure what to do. The alarm continues to shrill.

"Really, man, can you turn that off, it's giving me a headache."

"No shit! And no, I can't turn it off, because the keys are in the house!"

It goes on for another minute, before stopping on its own. At least I think it was on its own. It may have been Willow pushing the button. Either way, it's a relief.

I grab the blanket from the back, then brush as much glass as possible off the front seat, and climb in. Zach gets in on the passenger side and pulls the blanket toward him.

"You get half, man. That's how blanket sharing works."

"I barely have any, look?" He holds the blanket up.

"That's how much I have." I do the same.

"The only thing getting blanket is the center console," Zach gripes.

"Let's get in the back seat," I say. "Then we can sit closer together and get more blanket."

"Barely broken up with the girl and already hitting on the best friend," Zach mumbles.

"I'm not hitting on you," I say. "And Willow and I are not broken up. I will explain everything in the morning. And she will understand."

"You better hope so."

"Trust me, I do. So much."

40

——————

WILLOW

I LISTEN TO THEM ARGUING IN THE FRONT YARD. IT'S NOT HARD to hear them with how quiet the area is. If I wasn't so angry, I would probably laugh.

I hear something smash, like glass, and then the car alarm goes off. I look out the window and see that they are arguing again, both have arms flying in the air as they talk. It looks like the driver's side window on Mason's Jeep is broken.

Jesus. Idiots.

I grab his keys and click off the alarm, so at least that stops. The remnants of their little party still on the coffee table. A near-empty bottle of tequila, salt everywhere, lime rinds, shot glasses, an empty bag of chips, and a cooking competition on the TV. I grab the TV remote and click it off, then wipe up the tequila mess. I'm surprised to see the kitchen is completely clean, as is the back patio. You can't even tell there was a party here today. I open the fridge and see a small number of leftovers and smile. It means Mason used my to-go containers and made everyone take food home.

I dump the rest of the tequila down the sink, throw the bottle into the recycling bin, then grab an afghan and cuddle on the couch with Princess Tinkerbell.

"What went wrong today, P-Tink?" I ask her. She licks my hand in return.

"Why did Mason and Zach get to have a tequila party when I'm the one who's pissed off? Huh?" I scratch behind her ears and she immediately rolls over and displays her belly. So I scratch that too.

I'm angry that my family came and messed up what was a perfect moment. Mason's and my perfect moment. For once, I just wanted to set them all straight. Tell it like it is. And for hours I tried to do just that.

But everything I said was ignored by Cassandra and AshLynn. They believe what they want to and that's that. They tag teamed me the entire pointless conversation. I waited for my father to come to my defense. For him to say anything at all, but he just sat there. He didn't join in with anything they said, but he didn't counter it either. It was like he just tuned out completely.

We didn't just talk about Mason, they lost steam with that soon into our time together. Then they went on to money, specifically the money that my grandmother left me that should have been "family" money. The fact that my dad took my entire inheritance from my mother as "family" money didn't matter to them. It should all be "family" money.

Of course, talking about money led back to talking about Mason and how he is only with me for my money. My counter argument was that he has money of his own. A net worth of millions in real estate holdings and other equally sound investments. That's when things got really ugly. Because then AshLynn's brief fling with Mason—which apparently was fake all along—became the love story of the century and I ruined it. And now I'm tromping all over it with my wanton behavior. Not to mention, that I've flat-out ruined my relationship with my poor sister. And she will never forgive me.

Ever.

Ever.

She actually stomped her foot when she said that. Which made me laugh. Which made Cassandra livid. Which made her turn red. Red like I've never seen. Really, I've never seen her face be anything other than cool motionless ivory. I think she broke her Botox. Why AshLynn couldn't be bothered to admit the engagement was fake all along is beyond me.

Which was when my father finally stepped in.

"Enough," he'd said. It wasn't loud, but it was finite, and it made everyone stop. He still didn't stick up for me, but he didn't stick up for them either.

"You both have your opinions. And they are different. That's it. End of discussion. AshLynn, there will be other boys who will break your heart. Willow, there will be other boys after your money. Deal with it. Both of you. I love you, but I'm done. I don't want to hear any more of this. Understood?"

I'd nodded. Then I kissed my dad on the forehead and left. Their hotel was in downtown Seattle. I hung out in the bar for a while drinking coffee and sorting out my thoughts. Then I bought a jacket and some sweatpants from the gift shop and charged them to my dad's room and walked around downtown. Went back to the hotel, ordered a town car, charged it to my dad's room too, and had the driver bring me home.

I cried the entire way. For the loss of my relationship with my father. The loss of my mom and my grandmother. And even the loss of AshLynn and Cassandra. Or at least the loss of the *idea* of a stepmother to take the place of my mom and the *idea* of a sister. Because the reality with them was only good for a short time. I still don't know why it changed. Why everything changed. And coming to terms with all that was emotionally debilitating. All I wanted to do was go home and see Mason and P-Tink. Forget about AshLynn and Cassandra and all the bitterness wrapped up in them. Go home, let Mason prop me up and put me back together, in the way that only he can.

Instead, I open the front door and hear Mason and Zach talking about how the entire relationship with AshLynn was fake. He lied about it all, then and now. And I just want to know why? Why did he do that for her if he didn't even know her? And why lie to me about it? It doesn't matter what, I'm always second to her. I spent all afternoon being reminded how much better she is than me.

I can't do it anymore. I just can't. I thought I had it all figured out by the time I headed home. But apparently not. And now I don't even have anyone that I can talk to about it. Because I just kicked out the only two people I would ordinarily talk to. I go to grab my phone, thinking maybe I will call one of the girls from today.

Which is when I see the ring. I don't even remember taking it off. But I must have, maybe subconsciously, when I knew I would be talking to my family. Which is stupid since it's a huge diamond, from Mason to me, and that would have only aided in my arguments with Cassandra and AshLynn today.

They would have assumed you paid for it anyway.

True.

Which deflates me even further. I didn't even think that was possible. But it makes me realize I don't want to talk to one of the girls from today. I want to talk to Mason. And Zach. I want to forget about what they said about AshLynn and have everything go back to the way it was this morning.

But I can't forget.

At least not right now. It's all too raw. The arguments with AshLynn and Cassandra too fresh, and the lingering insecurity from that too overwhelming. The fact that my dad just sat there and did nothing the entire time they harped on me. For hours he let them rant. The favoritism could not have been clearer than it was today. There is no way for me to go on pretending he treats AshLynn and me equally.

Sigh.

I flop back down on the couch with P-Tink and let her lean her big body against me. My ring twinkles in the light. Not that I've put it back on my finger. But I am holding it in my hand, turning it back and forth studying it.

It's perfect.

And huge. The center stone is at least two carats. With another carat of small round brilliants surrounding it, and probably another carat more floating between two bands down the sides.

When did he even have the time to do this without me knowing? We've been so busy with the house and then planning the party. To say I was shocked when he proposed is an understatement.

He knows AshLynn is a sore spot for me. If they weren't ever really engaged, why didn't he just tell me that? I know I told him I didn't want to know.

Remember you promised him you'd talk to him before you spoke to AshLynn. Maybe you should go ask him.

Maybe I will.

I get up and head to the front door.

41

———

MASON

Zach and I huddle in the back seat. I stick my hands in my armpits to keep them warm and hold the blanket up over me by tucking it under my chin.

"When did it get so fucking cold?" Zach asks.

"I don't know. Maybe you should go ask for another blanket."

"Maybe you should."

"She doesn't want to see me, dude. She left me, remember?"

"She used the word *fuck*, remember?"

"How do I fix this, Zach?"

"I don't know, man. I especially don't know when I'm cold and coming down off a tequila high."

"Why did we drink so much?" I ask.

"I blame you," he says.

"Me? You're the one who brought the tequila into the living room. With the limes and shot glasses and shit."

"Yeah, but you're the one who got dumped. Necessitating the tequila."

He has a point.

Fuck.

"Maybe you should go apologize," Zach suggests.

"Do you think it will work?"

"No, but it would give me more blanket."

"Asshole."

"But I'd be a warm asshole."

"Okay, what do they say to do in the tundra? You know, to stay warm and alive."

"Get naked."

I scoff. "Can you imagine how much trouble I'd be in with Willow if she thought I was cheating on her with you?"

Zach laughs. "You? What about me? I'd be the one who betrayed her by seducing her fiancé."

"Maybe I would have seduced you," I say.

"Not a chance," Zach says.

"I've got moves."

"Not gay moves."

"Gay moves are different?"

"So different."

"Like how?"

"We're more direct. There's no subterfuge like with you hetero men."

"I don't use subterfuge."

"Of course you do, you all do."

"All men who like women?"

"All heterosexuals period. Men and women. It's all you do with your touched-up profile pictures and exaggerated occupations, fake hobbies and changed names."

"And gay guys don't lie on their profiles?"

"No. We don't."

"Huh." That surprises me.

"We use *Grinder*. To hook up. That's it. I see a guy is a mile away, he's a bear who's into twinks, but likes to be a bottom. Boom. I hit him up. Few minutes later we are both getting off in exactly the way we want and anticipated."

"Interesting."

"Jealous?"

"No." I scoff. "Well, maybe. It just seems so simple."

"It is."

"So, stuff like this never happens in a gay relationship?"

"Who said anything about a relationship? I'm talking about fucking. If we switch to talking about relationships, it's a whole different story. Gays are DRAMA with a capital everything."

I laugh again. "Okay, okay. I get it." I pause for a minute before asking another question, "How come you're not in a relationship, Zach?"

"Did you not just hear me?" he asks. "Gays are drama. And I am a queen."

I gasp and feign shock. "I can't believe you would be dramatic."

"Fuck off, dude." He pauses, then continues, "I'll be honest, at this point in my life, I don't believe in them. Mostly because I would want a relationship to be monogamous."

"Nothing wrong with that," I say.

"Except that I don't believe it's possible to be monogamous."

"I'm monogamous with Willow."

"For now."

"No, not just for now. Forever. Anything that I might benefit from by cheating would not be worth risking losing her over."

"Okay, Mister Ray of Sunshine, let me rephrase. I can't be monogamous."

"That's different."

"Yes. I can't expect fidelity from a partner I'm not willing to be faithful to."

"How do you know you can't be faithful to someone if you haven't yet met the someone you're willing to be faithful to?"

Zach yawns. "I'm going to pretend that question makes sense while I lay my head on your shoulder. I'm not hitting on you, stud-mc-muffin, just tired."

I rest my head on his, grateful for the added warmth the closeness brings.

I must fall asleep, because the next thing I know, Zach is screaming like a little girl and someone is shining a flashlight in our faces.

I hold my hand up to block the light from my eyes. "Willow?"

"No," a deep voice answers. "Mason, is that you? What are you doing out here? Is that Willow with you?"

I recognize that voice.

"Mister Brooks?" Zach croaks.

"Zachary?"

I clear my throat. "It's Mason and Zach, Jonathan. We are the only people in the car."

"What the hell are you doing in the car?"

"It's a long story," I say at the same time Zach says, "Your daughter kicked us out."

"Why not just go home?" Jonathan asks as he opens the driver's side door and takes a seat. "Did your window break?"

"We were pretty drunk when she kicked us out," Zach says. "We broke the window to get in the car."

"Must you be so honest?" I hiss at him.

"There are keys for such things," Jonathan says.

"I know," I say. "Our keys and phones are in the house with Willow. Which is the only reason why we are in the car."

Jonathan nods. "You both look like hell."

"Thank you, sir," Zach says.

I run my hands through my hair. It feels dirty even though I just showered this morning. Or maybe that's me. Maybe I feel dirty because I know I've just hurt the most important person in my life with a callous comment that never should have left my mouth.

"You love her?" Jonathan asks looking at me.

"With everything I have."

"It's my understanding that you are quite well off financially," he says.

"I do okay."

He looks at me thoughtfully.

Then nods and says, "I'm going to talk to my daughter. I'd be happy to bring you out your phones and wallets or whatever you need to give me a few hours alone with her, if you don't mind."

"Is she going to be upset after she spends this time alone with you?" I ask.

Jonathan looks down and shakes his head before looking back up at me. "I hope not. I've not been a good father to her for quite a while. I want to apologize to her for that. I want to mend what I am now realizing is a very broken relationship with my firstborn, and I'm afraid I am primarily to blame for that."

I stare him down. He doesn't look away.

I nod my approval. "If you could bring my keys and wallet, I would appreciate it. I will give you time with Willow, but I will be back first thing in the morning, if not sooner. After that I'm not leaving until she is convinced that there is nothing in this world more important to me than her."

"Hoorah," Zach says from under the blanket. Which makes me laugh since he was never in the military, but also makes me feel good that I have his support.

Jonathan steps away from the car, then turns back and leans his head in. "Is there room for one more under that blanket if she's not willing to talk to me?"

Zach pokes his head out. "I'll keep you warm, Johnny." He wiggles his eyebrows, making me laugh.

Jonathan, to his credit, laughs as well, shuts the car door, and heads toward the house.

42

———

WILLOW

I TELL P-TINK TO STAY IN THE HOUSE, THEN OPEN THE FRONT door, and shriek in surprise at the man ready to knock.

"Dad?" I ask.

"Willow, I was hoping we could talk. May I come in?"

"Uh . . . sure. I was just, um . . ." I want to ask him if Mason is still out there. It's important to me that he's still there. Somewhere in my mind it proves that I come first.

"Mason and Zach are in the back seat of that car if you are wondering," my dad says. "I said I would bring them their keys and wallets."

"Oh, are they leaving?" Dread fills my body and weighs down my heart. Mason is leaving. Our first fight and he's through.

"I asked them to leave us for a few hours. I hope that was okay."

"You asked them to leave?" I confirm.

"Yes. They would not be leaving otherwise. Or at least Mason would not be. He said that he would be back first thing in the morning though. And then after that he wouldn't be leaving again until he'd convinced you that you're the most important thing in the world to him."

My heart soars and I can't stop the smile that takes over my face. Both of which have seem to forgotten that we are mad at Mason. I get the wallets and keys for my dad to take to Mason and Zach. As an afterthought I add shoes and jackets to the pile.

"Would you like coffee?" I ask him.

"I would love it," he says. "I'll be right back." He leaves to give the boys their things.

I've got coffee brewing by the time he returns.

"This is for you." He hands me a small piece of paper. It's a receipt that's been ripped in half. On the back Mason has written:

I love you. Only you. Always you. Please allow me to explain. I did something stupid, but it doesn't change how I feel about you. Just five minutes. Please.

Love, M

PS—Zach says he loves you and don't be mad

I read it twice, then tuck it in my pocket. Dad and I both get a cup of coffee, then return to the living room. I sit in my favorite chair where I feel most comfortable. My dad sits across from me on the couch. I wait for him to start.

"I owe you an apology and an explanation," he says. I do my best to keep all emotion off my face and sip my coffee.

"I've done you wrong, Willow, for a long time. And I'm sorry. I have no reason or excuse other than I was weak." He places his palms up and shrugs his shoulders, then leans forward, elbows to knees. "When your mother died, a part of me did as well. I know you know that, and I know the same is true for you."

He takes a deep breath and lets it out slowly before continuing.

"But, while it made you stronger, it made me weaker. Infinitely weaker. I felt incomplete and unfinished. Like I didn't belong in my own skin. Or my own life. I didn't know how to give you what you needed, and I didn't want to make the effort to learn how. I just allowed myself to wallow."

His voice breaks, making me want to go to him. Comfort him. But I force myself to stay seated. If I stop him now, if I make it okay now, I may never get the whole story from him. And I desperately need to know why he's done the things he has.

"It wasn't until I met Cassandra that I even started to breathe again."

He looks at me, as if seeking reassurance. I nod and smile halfway so he will continue.

"And when AshLynn was born, it was like my chance to do it all over again. Not just fatherhood, but as a husband and a man. I failed your mother in so many ways, Willow. So many. But she accepted and forgave. Over and over again. I didn't deserve it. You have no idea how little I deserved that from her. Which in turn made me feel small and ineffective. It was emasculating when it should have been empowering."

"Are you blaming her for your shortcomings?" I interrupt.

"No." He shakes his head vigorously. "Not at all. Make no mistake, it was all me who felt this way. My own insecurities magnified, I felt guilty and insufficient. I'd taken your mother's last name for god's sake. There weren't many ways for me to prove my manhood as far as I was concerned."

It never occurred to me how that may have made him feel, emotionally. I always just assumed it was a good business opportunity for him, so he took it. To realize that it was probably both good and bad in equal measure is a little mind-blowing.

"With Cassandra, I could reinvent myself, become an entirely new Jonathan Brooks, one who didn't rely on his wife for everything."

He hangs his head with a sigh. And stays that way for a few minutes. I finish my coffee and am about to say something when he looks up again. The pain so evident in his eyes, it takes my breath away.

"Except I'm not a new man, Willow. I'm the same man only now instead of a wife who supports my every move, I have one who critiques it." He lets out a short and bitter laugh. "Which is just as emasculating. I avoided you because the reminder of your mother was so strong and my longing for her overwhelming. Then I avoided you because you represented my epic failure as a man when I had a chance to do it all over."

I see tears start to slip down his cheeks. Making my own eyes water.

"And I've come to the realization that I'm just not a strong man. As much as I may want to be or try to portray myself as. I've accomplished things that should make me feel strong, like Brooks International."

He names the company that he's built from the ground up. And he should be proud of that, it does very well. So, I tell him so.

"It does do well. But not through any effort on my part. I got lucky with who I hired in the beginning. That's all. It's the people under me that make it all work. Make it grow and be a success. If it were left up to me, I'd probably have run it into the ground by now."

"Dad—" I start.

He holds up his hand to stop me. "But, that's not what I came here to say. And I'm not looking for your pity or any atta-boys. Regardless of the reasons, I've not been fair to you and I'm sorry for that. And today, when I sat there for hours and listened to you argue with Cassandra and AshLynn about things that have no purpose being argued over, I real-ized how long I've let that go on. I'm not sure when the divide started between Cassandra and AshLynn and then you, though I think it was always there and I'm just ignorant. But after you left today, it became so clear to me how long it's been a problem and how often I've fostered it whether intentional or not."

I wipe at the tears streaming down my face. My dad pulls his handkerchief out of his pocket and leans over the coffee table to hand it to me. I smile my thanks.

"I talked to Cassandra and AshLynn before I came over here. And told them a lot of the same things I'm telling you.

I also told them there are changes that need to be made in this family. Changes regarding their perceived entitlement and especially changes with their behavior toward you and me. I think they understood. At least to the best of their ability to empathize with another person."

I cry-laugh at that and blow my nose.

"I'm making you a promise now, Willow, to be a more supportive father to you and pay attention to your needs. To speak up when necessary and not allow Cassandra and AshLynn to steamroll you and your life. I only hope I'm not too late." He stands and holds a hand out to me. I move toward him, but instead of taking his hand, I pull him into a hug.

"Thank you, Dad. I appreciate your honesty, it could not have been easy to open yourself up like that."

"Thank you for listening to me. I love you, kiddo."

"I love you too."

He kisses me on the top of my head. "Well, I'm sure it's been an emotional day for you, I didn't mean to add to that."

I wave my hand in the air, gesturing that it's fine.

"I'm going to head out."

I nod in response.

"You've got a really good guy there, Willow. I don't know what he did tonight to make you mad, but I do know how much he loves you. Maybe cut him some slack if you can, huh?"

I smile. "I will."

"I'll call you tomorrow before we head back to Southlake to say goodbye."

"I'd like that," I say as I walk him to the door. He hugs me one last time and then leaves.

I flop back down on the couch. "Can you believe this day, P-Tink?" She yelps in response.

I feel exhausted and exhilarated at the same time. But still turn off the lights and get ready to go to bed. As I'm heading down the hall, I hear a knock on the door.

"Dad, what did you forget?" I ask as I open the door. Only instead of my dad, it's Mason.

"Hey," he says. "Can I come in?"

43

———

MASON

Willow steps aside to let me in.

Oh, thank god! One hurdle down. Now to convince her why I did what I did.

"Your dad was here, are you okay?" I ask. She looks like she's been crying. Probably because I'm the world's biggest asshole. Or else her dad is.

She nods in response to my question. "We talked. It was good. Really good. He said a lot of things I needed to hear." She sits down in her favorite chair. I sit on the coffee table in front of her and take her hands in mine. She doesn't pull away.

So far, so good.

"I am so sorry about AshLynn and not telling you the truth. I was embarrassed about something that happened, that she caught me doing, and at first I didn't want you to know. Then, as more time passed, I couldn't figure out how to tell you without making you angry that I hadn't told you before." I pause in case she wants to say something, but she stays silent.

I continue, "The first night we were here, after AshLynn and I arrived, you remember we ordered pizza?"

She nods.

"I went outside to play ball with P-Tink. Only we lost the ball. When I was looking for it, I saw you, through your bedroom windows, just out of the shower. The curtains you had up hid nothing. You were putting lotion on that beautiful body of yours."

She gasps.

"I watched you from the time you got out of the shower, until you got dressed. I fell in love with you that night. Not just because you are beautiful, but because of how I felt when I was with you. When you look at me, and now that we've been together, for so much more."

"I don't understand what this has to do with AshLynn," she says.

"I'm getting to that," I tell her. "As you were dressing, AshLynn caught me watching you from the beach. She threatened to have me arrested for voyeurism if I didn't pretend to be her fiancé."

"I'd like to say I'm surprised," she says. "But I don't think I am."

"Yeah, well, I sure was. I knew I had feelings for you, I didn't want you to get creeped out knowing I'd seen you. And I was only supposed to have to pretend for an hour or so, it was never supposed to go as far as it did."

"Why did it go so far?"

"AshLynn thought she could get her inheritance if we were engaged. And she claimed to have a picture of me touching myself while watching you."

Willow smirks. "Did she?"

"No."

"Wait, how were you even together in the first place then?"

"I met her at the bar in the hotel where I was staying. I bought her a couple drinks, she told me she was stranded, and needed a ride to Seattle. I was coming here anyway and before I realized what I was doing, I offered."

"So, did you guys . . .?"

"No, we did nothing, no kissing, no hand holding, absolutely nothing. I felt bad for her because her boyfriend had just abandoned her at the wedding she was at, when she'd thought he was going to propose. Apparently, she'd told everyone he was going to and was humiliated when he didn't."

"Boyfriend?"

"Yeah, Brian I think his name was. They hadn't been together long. They met a week or so before at the bachelor/bachelorette party."

"Leave it to AshLynn to think she can get engaged to a guy she's known a couple weeks."

"I wanted to marry you after a couple hours," I tell her.

"No, you didn't," she says.

"Yeah, I did. And as far as I knew today, you accepted my proposal, then left me. You took off the ring I'd just given you and left in the middle of what was about to be an engagement party, to go with your family. Who, as far as I'm concerned, do not deserve any time or consideration from you."

She opens her mouth to say something, but I silence her with a finger against her lips. She kisses it lightly. I take that as an extremely good sign. A sign that makes me want to pull her in my arms and kiss her for real. But I need her to know how the conversation went down. And to know that it's her, first and foremost, before everyone else.

"Zach mentioned he felt like you'd left him too," I continue. "He said that he had lingering insecurities from when you were younger about you choosing your family over him. Which led to us talking about your issues with AshLynn. Both of which were mere sentences, it's not like they were full-on discussions. Then he asked what I'd ever seen in AshLynn. And that is when you walked in." I lift her hands and kiss each palm before lowering them back to her lap, still holding them in mine.

She nods in response. Then takes a deep breath and lets it out slowly. "I don't remember taking off the ring. I didn't realize I'd done it until after I was home tonight and I grabbed my phone for something. I'm sorry I did that to you. There was no hidden meaning or ulterior motive with it."

She lifts my hands this time and kisses the backs of each. I grip them a bit tighter. I don't like the idea that she just took off the ring without remembering, but I think I understand why it happened.

"I needed to clear the air with my family once and for all. Or at least try to. I needed them to know how I felt about everything. And that this thing between you and me is real. If they want a place in my life, they have to accept that."

She pauses.

"How did that go?" I ask, keeping my voice soft.

"Not good." She laughs bitterly. "It was mostly my dad sitting there saying nothing, and Cassandra and AshLynn trying to convince me how right they are and wrong I am."

I scoff. "About what?"

"Everything. Anything. It didn't matter, they ran the gamut of topics."

"That was like seven hours that you were gone, baby. You must be wrecked." I brush the hair back from her face and cradle her cheek. She turns her face into my palm and kisses the heel of my hand.

"I left after three hours."

"Where did you go?"

"I bought some clothes from the gift shop, charged them to my dad's room, then walked around a while, had a cup of coffee, and just thought about everything that had happened. Trying to wrap my head around it."

I nod in support.

"Then, I ordered a town car, charged that to my dad's room too, and had it bring me home."

"Which is when you walked in on me confessing my greatest sin."

"No," she says. "I walked in on my fiancé confessing his greatest sin." She smiles.

I smile back.

"Then my dad came over." She looks off to the side, as though thinking about what happened.

"But that went well?" I ask, even though I'm already sure that it did. Based on what Jonathan told us and based on how Willow is acting now.

She nods. "Really well. He apologized for everything. Which was amazing. He explained himself and why he did some of the things he did. It was so incredibly revealing. Even promised some changes."

"How do you feel now?"

"Better." She smiles and ducks her head. "Will you do it again?" She peeks up through her lashes.

"Do what, baby?"

"Ask me again."

"All day, every day." I kneel between the chair and coffee table at her feet.

"Wait." She gets up and goes to the counter, coming back with the ring, and hands it to me.

I take her hands in mine and look at her. This beautiful woman who for some reason has blessed me with her love and affection. "Willow, I can't fathom going a day without you by my side. You make me a better me just by being you. You are the sun in my day and the stars in my night. Will you do me the honor of making me the luckiest man alive and agree to marry me?"

She smiles big. "That was different from before."

"I have a few different versions. In case you said no the first time, I planned to keep asking until you said yes." I wink and stand before her.

She blushes that beautiful pink color that I love so much, then holds out her left hand for me to put the ring on her finger.

"Yes," she whispers. Tears stream down her cheeks. "Yes. I will."

I take her face in my hands and kiss her softly. Putting every single feeling of love and devotion that I have into that kiss. She wraps her arms around my neck and pulls me in tighter. The kiss goes from soft and loving to hot and possessive. My hands run down her body to cup her ass, her body melts against mine. When her legs wrap around my waist, I turn and sit in the chair she vacated as she straddles me.

My body heats, I can't remember a time where I've been so turned on. So desperate for a connection than I am now.

"I need you, baby, I need to be inside you," I breathe into her ear. She nods and rises off my lap, not breaking the kiss, while we both push her sweatpants down her thighs and past her knees. She kicks them off her feet as I lift my ass to push my own sweatpants down my hips, barely freeing my cock before she's sinking all the way down onto me.

"Oh god, Mason," she moans as I bottom out.

My left hand moves under her arm, up her back, and over her shoulder to hold her in place as I grind up into her. Skin on skin, her heat envelops me, while my other hand finds her clit and I start to work it with my thumb.

"Oh dear god," she cries. "Oh, Mason, oh don't stop."

"Never, baby. Never."

Her orgasm takes over, faster tonight than ever before. Which is good, since I'm about ready to blow. Willow cries out my name as I growl out hers, pumping my release into her as her muscles pulsate around me, squeezing out everything I have.

My hold on her tightens and I never want to let go. Her body melts into mine and we sit there, breathing heavily, my hands running over her back. Not quite believing I have her back in my arms after today.

A day filled with such highs and lows. My girl has had a hellish day.

"Thank you," I say. "Thank you for agreeing to marry me, for giving me another chance tonight, for hanging out in my mom's bookstore on that fateful day way back when, thank you for loving me, and for making me a better man."

She laugh-cries. "It's me who should be thanking you. For being so patient with me and for loving me as I am. I don't know how I ever thought I was happy before you came into my life. But I am now with you. And I'm happier than I ever thought possible."

Willow sits back slightly and looks around. "Hey, what happened to Zach?"

"Your dad had his town car take him to the docks and he caught a water taxi home."

"What did you do? Just stay outside?"

"After your dad asked us both to leave, I stayed in my Jeep because I wasn't going to go anywhere until I knew you were okay. Either from the havoc I wreaked on you today, or from your dad's visit. When I saw him leave, I took a chance and came to the door."

"I'm glad you did," she says.

"Me too."

"He told me what you said. And gave me your note." She smiles. "It was on a receipt, what happened to your notebook?"

"I didn't have it with me. I was glad I had pencils in my glove box. Otherwise I would have been writing on your dad's arm with a construction Sharpie."

She laughs.

"Promise me, Willow, that you will never doubt my love for you. You are my heart and my soul. There is no one else for me. Just you. Always you."

Tears fill her eyes again. I touch my nose to hers, then move to nuzzle her neck.

"I won't," she whispers.

P-Tink lets out a yelp from the floor and starts kicking her legs.

"Aw, she's dreaming again," Willow says, yawning.

I reach down and pet the dog's belly. She settles and sighs. Then I pick up my girl and carry her to our bedroom, and tuck her in, where she settles and sighs. I turn off all the lights and check the doors and windows to make sure everything is locked, set the alarm, and head back to our room.

Willow is already asleep, curled on her side with one hand —her left hand—resting on the pillow by her head, her ring back on her finger where it belongs. P-Tink comes in and settles herself at Willow's feet on the bed.

That's my whole world right there.

Outside of my mom, the only two things who matter. I have to take a breath as my chest fills with pride and gratitude.

I watch her for a moment more before I shed the remainder of my clothes and crawl in behind her. She nestles her butt back against my cock when she feels me beside her. I wrap her in my arms and pull her to me, she sighs. I take a minute to thank whatever powers were at work to bring this woman into my life. I allow myself one tear of happiness and gratitude before I kiss the top of her head and succumb to sleep myself.

EPILOGUE

FIVE YEARS LATER

Willow

Mason steps up behind me and wraps his arms around my waist, nuzzling my neck with his chin, his whiskers tickling the soft skin making me giggle. He's been experimenting with a full beard lately, instead of scruff. I'm still torn between which I like best.

"Mmmm, you smell good."

"That's cake frosting you smell." I dip my finger in the frosting bowl and hold it up over my shoulder for him to taste. He pulls my finger into his mouth and sucks hard. The feeling is titillating. Warmth floods my center and my panties dampen.

"She's smart, she bakes, she's beautiful, and great in the sack, is there nothing you can't do, woman?" he asks as he moves his hands up to grab my breasts, pressing his pelvis against me.

"She down?" I ask.

"Like a champ." He turns me around to face him and claims my lips with his. He tastes sweet, like chocolate frosting.

I moan into his mouth. He pushes the frosting makings aside and lifts me to the counter, pushing my dress up to my waist and stepping between my legs, pulling me closer. I wrap my legs around his waist and my arms around his neck.

Mason stops the kiss after a minute and looks at me, our foreheads touching. "You know what this means?"

"We have time for a quickie?" I ask.

"Maybe even time for an in-betweener." He wiggles his eyebrows. Our term for something in between marathon lovemaking and a wham-bam-thank-you-ma'am. As he would call it.

"I like where your head is at," I tell him. He lifts me from the counter and starts to carry me down the hall, while I nibble at his neck and whisper about the other places I plan to nibble.

The front door crashes open as we are halfway down the hall.

"Daddy! Daddy! Guess what?"

Mason groans and stops. I lower my legs from around his waist.

"Daddy! Where ARE you?"

Little legs run from the front door through the living room and kitchen, to the back deck and then return the same way, before pausing in the entryway. "DADDY!"

"I'm right here, bud." Mason heads toward the entry while I straighten my clothes and follow.

Dash looks up at Mason. "Wow, that was a close one, Daddy, I couldn't find you and I HAD to tell you what happened."

Dash, our four-year-old son, has been trying to work idioms into his everyday conversation, thanks to Zach. But he doesn't quite have a handle on their proper usage yet.

"Wow, that sounds crazy. What happened?" Mason picks him up so they are eye to eye.

"Well." Dash pauses for effect. "When we got to the store, there weren't any Saturn Twenty-Sevens left. Right, Uncle Zach?"

Zach nods in agreement. I head over to him and give him a hug hello. "Thanks for coming back early," I mumble in his ear.

He brings one hand to his chest and feigns shock. "Did I cock-block you, Willimena?"

"You know you did," I say drily.

"You've already got two. Isn't that enough? I thought you heteros only had sex to procreate?"

I backhand him in the stomach.

Dash is still telling Mason the harrowing story of how the store clerk had to get the very last of the Saturn Twenty-

Sevens from the back as there weren't any more on the shelf. Mason responds in kind with shock and awe. We already know Zach had called ahead and paid over the phone to get around the demand for the latest movie franchise character frenzy—Saturn Twenty-Seven. Which is all Dash has talked about for months.

"And the lady told me, it's the very last one ANYWHERE. Isn't that cool, Daddy?"

"That is way cool, dude. You are a lucky birthday boy, that's for sure."

"I know!" Dash runs out to the back deck to play with his new toy.

Mason looks to Zach. "Thanks for coming back early, man."

"The little woman already thanked me. And you're welcome." He looks around. "Where's my little princess?" he asks of our daughter, Zoe.

"Napping," Mason says.

"Oh dear, that is tragic," Zach says. "You really did have a moment for some afternoon delight, didn't you?"

"Doesn't happen often, man." Mason sighs.

"If I were a better friend maybe I would distract the little man and give you twenty minutes."

"I only need ten," Mason says.

Both Zach and I look at him, eyebrows raised.

"I know how that sounds," Mason says. He turns to me and says, "Trust me, baby. I'll make it good." He grabs my hand and pulls me down the hall to our bedroom.

"I didn't say I was that better friend," Zach calls behind us.

"Ten minutes," Mason says. "Thanks, man." He shuts the bedroom door and locks it. Pushing me up against the back of the door, hands on my breasts, hips grinding against mine, lips taking control.

A moment later, he softens his grip and kiss, steps away from the door, leads me to the bed, and pushes me back gently.

"We have time for the bed?" I ask, smiling.

"The door's locked, what's he going to do? Knock?"

"Yes." I laugh.

Mason crawls over me, kissing his way up my body. I shiver in anticipation as his lips ghost over my thighs. He pushes up the bottom of the sundress I'm wearing and licks me through my panties.

I grab his head to hold him there.

He does it again. Then nibbles at my clit.

"Oh, Mason," I sigh. He pulls my panties to the side and pumps two fingers in and out.

"Jesus, 'Low. So wet, you feel so good." He curves his fingers as he moves them in and out of me, and takes my clit into his mouth, alternating between sucking and licking. I can feel my orgasm starting. Mason moans in appreciation. My thighs lock around his head as I come. He licks me all the way through, not stopping until I push him away.

"I can't, it's too sensitive," I say weakly.

"You can, and it's not," he says as he pulls my panties down and quickly sheds his shorts and boxer briefs.

He's inside me with one thrust. "Oh god, Willow," he moans.

I wrap my arms and legs around him, pulling him closer. I love the feel of him inside me, over me, with me. He pistons his hips, rotating slightly, hitting my clit with each thrust.

"You feel so good," I moan in his ear. He sucks on my neck and bites down lightly. Sending a zing straight to my center. "Oh god, Mason."

He grabs one leg and slings it over his shoulder, opening me wider, thrusting harder, hitting that one spot.

"Oh, Mason, I'm going to—"

He rocks into me as I find my release again, crying out his name. My body tensing, heating, tightening, letting go. He's not far behind, growling out his own release as he pumps into me.

He rolls off me and pulls me with him. We sit there for a moment, enjoying the afterglow, trying to catch our breath.

"Fuck, I love you, woman. So much." He kisses the top of my head.

"I love you," I murmur to his chest, turning to kiss it.

His hold on me tightens. "I want to stay like this all day."

"Think Zach can handle the party on his own?" I ask.

He scoffs. "Totally. Between him, your dad, and my mom, they've got it covered. No problem. We can stay here, and I can ravage your body over and over." He leans in and fake bites at my neck with a growl, which in turn makes me squeal.

Mason checks his watch. "Seven and a half minutes. That might be a new record." He puffs out his chest with pride.

I sit up. "Most men don't brag about their speed with sex, hot stuff." I pat him on the belly.

"Ah, but most men didn't get their wife off twice in said time, all with a four-year-old outside, a two-year-old napping, and a party starting in a couple hours. That is immense pressure to perform under. I'm pretty much a fucking god." He stands to strut around the room, naked. Making me laugh again.

He gets a warm washcloth and brings it back to clean me with.

"Thank you." I smile.

"It's the least a god can do for his goddess." He kisses me hard, then moves to get dressed, whistling as he goes. The tune familiar.

I change my panties, shake out my dress before putting it back on and fix my hair. Mason stops whistling before opening the door.

He turns to me. "Was I just whistling—"

"Yep," I say.

"Dammit. It's hard to be a sex god when you start whistling The Wheels on the Bus afterward."

"I feel your pain."

He shakes his head at himself and leaves the room. I straighten the bed linens, laughing intermittently, feeling happy and lucky. Really freaking lucky.

Mason and I had a little bit of a rough start, and discovering I was pregnant early on in our relationship didn't help. We weren't even married yet. But he took it in stride and made sure both the baby and I knew how wanted and loved we were.

We got married right before I started to show. At the courthouse with just Zach and Caroline, his mom, in attendance as witnesses.

He flipped another house during the pregnancy so he felt more comfortable taking time off after Dash was born. Neither one of us worked for the first six months, which I know is rare and we were lucky to be able to do. Mason took on a couple more projects after that. And slowly transitioned to renovating more commercial properties than residential.

I still don't really have a job outside the house and raising the kids. I help Mason with the designs on his properties, but that's about it. Mostly because even this close to forty years old, I still don't know what I want to be when I grow up. And maybe I never will. At the risk of sounding old-fashioned, being a wife and mother fulfills me in a way I've never felt before. I'm really content to be at home with my kids. Dash was born about five months after we were married. And our daughter, Zoe, about two years ago.

Don't get me wrong, we get a lot of help from Zach and Caroline and Abe with the kids. And I have a housekeeper who comes in twice a week. Which takes a lot of pressure off me and I'm grateful for that. I know I can afford a lot more, but I don't want to live a lavish lifestyle. I enjoy the relative simplicity of what we have now. We live on Mason's income, and anything I do spend of my money is just from the interest collected. Most of which I put away for the kids' college, or donate to Zach's new foundation, Captain Cupcake Cures. Devoted to teaching kids anti-bullying and acceptance, much like his books.

I head into the kitchen to finish the frosting and check the portable monitor screen to make sure Zoe is still sleeping. Then I watch Mason with Zach and Dash running around outside while I frost the cake. They are all goofing off with Dash's new toy, while P-Tink runs circles around them with the occasional bark. The sun is shining today, and the weather is warm. It's the perfect day for a birthday party.

Dash looks up and sees me through the window watching them. He waves and then blows me a kiss. Mason, seeing him, does the same. As does Zach, never one to be left out.

It doesn't get any better than this.

Mason

I watch as Willow laughs at something her dad says. They've come a long way since my first induction to the Brooks family. Though she's Willow Brooks Cartwright now. I was surprised when he flew out for Dash's birth, sans Cassandra. But when he came again for Dash's first Christmas and again for his first birthday, I started to feel more relaxed about it. We see him now about six times a year. Sometimes with Cassandra, but most often not.

While AshLynn has refused to "forgive" Willow for the transgression that is me—ridiculous though it is—Cassandra has been a bit more lenient. Not much, but a bit. They still don't know the engagement was fake, and neither Willow nor I plan to tell them.

Jonathan has mellowed quite a bit with his risky business decisions and his spending habits, and his life seems to have calmed over all. Which makes Willow happy. And as long as 'Low is happy, then I am too.

Zach approaches with Zoe in his arms. "Someone needs changing, wish me luck."

"Zoe poop!" my daughter yells, bouncing up and down in Zach's arms.

"Good luck," I call after him.

Zoe took to Zach immediately. From the minute she was born, and they cleaned her up under the heat lights, he was there talking to her, letting her grab his finger, and telling her everything she needed to know about life. He is by far her favorite of all of us. And she his. I thought Willow would feel slighted by it. Instead she feels grateful for the extended family we've provided our children and that they have a "choice" of adult to bond with.

I take another sip of my beer and look around at the party. The deck and beach are filled with people. Our friends with their kids, Dash's entire preschool class and their parents, Mom and Abe, Zach and his partner, Michael. We do parties like this a few times a year, and Willow thought she would hate it. But she shines. Every time. She's in her element talking to people and making them feel at home, and I am happy to let her do it.

Dash is in the bounce house with a bunch of his friends, having the time of his life. P-Tink travels from person to person, nudging them with her nose, hoping for either dropped food or belly rubs. Or both.

Michael enjoys staying busy. Filling drinks, taking empty plates, providing refills, prepping and replenishing food. He's a sous chef in a French restaurant downtown, every aspect of hosting a party makes him happy.

Which leaves Zach to play with Zoe. A task he takes seriously. In addition to diaper changes, he carries her with him everywhere at most parties. And she is perfectly content to stay in his arms and hang on his every word. He tells her interesting facts about each guest, about their conversations, sometimes in front of them, sometimes not. Most times offensive and inappropriate I'm sure, but it's their thing. Zoe is an old soul in a toddler's body. She and Zach connect in a way that most of us don't understand.

Willow is convinced that Zoe is their friend Marlie come back to life. Much the same way that P-Tink is Granny Violet incarnate. I don't pretend to understand a lot of that stuff, but as long as Zoe isn't negatively affected by Zach's comments or actions, I'm totally okay.

Speak of the devil.

"Tell Daddy what you just told Zachey," Zach says to Zoe.

Zoe sighs, then places her little hands on either side of Zach's face, forcing him to look her in the eye. "You is good boy."

"See?" Zach looks at me triumphantly. "Princess Zoe has spoken."

"Piss Zoe poken," Zoe says.

"I am a good boy," Zach says. "I'm going to have T-shirts and hats made. Maybe some buttons, like those ones they use in campaigns. Soon, everyone will know."

"Eryone, Daddy." Zoe nods in agreement.

I kiss my daughter on the cheek. "You're a good girl, Zoe."

"Zoe good girl," she says.

"Okay, well, we're off to conquer the world," Zach says. "Onward, Princess Zoe."

"O word," Zoe parrots.

I check the meat on the grill and grab a fresh beer from the cooler.

"I'll take one of those," Jonathan says from behind me. I grab him a beer, open it, and hand it to him.

"Thanks," he says moving to stand beside me.

We are silent for a moment before he speaks again. "I don't think I've ever thanked you, Mason. After all these years."

"Thanked me for what?"

"For changing my life," he says casually. As though changing a life is an everyday occurrence.

"Excuse me?" I ask almost choking on my beer.

"Whatever nonsense it is that happened between you and AshLynn set off a chain of events that has irrevocably changed my life for the better. Even if I didn't realize it then, I do now. And I owe it to you. So, thank you. I'm indebted to you." He raises his beer and tips the bottle at me in affirmation before walking away. I stand there, fully aware that my mouth is hanging open in shock, but not yet having shut it.

Willow wraps her arms around me from the side. "You okay? What was that?" she asks.

"That? With your dad?"

"Yeah," she says.

"That was your dad shocking the hell out of me. But in a good way."

"He finally thank you for changing his life?"

"Yeah, he did." I look down at her. "How'd you know?"

"He's only been talking about it for years. I figured he'd do it when he was ready."

"Yeah . . . that . . . well, I guess he was ready."

"Good," she says as she smacks my ass.

"Watch it, woman," I growl. "I'll drag you back into the bedroom and show you just what a good spanking will get you."

"Save it," she says. "Your mom and Abe are taking the kids for a sleepover. We have the bounce house until tomorrow. I've got big plans for later." She winks and walks away. I watch her ass sway as she goes, feeling myself harden as I do.

I silently thank the powers that be, much like I do every day, for giving me everything I never knew I wanted, making me happier than my wildest dreams.

***

Did you enjoy I Heart Mason Cartwright? Please leave a review - I would super appreciate it. I'll be your best friend. Unless you already have one, then I'll totally be the backup.

And, if you like free shit, subscribe to my newsletter.

THANK YOU FOR READING!

If you enjoyed this book, please consider leaving a review. Hell, even if you didn't enjoy it please consider leaving one. That way I'll know what to change for next time.

If you want to know more about my books and new releases, join my newsletter!

SNEAK PEEK - POUR DECISIONS

Chapter One

My eyes have a hard time opening. Last night's mascara holds my lashes together, making them stick like glue. I use my fingers to pry open the right, blinking rapidly to adjust to the light. It's dim, but still an intrusion from the black void of a moment ago. My head raises and my left eye mimics the right. My vision blurred and hazy. A sea of white surrounds me, accompanied by the faint smell of sex, sweat, and bleach.

I'm not good with mornings. I don't like them; they don't like me. As though in testament to such, my stomach protests as I sit up slowly. Could be that its morning, could also result from too much alcohol and not enough food last night. My head spins as I take in the surrounding room. I'm in a hotel room, that much I remember. It's a nice one, spacious and well furnished. One of those with separate bedroom and living room areas. A ceiling fan rotates above my head. I can't recall ever seeing a ceiling fan in a hotel bedroom before.

Blackout curtains cover the window while the faint hum of the air conditioning dances around my ears. A quick peek under the sheets shows my naked body glaring back at me while snippets of last night's festivities pepper through my mind. My girlfriend's and I venturing out to the Villa Royale hotel for drinks. What started as a low-key happy hour stretched into four, then five. Or was it six?

Dancing. Oh god, so much dancing my legs ache.

I'd gotten word early afternoon about my nomination for the West Coast Winemaker's Association (WCWA) Innovation Competition (WCWAIC). My friends Tess and Megan thought it would be a good idea to take me out for drinks and we came to the same hotel that is hosting the WCWAIC starting tonight. My face grins at the memories, my body stretches languorously, and my throat groans at how good it feels. All the parts working independently, yet simultaneously, while—

Oh. Wait.

My legs aren't the only part of me that aches.

I trail my fingers down between my legs and push gently at the sore, swollen tissue, remembering how thoroughly and completely that delicious man fucked me last night. Multiple times if the condom wrappers on the nightstand are any sign.

Wait again.

The man.

I glance to the other side of the bed, relieved to find it empty. My sleep-addled brain finally catching up to the fact that the only light in the room is filtering through the cracked bathroom door, where the shower is running. And all the pieces come together in a linear fashion.

The competition.

My nomination.

Tess, Megan, and me celebrating.

Copious amounts of drinks.

The gorgeous guy.

All that dancing.

Fantastic sex.

Aw, fuck!

I need to go now before the guy gets out of the shower and we have to do that awkward morning after thing that everyone talks about. Where you don't know if you should go to breakfast, maybe have sex again, trade numbers, or avert your eyes and go your separate ways. Not that I would know. This is my first one-night stand ever. But I've heard enough stories to be frightened.

I scramble from the bed and begin the hunt for my clothes. The room isn't cluttered, far from it, but I'm still having a hard time identifying things. I grab my fishnet stockings and try to pull them on while standing.

Oh, they're ripped.

Wow, really ripped.

Especially in the crotch.

Nicely done, Morgan.

I mentally pat myself on the back, before realizing I didn't need them on anyway. What better way to make the proverbial walk of shame look even more embarrassing than by wearing the ripped stockings from the night before

I shove them along with my bra into my purse. Searching for my underwear while trying to zip the back of my dress at the same time. Right arm over my right shoulder, left arm bent behind my lower back and moving up from the bottom. Both trying in vain to reach the zipper pull or each other. Clearly, dresses were designed by sadist contortionists with no concern for how normal people dress in short amounts of time or otherwise.

Grabbing my shoes and purse in one hand, all the while holding the front of my dress to my chest, I quietly slip out the door into the hallway. Then toe on my shoes as I hit the elevator call button and continue to try unsuccessfully to zip my dress. The telltale ding signals the elevator car and the doors open to reveal a tall blonde woman in gym clothes, toweling non-existent sweat off her face, just as I'm pushing my heel into my shoe.

I nod my head as I enter, and give her a small smile, trying to pretend everything is normal. My dress isn't half hanging off my body, and I'm not—

OHMIGOD!

The reflection in the mirrored walls of the elevator car show someone who can't possibly be me. I mean, it's my dress, but no way is that nest of tangles and disarray my hair. And the raccoon eyed face with streaked eye makeup belongs to a stranger.

I can't help but gasp once I see myself. My free hand flies to my hair as I attempt to pat it down before licking my finger and running it under my eyes to get the smudge under control.

"Crazy night, huh?" the girl asks. She looks nice when she smiles at me.

"You have no idea." I smile back, a feeling of camaraderie developing, as though we're sharing in a sisterhood of sorts.

"Want me to zip your dress?"

"Oh, god, would you," I breathe. "Thank you so much." I turn my back to her, shivering slightly as her icy hands graze my skin.

"Looks like you had a good time." She gestures to my neck.

I lean in closer to the mirror, inspecting the number of hickeys on my neck.

My first one-night stand.

My first hickey on other parts of my body that aren't my neck.

"I did." I smile, pivoting to face the front. A flyer announcing the WCWAIC competition hangs from a bulletin box above the button controls and snags my attention. My heart does a little flip knowing that starting tonight, I'll be a part of that. And a competition like this one, where innovations in the wine industry are judged and awarded, could make a career for someone as small-time as me.

The car stops and the doors open, I make my way out to the lobby. Feeling proud for stepping out of my comfort zone and doing something so ordinarily out of character. Both in submitting to the competition and in a one-night stand.

"Bye," I say to the girl as we part ways; she in the direction of the juice bar and me toward the exit. But as proud as I may feel in that moment, I still wait until I'm a block away before pulling up an app and ordering a car to come and take me home.

Chapter Two

I pull up the messages on my phone to send a text to my best friend, Tess, and see all the pictures that she and Megan sent me the night before. Dozens of pictures of me on the dance floor with the guy from the hotel. And almost every single one they took is flattering. If it weren't for the fact the girl in the photos is wearing the same dress I am, I might not believe it's me.

This girl looks . . . hot.

Confident.

Sexy.

I'm not any of those things in my everyday life. Look up shy, mousy, and wallflower with social anxiety in the dictionary and there I will be. Which often makes me wonder how different my life would be if I were confident and sexy. Would I have a boyfriend? A better career? Might I have finally moved out of my mom and grandma's house to live on my own?

Cause none of those things are true now.

I'm working on the career part though. This award will help that along. If I win, that is.

Tess' words from last night ring through my mind.

When.

Not *if.*

When I win this competition, the recognition will help to further my career. The WCWAIC award is for showing innovation in wine making and selling techniques. Coming up with something that benefits the end user, i.e. the wine drinker, in a way that's not been done before. It's rare that a competition like this comes up, where the primary goal isn't focused on something more traditional, like "Best Cabernet Sauvignon" or something along those lines. There's just this one for the west coast, and then I think one of the big wine magazines has a national one.

Winning should mean more sales, which means more money, which is all I need to get a place of my own. While I may love my mom and grandmother, I don't need to be living with them any longer. I'm going to be thirty years old next year, I should have been out of their house six years ago. But they live where my grapevines live and I really love my vines.

I flip through more of the pictures with me and the guy who is so totally out of my league. As he kisses my neck, grabs my hips, laughs at whatever I'm saying. This girl has him captivated. How did I do it?

I dial Tess, hoping she's awake.

"Toot, toot, and beep, beep," she answers in a sing-song voice.

"What?" I ask, laughing.

"Bad girl. Talking 'bout the bad girl, yeah," she sings the Donna Summer song from seventies into the phone.

"I am not a bad girl, take it back!"

"I will not take it back. Last night was awesome! I've never seen you cut loose like that. You were having so much fun! Did you spend the night with him? Was the sex good? What did he say this morning? Did you exchange numbers? Are you doing the LYFT of shame home right now? Are you going to see him again?" She rattles off questions.

"Um, let me see." I tap my finger on my lips, pretending to think, even though she can't see me. "Yes. Yes. Nothing. No. Yes. And I doubt it."

"Nooo! Why?"

"Which of those responses are you asking why to?"

"Exchanging numbers. Seeing him again. Did you say anything to him?"

"No! I snuck out while he was in the shower."

"Morgan!"

"Tess!"

"Come on. Really? This has got to be your first one-stand in—"

"Ever," I interrupt.

"No," she gasps.

"Yes," I affirm, nodding.

She's silent for a moment. "I guess you're right. Well then, all the more reason why you should have embraced it. Jumped in the shower with him. Left your number in his wallet, a lipstick print on his boxers."

"I don't think so," I say.

"Spoil sport. Fine, let's get back to the sex then. You said it was good?"

"Better than," I whisper into the phone. I catch the LYFT driver's eye in the rear-view mirror and turn my head to the side, covering my mouth with my other hand. "Mind blowing." I lower my voice, not wanting him to hear.

"What?"

"Mind blowing. Like what we see in movies," I mumble.

"You guys watched a movie? Like porn?"

"No," I sigh. "I said like what we see in movies."

"Wow, like porn movies?"

"No, just normal movies. Or, I don't know, maybe porn," I giggle. This time when the driver looks back at me through the mirror, I meet his gaze and stare hard. Screw him for listening in. It's my conversation, not his. And it's private. Though, I probably shouldn't be having it in *his* car then, but whatever.

"I knew the sex would be great. He was so good looking!" Tess enthuses.

"Is that all it takes?"

"Pretty much. The better looking they are, the more sex they've had. And the more sex they've had, the better they are at it."

"What about that whole *average-guys-try-harder-in-bed* theory you had before?"

"Morgan, let's face it, anytime you get the opportunity to sleep with a hot guy over an average guy, you need to take the hot one. You never know when you'll get a chance again."

"Gee, thanks. You're quite the ego booster this morning."

"Oh, you know what I mean. Things like that don't happen to girls like us."

"Who are girls like us?"

"You know, average girls. We're cute, smart, successful, but there's nothing crazy extraordinary about us."

"And the ego boosts just keep coming," I say drily.

"Says the girl who just left the hot guy's bed."

"There is that," I say, tempted to blow on my fingernails, then shine them on the chest of my dress. Last night was like a coup for ordinary girls everywhere. Because the guy wasn't that drunk.

Riggs.

That's his first name. I didn't ask for his last. Even his name is sexy. I shiver at the memories of his hands roaming my body, his lips murmuring beautiful words, his eyes worshiping in their quest to see everything about me at once, yet still retain each detail. I should be on cloud nine after last night. And part of me is. But the part of me that didn't leave my number, or get his, and who snuck out while he was in the shower, that part of me knows I'll never change.

Always preferring the sidelines to center stage; the wall to the middle of the room; the backseat to the driver. Probably because my mom and grandmother are such drivers. There's not room enough for three of us in the same house. It's barely tolerable with the two of them. Which reminds me, I never did text my mom or grandma to say I wouldn't be home. Not that I have a curfew or anything, I'm a grown woman. But they worry when they don't know where I am or what I'm doing.

The driver turns onto the long dirt drive leading to our house. It's impressive when you don't realize that we're at the tiny square house to the west and not the multi-level chalet straight ahead. But that's a story for another time. Right now I've got to square my shoulders and prepare myself for the onslaught of questions the two pains in my neck are going to shower me with the minute I walk in the door.

"Hey, we're pulling up to the house, I'll call you back in a bit," I tell Tess.

"Later, bad girl."

I chuckle as I click to end the call and gather my purse, looking around to make sure I haven't left anything in the back seat. "I can tip through the app, right?" I ask the driver, even though I already know the answer to that.

"Yep," he nods once as he answers. It's a dumb question but I don't know of another way to let the driver know I plan to tip them. I don't want them driving away thinking I stiffed them until later when they get their paycheck or whatever and realize I did tip them. I mean, by then they may not even remember who I am or what day it was they drove me.

This way they have it on their mind, hopefully for a couple days, and then make the connection that I'm the girl who left the tip. Not that I'll ever see them again, but that's not the point. I want them to have the instant gratification of knowing I appreciated them and the service they provided, and that I plan to reward them financially.

I slip inside the front door as quietly as possible in hopes my mom and grandmother are still asleep or at the very least, preoccupied somewhere else. Which turns out to be futile. The familiar voices of the cohosts for a popular morning show are already echoing through the room, followed swiftly by the tenors of my mother and grandmother as they argue the points of the story that just aired. It won't matter what it was about, they will never see it from the same point of view. Even if one of them has to argue against their personal beliefs, they will over agreeing with the other. It's not something I understand or even try to.

"There you are!" my grandmother exclaims. "Come here right now, young lady."

I bow my head slightly and walk toward them, ready to be shamed for staying out all night without calling and then walking in looking like . . . well looking like a hot guy fucked me hard all night long.

"Morning, Grandma." I lean in to give her a kiss on the cheek. She smiles, but it's fast, and her face turns hard again.

I brace myself for whatever punishment is about to verbally rain down.

"You tell your mother that Tom Selleck's mustache is real. That man does not need to use a hair growth treatment on his face. He is all man. A real man. And real men can grow a proper mustache."

"It's too lush, Morgan. Look at it, no one has hair like that, facial or otherwise. He's got to be using extensions or some sort of potion. And it's definitely dyed."

I look back and forth between the two of them, not quite believing what I've walked into. They've rewound the program and have it paused on the man in question. I have to admit, his mustache looks lush, and very dark. Almost too dark. I squint at the screen, trying to see if anything looks amiss. But Tom Selleck looks just as he should, other-worldly handsome with all that thick, dark hair above his lip and atop his head.

Both women lean toward me from their chairs, waiting to hear my answer. As though this will be the time I will produce a tie breaker. I won't. I never have, and I probably never will.

"Hasn't it always looked like that?" I ask, trying to take the middle road. "Lush and full? Like, since he was young."

"Ha," they both say, even though I've proven neither point.

"Okay, well, I've got to go get ready for my day and plan out tonight." I wave over my shoulder as I head down the hall. Still wondering why no one said a word about my appearance or the fact that I was out all night.

Get your copy of Pour Decisions now!

ACKNOWLEDGMENTS

Mason's story was lurking in my brain for a while, so I'm excited to finally share him with you!

He was a true labor of love towards the end. Early feedback on the first draft was not good. So, a little over a month before the release I started to rewrite the entire thing. Gah! Soon after that, my father passed unexpectedly. And let me tell you, it is hard as fuck to write rom-com when you're sad.

But I found that I have an amazing team of people that help and support me. Without them, this never would have happened. In no particular order, I want to thank:

Rachel Radner - Once again you prove to be an invaluable source of knowledge and support in my life - my writing life and my real life. Thank you isn't enough, but thank you anyway.

Gabriella Scavella-Bell - I know you liked the first version better. :-) But, I appreciate you sticking with me during the re-writes. You are an awesome sounding board with great ideas and infinite patience.

Stephie Walls - My bestie, I doubt you even know the impact you have on me. You are my inspiration and my hero. I promise to always stalk Charlie Hunnam at airports to get his picture for you just to prove my devotion.

Linda Russell, Foreword PR - My guardian angel. You talk me down off the ledge every time, and always with a smile. It's amazing really. Thank you for your never ending support. And for not getting upset when I message you at all hours because I forget about time zones.

Kristie, Vanilla Lily Designs - Thank you doesn't begin to cover what I want/need to say. Thank you! Thank you! Thank you!!! You are awesome!!!

Missy Borucki - OMG, I'm pretty sure I would die without you at this point. Doesn't matter where you are or what you're doing; if I need you, you're there. Thank you. Thank you. Thank you. You complete me. Jerry McGuire style. (LOL) And, Highway to Hell = fucking brilliant.

Judy Zweifel, Judy's Proofreading - You are awesome. I look forward to letting you clean up my messes many more times to come.

BETAs - Angie, Rochelle, Eileen, Sue, Jami, Gabby-Dabby-Doo - COULD NOT have done it without you ladies. Hands down, just never would have happened. Thank you so, so much!

ARC Readers - An author's road to success is paved by reviews. Thank you for taking the time to help me with mine. And, **Sonja Tonjer** - you saved my ass. Can I send you all my ARCs?

My Dirty Darlings - Best reader group EVER! You guys just fucking rock. (Click to join my reader group)

BW - Thank you for understanding when I shut out the real world to play in my imaginary ones. You selflessly give so much to help me live my dream. I chose you, you're mine, no one else can have you, and I'll never regret it.

ABOUT THE AUTHOR

Denise has been reading since before she could talk. And to this day, escaping into a book is her go-to activity before anything else.

She likes to write about sassy women and semi-flawed alpha-esque men (hard on the outside and just a little soft on the inside.) Denise's female characters always have strong friendships, potty mouths, and like to drink—a lot.

Denise is loyal to a fault, a bit too sarcastic, blindingly optimistic, and pretty freakin' happy with life overall. If she couldn't be a writer, she'd be a singer in a classic rock band. Right after she learned to carry a tune. She has more purses than days in the month, an obsession with colored ink pens, and a slightly unhealthy bracelet habit.

Home is in the Pacific Northwest where she lives with six special needs Siberian Huskies and a husband (BW) who has the patience and tolerance of a saint. And, lest she forget, Denise also lives with too many to count characters inside her head, who will eventually have their stories told.

For more about Denise visit her website at: www. DeniseWells.com

Or follow her on any of the social media sites below.

facebook.com/DeniseWellsAuthor

instagram.com/DeniseWellsAuthor

bookbub.com/authors/denise-wells

goodreads.com/denisewells

pinterest.com/denisewellsauthor

patreon.com/DeniseWells

tiktok.com/@denisewellsauthor

ALSO BY DENISE WELLS

<u>STANDALONES</u>

The One I Can't Have, a steamy age-gap novella in **AB Worlds Age-Gap series**

The Three Way, a steamy novella in the **AB Worlds Valentine's Day Series**

Forever Wicked, a steamy novella in the **AB Worlds Halloween Party Series**

Summer Shivers, a romantic thriller in the **Summers in Seaside Collection**

Overdrive, a steamy enemies to lovers romance **in KB WORLDS - DRIVEN COLLECTION**

Pour Decisions, a romantic comedy novella in the **Girl Power Collection**

How to Ruin Your Ex's Wedding, a steamy romantic comedy

I Heart Mason Cartwright, a steamy romantic comedy

Love Off The Rocks, a romantic comedy short

Rebel without a Claus, a steamy, gay romantic short

Breaking Dylan, a coming of age story

<u>AGENTS AND ASSASSINS TRILOGY</u>

Fearless - Book One, a steamy romantic thriller

Careless - Book Two, a steamy romantic thriller

Ruthless - Book Three, a steamy romantic thriller

<u>SAN SOLOMAN</u>

Keeping Kat, a steamy second-chance firefighter romance

Romancing Remi, a steamy enemies to lovers romance

Loving Lexie, a steamy cowboy enemies to lovers romance

Seducing Sadie, a steamy firefighter romance

Trusting Tenley, an emotional second-chance at love romance

ANTHOLOGIES

High EX-Pectations, a romantic comedy short in the **Imperfect Date Anthology**

CAUGHT UNDER THE MISTLETOE - A Holiday Affair to Remember, a romantic comedy holiday short

STORYBOOK PUB CHRISTMAS WISHES - Mistle Oh-No, a romantic comedy holiday short

STORYBOOK PUB - Breezy Like Sunday Morning, a romantic comedy short

LIMITED RELEASES

GIRLS JUST WANNA HAVE FUNDAMENTAL RIGHTS - Charity Anthology

SEEDS OF LOVE A Charity Romance Anthology to benefit Ukraine - Charity Anthology

HOT AS F$#K SUMMER ROMANCE ANTHOLOGY - SULTRY SUMMER NIGHTS

LOCKED AND LOVED: An Isolated Romance Collection

SUMMER WITH YOU: Summer Shorts Collection

JUST A LICK Collection

LOVE LETTERS Collection

STOCKING STUFFERS Anthology